THINGS  WHAT THEY SEEM....

Two bestselling authors bring you two riveting romances in one volume!

TWO HEARTS
by Maggie Shayne
• Jack McCain is a government security agent—
or is he?
• Grace Phelps is a socialite heiress—
with a secret?

"Brilliantly inventive, Maggie Shayne is a definitive voice in contemporary romantic fiction."
—*Romantic Times Magazine*

A LITTLE BIT DANGEROUS
by Marilyn Pappano
• Mary Katherine Monroe is a riverboat waitress—perhaps....
• Chance Reynard is head of security for a riverboat casino...or so everyone thinks!

"One of the best authors in the genre today."
—*Romantic Times Magazine*

**When love goes under cover,
the unexpected happens!**

Dear Reader,

The 20th anniversary excitement continues as we bring you a 2-in-1 collection containing brand-new novellas by two of your favorite authors: Maggie Shayne and Marilyn Pappano. *Who Do You Love?* It's an interesting question—made more complicated for these heroes and heroines because they're not quite what they seem, making the path to happily-ever-after an especially twisty one. Enjoy!

A YEAR OF LOVING DANGEROUSLY continues with *Her Secret Weapon* by bestselling writer Beverly Barton. This is a great secret-baby story—with a forgotten night of passion thrown in to make things even more exciting. Our in-line 36 HOURS spin-off continues with *A Thanksgiving To Remember,* by Margaret Watson. Suspenseful and sensual, this story shows off her talents to their fullest. Applaud the return of Justine Davis with *The Return of Luke McGuire.* There's something irresistible about a bad boy turned hero, and Justine's compelling and emotional handling of the theme will win your heart. In *The Lawman Meets His Bride,* Meagan McKinney brings her MATCHED IN MONTANA miniseries over from Desire with an exciting romance featuring a to-die-for hero. Finally, pick up *The Virgin Beauty* by Claire King and discover why this relative newcomer already has people talking about her talent.

Share the excitement—and come back next month for more!

Leslie J. Wainger
Executive Senior Editor

Please address questions and book requests to:
Silhouette Reader Service
U.S.: 3010 Walden Ave., P.O. Box 1325, Buffalo, NY 14269
Canadian: P.O. Box 609, Fort Erie, Ont. L2A 5X3

WHO DO
YOU LOVE?

MAGGIE
SHAYNE

MARILYN
PAPPANO

Silhouette®
INTIMATE™MOMENTS®

Published by Silhouette Books

America's Publisher of Contemporary Romance

SILHOUETTE BOOKS

ISBN 0-373-27103-4

WHO DO YOU LOVE?

Copyright © 2000 by Harlequin Books S.A.
The publisher acknowledges the copyright holders of the individual works as follows:

TWO HEARTS
Copyright © 2000 by Margaret Benson

A LITTLE BIT DANGEROUS
Copyright © 2000 by Marilyn Pappano

This edition published by arrangement with Harlequin Books S.A.

® and TM are trademarks of Harlequin Books S.A., used under license. Trademarks indicated with ® are registered in the United States Patent and Trademark Office, the Canadian Trade Marks Office and in other countries.

Visit Silhouette at www.eHarlequin.com

Printed in U.S.A.

CONTENTS

Dear Reader,

When Silhouette approached me with their idea for the theme of this special 2-in-1 project, *Who Do You Love?*, I was particularly pleased, because I had a story idea on the back burner that fit perfectly. I'd been waiting for just the right time to develop it, and this project was my cue. Secret identities, hidden agendas, lovers in disguise—these have always been favorite themes of mine. They beg the answers to some of life's deepest questions. What is love, really? What part of a person do you fall in love with? Is it the mask they wear, their career, their background, their manners? Or is it something deeper? The heart and soul that lie beneath all those things, perhaps. In "Two Hearts" I've been able to dig into these questions and more. I hope you like the answers I came up with.

Happy reading!

Maggie Shayne

Two Hearts
Maggie Shayne

MAGGIE SHAYNE,

a national bestselling author whom *Romantic Times Magazine* calls "brilliantly inventive," has written more than fifteen novels for Silhouette. Her Silhouette single-title release *Born in Twiligh*t (3/97) was based on her popular vampire series for Shadows, WINGS IN THE NIGHT.

Maggie has won numerous awards, including a *Romantic Times Magazine* Career Achievement Award. A four-time finalist for the Romance Writers of America's prestigious RITA Award, Maggie also writes mainstream contemporary fantasy.

In her spare time, Maggie enjoys collecting gemstones, reading tarot cards, hanging out on the Genie computer network and spending time outdoors. She lives in a rural town in central New York with her husband, Rick, five beautiful daughters and two English bulldogs.

Chapter 1

It was almost 8:00 p.m., and Jack McCain was a mess. He hadn't shaved in a week, and he reeked of the stale beer JW had poured over his tattered pea coat and moth-eaten knit cap. The jeans he wore were slick with age and damn near black with grime down the fronts of the legs. The sneakers—yeah, he still called them that—were of the sort that seemed to talk to you when you walked, the toes opening and closing with every step. The socks underneath had holes in them.

He sat on the sidewalk, in the shadows between a couple of overly ripe trash cans, on a spring evening in the bad part of town. The sky was mud-colored, partly from the encroaching darkness, partly from the gray smog and rain clouds that hung over everything. The streetlights, the few that were working at all, were like weak, hazy eyes on the brink of death. They barely penetrated the gloom.

In his hand he had a bottle wrapped in a brown paper bag. Iced tea, not whiskey, but the look was right. His .44 Magnum was in a shoulder rig, resting heavy against his right side. Jack was a southpaw, so the mike was sewn into the cuff of his right sleeve. The earpiece was attached to the cap he wore. JW was on the other end, wearing headphones and waiting to send in the troops.

Just like he'd been waiting…for three solid weeks. The crack house Jack was watching was doing a steady business. But they were waiting for the supplier. Word was he'd be showing up in person for some major funds to change hands. He hadn't yet, but Jack figured he would. And soon. His radar was buzzing tonight.

It was off, though.

The guy who showed up instead was maybe fifty. Big guy, a little overweight, but solid-looking, shoes smacking over damp, broken sidewalk. From the cut of his suit Jack knew he didn't belong in this part of town. He was upper-crust. He wasn't the dealer. Jack knew that the same way he knew so many other things he shouldn't. He'd acquired a sixth sense from years of being a cop. A kind of radar. It wasn't something most of his colleagues talked about much. Sometimes he would just…*know.* This guy—he was one of the good ones. And he was headed for trouble.

He traversed the sidewalk, looking from the slip of paper in his hand to the numbers on the buildings he passed. An old newspaper page blew past his feet, past shoes that cost what five pairs of Jack's own would. And the ''boyz'' on the corner in their oversize clothes and stolen Nikes, looked up. They had radar, too. They smelled his money, and they'd pegged him for an easy mark.

Jack tipped up his bottle, pretending to slug back some whiskey while he talked to his worn-out cuff. ''We got a man about to get rolled here. Send a black and white.''

There was pause. Then, ''They're thirteen blocks out. Two minutes, Jack.''

The boyz—there were five of them—were already approaching the man in the expensive suit. Their victim spotted them, and his eyes widened. He got that expression on his face that comes when the clouds part and you realize you just walked right out in front of a speeding bus. He looked behind him, then turned to go back the way he'd come, but they were on him within a second. They surrounded him like a pack of freaking wolves. No. Dogs. Mean, ugly, mongrel dogs that have been kicked too often and fed too seldom. One of them looked around, and Jack slouched lower, closed his eyes.

"This guy doesn't have two minutes," he told his sleeve.

"Don't blow your cover, Jack. We've worked on this too long to—"

Jack didn't hear any more. His focus was all on the little group of Boy Scouts across the street. One had pulled a blade and they were backing the older man up, talking to him as his back pressed to the wet brick wall of the building behind him.

He reached for his wallet, then clutched his chest instead.

Jack shot to his feet and was across the street so fast he didn't remember his sneakers hitting the pavement. The Magnum was in his hand and he was yelling "Freeze" before he even thought about it.

One of the boys saw him coming and yelled, "Cop!" and then they scattered.

The man in the suit sank to the ground slowly. Jack brought his wrist up once more as he ran the last few steps to where the victim lay. "Get an ambulance out here, and tell that black and white to pick up the five little pricks they're about to see running like hell between Austin and Main."

"You got it, Jack."

Jack glanced around to make sure he was clear. He was. He could hear the siren now. No one would mess him up. Then he knelt beside the man in the suit.

The older man squinted at him, breathing quickly and too shallowly, Jack thought. "What are you, Super-Bum or something?"

Blinking, pretty much stunned that the guy could find anything humorous at all in the situation, Jack forced a smile. The older fellow was pale, and sweat beaded on his forehead. "Not exactly. I'm Jack McCain," he told him. "I'm a cop."

"Harry Phelps," he said, and a vague familiarity tickled Jack's brain then faded. "You were working undercover, huh?" the man asked.

Jack looked at the crack house, one house over, saw the faces peering out the dirty, broken windows from behind the rags that passed for curtains. "I was."

"I blew it for you."

"Doesn't matter. Do you have a heart condition, anything I should know to tell the paramedics when they get here?"

He made a face, tried to sit up, and Jack ended up helping him, because he wasn't quitting easy. "A touch of angina. I'll be…" He grunted, grating his teeth. "I'll be fine."

"We'll see what they say about that at the hospital."

"I can't…" He lowered his head as his chest, no doubt, sent another bolt of pain through him. "Have to get home. I'm expected… Hell, man, my youngest daughter is coming home from college tonight. Gracie. There's a party and—"

"The party can wait."

"You don't understand." The pain seemed to pass. Harry's face eased. "My wife will have every watered-down excuse for a man there—at least if they're single and have a pedigree."

"Your daughter's looking for a husband?" Jack asked, mildly amused.

"Gracie? Hell, no! But Mitsy can be…"

Jack was getting the picture. "Overbearing?"

"Like a bulldozer."

Jack smiled, finding he liked the old guy. "I can call your family for you. Tell them what's happened."

"And scare them half to death?"

The ambulance came around the corner, stopped in front

of them, and the back opened up. "I can be tactful," Jack told him.

"Yeah?"

"Yeah. I'll be at the ER when they arrive. I can talk to them there if you want, keep them calm while they wait for you."

His eyes narrowed. "Why will you be there? Waiting for some kind of reward?" he asked, one brow cocking up.

"You try offering me one and I'll arrest you. I'll be there to take your statement, you cranky old bastard."

The old guy smiled, right through the pain, he smiled broadly. And Jack decided he definitely liked him. He was tough as nails, and there wasn't a pretentious bone in him, despite the cut of his suit.

Harry reached up, clasped Jack's arm and squeezed it. "You saved my life just now, son. I won't forget it."

"It's my job." The ambulance crew pretty much shouldered Jack out of the way as they leaned over him. He spoke to JW via his wrist mike while they examined the old guy, but he never took his eyes off Harry. He was still in pain, but damn, he looked too tough to be in any serious trouble.

They lifted him onto the stretcher after a few minutes, and rolled him toward the vehicle.

"McCain!" the old man shouted.

The attendants paused, and Jack went back to the old guy. "I'm right here."

"Don't bother calling anyone," he said. "I have a cell phone. It'll be better if I do it myself."

"All right. My partner says they picked up three of the punks who did this, and one of them still had your wallet on him."

"Good," he said. "Kick their asses for me, will you?"

Jack grinned at him. "Not on duty, I won't."

"Hell, I'll have to do it myself then." He sounded as if he fully meant it. Jack bet he could do it, too. "You're coming to the hospital, then?" he asked.

Jack glanced at the attendants. "Mercy General," the paramedic filled in.

"Yeah. I'll be there."

"Do me one favor, son?"

Jack lifted his brows, leaned closer.

"Take a bath and put on a clean suit. You stink to high heaven."

He couldn't help but chuckle at that. "Get this character out of here, will you?"

The paramedics, smiling, as well, bundled Phelps into the back and took off, sirens wailing.

Watching them go, Jack had no idea that the course of his life would change radically that night. Some radar, right? He thought later that he should have known, should have sensed it somehow. That old man had plans for Jack. Big plans. And like some unseasoned rookie, Jack walked right into them, head-on.

He headed straight back to his tiny two-rooms-and-a-bath apartment over Mike's Bar and Grill. By the time he had showered, shaved, changed clothes and headed out again to go to the hospital, the better part of an hour had passed. And that damned dog from next door hadn't stopped barking the entire time. Jack knew hospitals. He figured he'd walk in to see the old gent biding his time in the ER, awaiting the results of his blood work or the cutting of the red tape that would get him a room.

He wasn't, though, and when Jack got his name from the ER admitting nurse, he finally figured out why. "Harry" turned out to be Harrison J. Phelps. The character was one of the richest men in the country. His name was as well known as Rupert Murdoch's or Donald Trump's. He'd been examined, diagnosed, and put into a private room with all due haste, and was even now visiting with his family doctor, who must have broken land speed records to get there.

Shaking his head slowly, Jack got the room number and

went to the elevator. At the sixth floor, he got off again. Jack was not usually the kind of man who worried too much about his appearance, and even less about what other people thought of him. Yeah, he had cleaned up for the old guy some, but he would have done the same for anybody. Now, though, that he knew who the guy was, he also knew he wasn't up to snuff. The suit was clean, in good shape, but even brand-new it wouldn't have fooled anyone into thinking it had any designer's name on the label—unless the designer was named JCPenney. Jack decided he'd keep his coat on. It was slightly more impressive looking. Nowhere near up to Phelps-style snuff, but it had cost a few bucks. It was a black trench coat, long enough to cover up most of the cheap suit.

Glancing at the numbers on the doors, Jack spotted the one marked 621, and tapped on it. The old man's voice called, "Come in," so he opened the door, stepped through, and got hit right between the eyes with the blinding light of an angel.

She was sitting in a chair beside Harry's bed, holding his hand in both of hers. And hers were long and strong, and elegant, her nails, short and neat. Jack's gaze slid up her arm to her shoulder, which was bared by the sleeveless dress she was wearing. It was pale blue, that dress, simply cut but elegant somehow. It came down to the middle of her thighs and from there on there was nothing but leg. She had long, long legs, and they ended in shoes that had pointy little toes and dainty little heels.

Jack swallowed hard, sliding his focus up her body again, knowing better, but somehow unable to do anything different. Her waist was small and her chest was small, too. Jack usually went for buxom babes with cleavage to spare—most of whom would come only up to this woman's shoulders—but there was something about her....

She wore pearls...tiny, perfect, pearls around her long, slender neck. Her auburn hair was tugged back into a smooth knot. Her skin…it was like cream. Her cheekbones made her seem born of royalty. And finally Jack looked at her eyes, and thought a goddess must have given birth to her. Big almond-shaped eyes, sizzling electric-blue, gazed back at him, and they were damn near as busy as his own, looking him over.

"About time you got here," Harry was saying. "This is him, Gracie. This is Jack McCain."

The girl blinked, and the next thing Jack knew she was out of her chair and in his arms. Tall, long and lean, she wrapped her arms around Jack's neck and hugged him close to her. "Thank you," she said softly. "Thank you for saving my father's life."

Jack blinked, pretty much bowled over at this point and trying real hard to keep in mind that this was a lady, a real lady, and not the type of girl he usually warmed his nights with. She was class personified. She was grace…they had certainly named her right. His hands were on her back, but not too hard, and he didn't dare move them. He felt as if he were holding something too clean to touch.

She smelled good. Like sunshine and wildflowers.

A throat cleared very slightly. Grace gently backed away, her blue eyes wet as she smiled up at him. Jack got the sense of other people in the room. It hadn't been Harry's throat-clearing just then. But for the life of him, he couldn't look away from the woman whose hands still rested slightly on his shoulders.

"I'm sorry," she said. "But when I think how close we came to losing him…"

"It wasn't that big a deal."

"Nonsense!" Harry boomed. "This young man saved my life. The killers had weapons!"

"They were muggers, Harry, and all they had was a pocketknife—"

"You should have seen him, Mitsy," Harry went on. "Onlookers actually applauded!"

Jack felt his brows pull together and for the first time he got that little niggling feeling at the back of his neck that told him something wasn't quite right. Gently, his hands resting at Grace's waist, he moved her to one side. "Harry, what are you—"

"I can't tell you how grateful we are, young man," a woman said. Jack looked her way, met her eyes, and saw an older, shorter version of Grace. She had to be the girl's mother.

"I was only doing my job, ma'am," he said.

The woman moved toward him, thrust out her hand. Jack took it. "Mitsy Phelps, darling," she said. "And exactly what do you mean, you were doing your job?"

"Ah, that's the same line he fed me, Mitsy!" Harry gushed from the bed. "His duty as a citizen, and all that!"

Again, Jack felt his brows pull together and his warning bells go off. He was not liking this.

"What line of work are you in?" Mrs. Phelps asked.

"I'm a—"

"Jack's in law," Harry said.

"Oh? A lawyer?"

"Not exactly," he told her.

"Jack's a…uh, security expert. I've been trying to lure him away from his current employer. I'd like him working for me."

"And who is your current employer, Mr. McCain?" Mitsy asked.

"Mother, really," Grace cut in, and Jack thought her voice sounded a lot like the bell ringing just before the champ went down in the tenth round. "Mr. McCain didn't come here to be given the third degree."

"It's all right," Jack said, amazed that he actually managed to get a word in. But when he said it, he looked at Grace again, and his vocal cords seemed to stop working. Her sparkling blue eyes had some kind of laser-beam force, or electromagnetic grip that just wouldn't let his go. And

they made him shiver with…something that was both ter-
rifying and delicious.

"Jack works for the government, Mitzy. And, uh, I'm
afraid that's all I can say on the subject, if you get my
meaning."

Jack heard the man, but vaguely. Then he heard his wife's
swift intake of breath, followed by her slow and awestruck,
"Ooooh."

Blinking, Jack realized that Harry was making him sound
like some kind of government intelligence expert instead of
a plain ordinary cop, and he wanted to know why. But he
decided to give him a minute on that. It was obvious he was
making a huge effort here, and he may very well have his
reasons.

"Jack…you don't mind if I call you Jack, do you?"
Mitsy Phelps said, reaching out to give Jack's hand a
friendly squeeze. "You simply must come by the house, and
let us thank you properly."

Yeah, right. And you might as well invite a jackass to the
Belmont, Jack thought. Out loud, he said, "Well, I don't,
uh, know if that would be—"

"Please say you will," Grace said.

Jack looked into those eyes. Laser beams. "Okay."

"You can come tomorrow night, for the party! I told you
about the party, didn't I, Jack? For Gracie's graduation from
college?"

Jack looked at her. God, she was gorgeous. "Ph.D.?" he
asked her, hoping like hell for a brief insane moment. Then
realizing it didn't make a damn bit of different how old she
was.

Her smile was bright and dazzling. "Just a B.A."

Jack swallowed hard. That would make her…twenty-two
or so. He was thirty-five. Not that it mattered, because she
was so far out of his league it wasn't even funny.

"Congratulations."

"Thank you. Will you come to my party?"

"I...thought it was tonight."

"It was...but that phone call of Daddy's kind of broke it up. Everyone will be back tomorrow night to pick up where we left off."

Jack looked at Harry again. "You think you're going to be ready for a party so soon?"

"I'm going home, son! Just as soon as my doc gets back in here with the paperwork. It wasn't a heart attack."

"But it soon will be if you don't start taking care of yourself," his wife said.

The older man shook his head. "Why don't you two beauties go and see what's taking Doc Emerson so long? Jack and I need to discuss a few things, anyway."

"Of course, dear." Mitsy went to the bed, leaned close, and kissed her husband's cheek. "Fifteen minutes?"

"I couldn't stand a second longer," he told her.

Grace went and kissed his other cheek. "We'll be right outside if you need us, Daddy," she told him. Then she went to Jack. She paused, staring at him, and then she kissed his cheek as well.

Jack tingled all over, from his cheek to his toes, and he figured there ought to be a law against the feeling, and he ought to be doing time for feeling it.

She left. Jack watched her go, turning around fully, unable to stop himself. The door swung closed behind her, and the deep laughter from the bed made the blood rush into Jack's face.

He turned slowly, eyed the man. "Just what do you think you're doing, telling them all that bull?"

Harry stopped laughing, dabbed at his eyes with the corner of the sheet. "Come here and sit down, son. I have a little proposition for you."

And every warning bell Jack's hard-knock life had built into him started ringing like crazy. But for some reason, he went, and he sat, and he listened.

Chapter 2

Jack sat there, listening to the old man talk, and he kept thinking maybe he ought to call one of the nurses because Harrison Phelps, millionaire, seemed to be delusional. He lay there in the bed, with a white sheet over his barrel-shaped body and his blue-patterned hospital gown, and just talked. He should have looked ridiculous. And his notions should have sounded ridiculous.

So why the hell didn't they?

"My Mitsy's done a hell of a job raising our daughters," Harry said. "A hell of a job. And for the most part, I've been perfectly happy to step aside and let her. Hell, I wanted the best for them, too. And what did I know about manners and clothes and piano lessons, anyway?"

"I'm sure you've both done fine by your kids, Harry. But I really don't have a clue where you're going with this. I just came to take your statement."

"Bullcookies. You came to see if I was all right, and to keep that promise you made me. I may not know about party dresses and manicures, son, but I'll tell you what I do know about.''

''What's that?''

''I know the difference between a polished-up pretty boy and a real man.'' Harry crossed his arms over his big chest, and gave his head a hard nod as if some major decision had just been made.

''That's really fantastic, Harry. But, um, about this statement.''

''That's why I didn't tell Mitsy you were a cop. She'd never let you through the front door if she knew!''

''I'm…not going to need to come to the house, Harry. We can take care of this statement thing right here, and then I'll be on my way.''

''Well, boy, you might not be quite as sharp as I thought you were,'' he said, eyeing Jack and frowning.

''How's that, Harry?'' Jack asked.

''How in the Sam Hill are you planning on seeing my Gracie again if you don't come to the house?''

Jack feinted backward slightly, as if trying to dodge a blow, but the blow seemed to land, anyway. The old bastard hit him right between the eyes. ''Well…I—I wasn't exactly planning to see her again at all.''

''She likes you, Jack. I could see that plain as day. She never once looked at one of those three-piece-suited phonies the way she looked at you.''

Jack lowered his head and tried to remain hard and cynical. Tried not to go soft inside at the very notion—because there was no notion. No chance. No way. ''If your daughter looked at me in any special way, Harry, that was only because you made me sound like some kind of hero who saved her father's life. Don't you think?''

''Nope. That had nothing to do with it.''

Jack licked his lips and lowered his head, trying to figure a graceful way out of whatever scheme the old guy was hatching. But he supposed, deep down, he wasn't trying very hard.

"You liked her, too. Sparks were practically flying across the room between you two! I'm not blind."

Jack's throat was very tight and dry. "I—your daughter is...an attractive young woman."

"So date her."

Closing his eyes slowly, Jack swallowed hard. "*Date* her?"

"Why the hell not?" Harry asked.

"Well, for starters, she's at least ten years younger than me."

"Is that all? I've got fifteen on Mitsy."

"Harry, this just isn't—"

"Hey, I'm not asking you to marry the girl, for Pete's sake! Just... Look, just come to the house tomorrow night for the party. At least do that much. Hell, the family would think it strange if you didn't! And Mitsy's gonna be shoving pretty boys in poor Gracie's face all night long. She ought to have at least one decent, honest-to-goodness man to compare them to."

Jack stared at him. He couldn't talk much. Basically he was speechless. But Harry wasn't.

"Gracie...she hates this kind of thing."

"What kind of thing do I hate, Daddy?" the deep, honey-rich voice of the woman asked from the doorway behind Jack.

He turned around, saw those eyes, electric-blue and almond-shaped, dancing over her father with concern and real love.

"I was trying to convince Jack here to come to your party tomorrow night."

Did those eyes light up just a little bit? Jack couldn't be sure. Hell, maybe it was wishful thinking on his part. If it was, it sure shouldn't have been.

"That would be...wonderful."

"Would it?"

Smiling slightly, she nodded. And Jack was trembling way down deep on some subatomic level. He could feel it, but it didn't show. As if it was his soul shivering in reaction to hers, not just his body.

"Yes. Will you come, Jack?"

Oh, man, when she said his name it was like electrocution. When he caught his breath again he said, "Only if you promise me a dance."

She smiled so suddenly it was like a flash of heat lightning. And her cheeks went warm and pink as she lowered her head. "As many as you want," she whispered, not meeting his eyes.

Jack's stomach was doing weird things, and it seemed as though his hands were in the way. He didn't know what the hell to do with them, so he stuck them into his pockets and felt like a school kid with his first crush. "I, um, I have to go."

"I'll see you tomorrow night, then."

"Yeah. See you then."

Jack left the room, but as he did he glanced back and saw that old man grinning from ear to ear.

He should have stayed. He should have asked the old guy just how far he intended to carry this ruse—this lie he'd dragged Jack into. He should have asked him just what the hell he was supposed to do if he ended up falling head over heels in love with his daughter. What then? She'd have to learn the truth sooner or later, wouldn't she?

He should have asked. But he didn't. Because it seemed like such a small lie...at the time.

"Dammit, Charlie, how could this possibly be happening?" Grace yanked yet another blouse from the closet, eyed it, and then threw it atop the mountain of clothing on the bed.

"How could what be happening?" Charlie sat there as if

she hadn't a care in the world. She wore a pair of black warm-up pants with a white stripe down the side, a New York Liberty warm-up shirt, and a baseball cap. Gracie had the exact same clothes, hidden way in the back of her closet. She and Charlie had bought them together on Charlie's fortieth birthday when Grace had taken her to Madison Square Garden to see a game.

Good old Charlie. She didn't look any older than Gracie did, except for the twenty or so pounds of adulthood she carried around her hips.

"How could it happen that my mother was actually right all these years?" Gracie wailed.

"Oh, yeah. Maybe in her dreams. What was she right about?"

"About me, Charlie. About how being a tomboy and a jock would ruin me, and how no decent man would ever look twice at me unless I acted more like she wanted me to."

Charlie leaned back on the bed, cocking one eyebrow. "And since when did you decide your mom was right about that?"

"You should have told me, you know. You were my nanny! It was your job to tell me."

"I tol' you what I knew, kid. To be yourself. To do what you love best, and to hell with the rest. And I sort of thought it had served you well. I mean, you were the lead scorer on the college basketball team, weren't you? And you did win that kickboxing championship last summer, right? And if I'm not mistaken, that box full of trophies hidden under the bed belongs to you, too, doesn't it?"

"Charlie!" Grace glared at her, putting a finger to her lips. Then she ran to the door and peered out into the hall. She looked up and down, saw no one. Sighing in relief, she closed it again. "You know better than to talk about any of that out loud."

"Jeez, Gracie, you're a grown-up now. Don't you think it's time you came out of the locker room already?"

Sighing, pacing, Gracie shook her head. "Mother was right," she said. "Last night, when I met Jack...I was wearing that stupid getup Mom bought me for the party, those dumb pearls at my throat, and my hair all tamed down and tugged back. And he... Oh, Charlie, the way he looked at me...."

Charlie rolled her eyes. "If you think he liked you like that, you wait till he sees you in your basketball jersey, sinking a three."

"No." She shook her head firmly. "No, he can't see me like that. I mean...he wouldn't have looked twice at me. No one ever has before. It was that whole image Mom made me put on that night. Don't you get it, Charlie?"

"No. I don't get it." Charlie got up, took Gracie's shoulders, turned her, and stared at her. "Your mother doesn't mean to do what she does, Grace."

"Mother doesn't...*do* anything."

"Yeah, she does. She withholds her love until and unless her daughters conform to her idea of perfection. She's done it to you all your life. For crying out loud, they were scouting you for the pros, Gracie! A dream come true! And what did you tell them?"

Gracie told herself that the burning in her eyes and the tightening of her throat had nothing to do with what Charlie was talking about. "Maybe that's not my dream," she said, sniffling.

"I raised you, remember?"

Gracie blinked. "It doesn't matter. I made the decision and that's the end of it."

"Damn right it is. Chances like that don't come along twice in a lifetime."

"Let it go, Charlie."

Charlie sighed, but she let it go. "So what's your point, kid?"

"My point is that I think I met the man of my dreams last night, and he's coming back tonight! I can't wear the same thing, and I suck at putting these kinds of clothes together. I need help, Charlie."

Charlie shook her head slowly. "I may be good at sneaking little girls out for phony etiquette lessons, helping them change into blue jeans, and taking them to the park to play ball, all without getting caught, kid. But I'm not good enough for the level of deception you have in mind."

Grace stared at her, blinking in shock at the judgment in her tone. "It isn't deception!"

"Yes, it is. And the worst kind. What we did, we did so you could be who you really were. But maybe I shouldn't have made it so damn easy for you. Maybe I should have made you stand up to your mother from the start, so you wouldn't be too afraid to do it now."

"I'm not afraid—"

"But even so, at least back then you were being yourself. What you're doing now is pretending to be something you're not. And no good can come of it, Gracie." She headed for the door.

"Charlie, if you don't help me, who will?"

Charlie shrugged. "Swallow your pride, and go talk to your big sister."

Then she was gone.

Gracie fell backward onto the mountain of clothes and closed her eyes. Dammit, she hated to go to Hope for help. All her life, she'd resented her older sister. For being feminine, and petite, and perfect. For being small and beautiful, and for falling into the image of well-mannered heiress almost naturally. Hope had been waved in Gracie's face constantly. "Why can't you be more like your sister, Grace? Why don't you ask your sister to take you shopping next time, Grace? My goodness, your feet are so big, Grace! Not tiny and cute like your sister's…"

"Oooooooooooh!"

There was a tap on the door.

Grace leaped to her feet and yanked it open. "Thank God, you came back, Charlie. I knew you… Oh. It's you."

Hope stood there in a cute pink sheath that perfectly matched her nails, her shoes, and her lips. Her hair was perfect, blond and gorgeous. Her makeup was flawless. Her eyes were big and innocent. "Yeah, it's me. I was listening in. So what's this about you coming out of the closet?"

Grace's eyes widened, then she blinked. "Locker room. Coming out of the locker room. Not the closet. God, Hope, leave it to a little priss like you to think just because I'm a jock I must be gay."

"I didn't say I thought that." Hope came into the room, looked around and frowned in distaste.

Grace scowled and turned away. "You shouldn't be listening to private conversations," she said.

"It's not as if I didn't already know."

Grace spun, wide-eyed.

"What, you think I don't go through your things enough to know what you're up to? What kind of sister do you think I am?" Hope asked.

Grace gaped at her. "You've gone through my things?"

"Monthly." Hope shrugged. "How else was I supposed to know what was going on with you? It's not like you talked to me or anything."

"I—I can't believe you! You rotten little prissy, short, snotty—"

"Yeah, yeah. I've heard it all before." Hope sighed, walked to the window, and stared outside. "I saw the yearbook. And I couldn't believe it was you. So I called the school, got the schedule. I saw the game against U.S.C., you know."

Grace was stunned into silence. She just stood there, staring as her sister turned to stare at her.

"That shot at the buzzer…I couldn't even believe that was my kid sister out there. And the whole crowd was on its feet." She shook her head slowly. "I was...I was so proud of you, Gracie."

Tears welled up and Grace tried to blink them away, but they kept returning. "You...came to the game?"

Sniffling, Hope nodded. "I got a copy of the videotape, too. It's hidden in, um, *my* secret box in the back of the closet. I'd have come to more if I'd known about them. Grace, why didn't you tell me?"

She shrugged. "I don't know. You know how mother is about...everything."

"Yeah. Yeah, I guess I can't even nag you on that one. Shoot, she doesn't know who I really am, either."

At that, Grace had to smile. "Sure she does. You're Miss Perfect."

"Yeah. Miss Perfect." Hope looked sad for just a moment, but chased the look away fast. "At least she's stopped pushing men on me now that you're home and she can target you instead. And speaking of men, what's this I hear about some guy you met last night? Wouldn't be this Jack McCain character Mom's been chirping about all morning, would he?"

Grace's breath left her in a rush. "Oh, Hope, if you could've seen him..." Then she frowned up at her sister. "Oh, no."

"What?"

"Well...if he sees you tonight, at the party, then he's not going to give me a second glance."

"Oh, hell, Grace, you just don't give yourself any credit at all, do you? Or me, for that matter. I wouldn't flirt with a guy you liked! Besides, he's not my type."

"You'll change your mind when you meet him."

"Trust me on this, hon. I won't."

Grace sighed. "I don't know what to wear. How to act, what to say. He's...he's like a cut above every other man I've ever met, Hope. He's like...got this air. Command, you know. Confidence and...a quiet strength. And there's an honesty about him."

"You *do* have it bad, don't you?"

"I just wish I'd paid more attention when Mom was giving us charm lessons and all that garbage."

Hope looked at the pile of clothes on the bed, pawed through some of them, shook her head. "Well, you're not going to find anything here. And you're about a foot too tall for anything I might have."

"I know," Grace moaned.

Hope shrugged. "How about I take you shopping?"

Grace blinked, and dabbed at her eyes. "You...you'd do that?"

"Sure. Look, I've been jealous of you for being stronger, for going out and doing what you really wanted even if you did have to sneak around to do it. I didn't dare even consider..." She gave her head a shake. "It's time we bonded, don't you think? We're adults now. And believe me, I'll be asking you to return the favor before too long. So let's go for it. We'll hit the best shops, and get you a makeover, and some nails, and in between we'll drink café au lait, and practice holding out our little fingers. Okay?"

Smiling broadly, Grace nodded hard. "Okay." She squeezed her sister's hand. "Thank you for this, Hope."

"Hey, don't think it means I approve of your little deception. Just that...I understand why you feel you have to go through with it."

"I can't imagine how."

"Just know this, little sister. Eventually the truth has to come out. You can pick the time, and the place, if you're lucky and don't wait too long. But if you don't, it will. The truth doesn't stay hidden forever. No matter what." She looked very serious, but then she smiled. "Come on. We'll get Daddy to let us take the Jag."

"I'm driving," Grace shouted.

"Not if I beat you to the keys, you aren't!"

They ran into the massive hall, footfalls echoing, laughter ringing.

Chapter 3

So he went to the party, and the first thing he did was spend ten minutes in the curving driveway wondering if he could find a hole in which to hide his car. Hell, his car wasn't bad. He'd been restoring it for most of the time he'd had it, but it still didn't look like much more than a twenty-year-old Mustang in sore need of a paint job.

These people lived in a mansion, surrounded by a tall fence, with automatic gates at the end of a driveway filled with Porsches and Beamers and Benzes. And in the middle of that looping, luxury-lined drive, there was a fountain.

A *fountain*, for crying out loud.

Jack was out of his league, and he damn well knew it. And if he'd had a lick of common sense he'd have kept on driving right around the loop and back out the front gates.

But he didn't. Because he made the mistake of looking up, and he saw this face at an upstairs window. And it was her face. And he couldn't look away, even when the lacy curtain fell in front of her to block her from view.

So he gave in. He let the valet have the Mustang to park

it, and prepared himself for his snooty sneer. But apparently, he was new to snootiness, because the valet said, "Wow, is this a seventy-five?"

"Yeah, that's right."

"Ni-ice," the valet said, drawing out the word.

Jack tossed him the keys, feeling marginally better.

He was an idiot, though. He felt like an idiot. He had gone to one of those swanky menswear shops downtown and bought a new suit. It had cost him almost a week's pay, not to mention that he'd spent his entire lunch hour with some foreign guy's tape measure in his crotch. The suit felt good, though. It looked good, too.

But hell, did he really think he was going to fool anybody? Class wasn't something you put on with a new suit. It was something that was bred into you. Well, it hadn't been bred into Jack. He'd spent his life with the scum of the earth, doing jobs that would make Little Miss Gracie Phelps's skin crawl. She was different. Above all that filth. Clean, and she ought to stay that way. Jack got the feeling that if he touched her he'd leave handprints. Stains.

But he was there, anyway, walking into that swanky mansion, into that crowd of what Harry had called "pretty boys," and waiters with trays full of snacks too pretty to eat and too small to do you much good if you did; and women with their hair sprayed unnaturally stiff and their nails unnaturally long and their waists unnaturally small. They reeked of money—all of them. Jack stood in the midst of them all, eyeing young men who probably had bigger bank rolls at twenty-five than he'd have when he hit seventy. And for a minute or two, he just watched.

The cop in him, he guessed. You served long enough, you started bringing it home. It wasn't just a job, after all. Jack could no more walk into a room without sizing up the occupants first, than he could let a stranger handle his gun. And when he watched, he was not a half-interested observer. He saw it all.

It was only a minute before he thought he understood a little better why Harry didn't want men such as these for his daughter. They had something in their eyes, in their faces— a competitive little mask that could go from gloating gleam to sneaky slant to petulant pout in about two-and-a-half seconds. There was so much petty jealousy floating around the room that the air was damn near green with it. And everyone pretending not to notice. They talked about jobs and cars and housing and golf in roundabout ways meant to assess the other guy's net worth rather than his personality. And they lied. Jack was a cop; he knew how to spot a liar. And he was surrounded by them.

"Jack!"

Harry's shout cut through them all like nobody's business, and when he shouldered through the crowd to clasp Jack's hand, Jack thought the looks flying their way could have sliced through his mamma's meat loaf. Sizing him up. Seeing right through the spit shine he'd slapped on for the party. That was okay. They'd taken far more pains than Jack had, and he saw through them, too.

He should stick the .44 in their smug, superior faces, he thought. Let 'em size *that* up.

Stupid thought.

"How you feeling, Harry?"

"Good as new," he said. "And yourself?"

"Frankly, I never did get your statement yesterday."

"I'll come by tomorrow morning, get that taken care of. But no business talk tonight. Come on, I want you to meet some people."

Well, he dragged Jack on through the crowd, introduced him to some of his big business buddies, telling them Jack was some kind of expert security consultant. Jack didn't have a clue what that was supposed to mean. So he damn near stammered when one of them asked him what, exactly, an expert security consultant did.

But Jack caught himself, saved himself, by simply telling the truth—a solution that he'd found usually worked.

He sipped his drink and leaned on the leather chair's soft back as if he belonged there. "When there's trouble afoot, they call me in. I...assess the situation through several means. Observation, interviewing the involved parties, and often times, gut feelings. Once I've decided on the best course of action, I...and, um, other members of my team, carry it out."

"Fascinating," said one of the men. "Tell me, McCain, is there good money in the field?"

Jack just smiled. "They don't pay me nearly what I'm worth."

The men around him released barks of laughter, and one of them slapped him on the back. "I like you, McCain." His cigar smoke smelled good when it wafted toward Jack's face. A little too good. Probably Cuban. If he'd been one of the shiny-faced little pricks on the other side of the room, Jack would have arrested him on the spot. But he wasn't. He was part of the inner sanctum. Harry's friends. Come to think of it, by dragging Jack into this little alcove where they'd gathered, Harry had made him a part of that clique, as well.

And the pretty boys out in the main part of the room didn't like that one bit.

"Any chance I could convince you to go over security in my corporation?" the smoker asked, puffing some more.

"I don't freelance," Jack said. "And my...employer doesn't think too highly of moonlighting."

"And who would that be? Your employer?"

Again Jack smiled and lowering his voice, leaned forward. The men around him leaned in, too. "I could tell you," Jack said. "But then I'd have to kill you."

Hands slapped knees, and they roared. Hell, fine. Jack had never done standup before, but if they liked it then he figured he could keep going all night. Glancing beyond the magic circle to the pretty boys relegated to the rest of the room, Jack saw looks of pure hatred sent his way. Uh-huh. Jealousy. He was eating it with a spoon.

But a second later all those pouting faces turned to the left and the men in Jack's circle fell silent. Jack knew it was her. He felt her coming close even before he looked. And then he turned around and saw her.

She stood on the stairs for just a moment, before coming the rest of the way down. And Jack thought he couldn't have been more starstruck if it had been Julia Roberts or Cindy Crawford coming down those stairs. She was grace, and poise, and elegance, and purity. And her dress...man, what a dress. As white as her soul, and as tight as Jack's throat. Halter neck, just hinting at the shadowy well between her breasts. It hugged her figure all the way down to the slit that revealed teasing glimpses of her endlessly long legs. Her hair was piled up. Diamonds dangled from her ears, and her toes showed in those white shoes with their spiky high heels.

She came down the stairs, and started right toward Jack. He almost smiled as he watched her approaching, and he wondered just what the hell this was that was hitting him so hard and so fast.

Then the pretty boys crowded in, blocking her from Jack's view. And she was smiling at them, answering their silly questions, nodding and looking interested in all they had to say, which was a lot. One brought her a drink and tried putting a possessive hand on her shoulder. Suddenly Jack felt like an intruder.

Then she looked past them, caught his eye, and sent him a message. One he read so easily that for a minute, he didn't move. Just stood there, thinking that was amazing. He and JW had been partners for five years before they'd been able to do that sort of thing—send an entire message with a single look. It shouldn't be possible with someone he'd just met, Jack thought.

"Excuse me," he said to the Old Boy network surrounding him. Then he went over there, shouldered his way through the handsome, hair-gel set of younger, richer, better-looking men who sent him nasty looks, and acted as if he were exhibiting the height of mannerlessness—but didn't shove back.

"Hello again, Grace," Jack said when he got to where she stood. "The way I remember it, you promised me a dance."

She smiled, shoved the drink she held into some blond beach boy's hand, and put her hand in Jack's. The others faded back, all but gaping as he pulled her close. He put a hand on her waist, she slipped hers around his neck, and moved against him, and they managed to dance themselves away from the hopeful crowd of phonies.

"Thank you," she whispered.

"No, thank *you.*"

"You rescued my father, and now you rescued me."

"You were doing fine. Could have had them all on their knees with a word."

She shook her head. "Oh, God, no. Not in a million years, Jack."

"What, you didn't see the way they were all drooling over you?"

Lowering her chin so he couldn't see her eyes, she sighed. "I've never been the sort of girl men do much drooling over."

"No?" She could have fooled him, he thought. He was drooling plenty.

"No."

"Well, you are tonight. You, um…you look…incredible."

"Really?" She seemed genuinely surprised, not fishing for compliments.

"Oh, yeah. How can you not know that? What, you don't have mirrors in this house?"

She smelled good. She *felt* good against him, just lightly touching, brushing, teasing but totally innocent.

They moved around, and other people began dancing, too. But when the dance ended, she didn't step out of Jack's arms. She seemed content to stay where she was.

"Gracie?"

"Hmm?"

He smiled, he couldn't help it. "Hon, our song's over. And there are about fifty guys waiting in line for the next dance."

Right on cue, some reed-thin, peach-fuzz-faced frat boy tapped Jack on the shoulder. "Don't forget, Gracie, you promised me a dance, too."

Gracie smiled at him, took a step, and then stumbled against Jack's chest. An event that sent bolts of heat sizzling through him and startled him at the same time. "Ow!"

Jack closed his hands on Grace's shoulders to hold her up and searched her face. "You okay?"

"Oh, darn," she said. "My ankle! Not tonight of all nights!" Several heads turned in their direction as Jack's innocent dance partner leaned on him, holding up one foot. "I'm sorry, Greg," she told the punk. "I was so looking forward to that dance, too." Then she looked at Jack again, putting her back to the guy as if he'd been dismissed and no longer existed. "Help me to a chair, would you, Jack?"

People crowded closer, one of them handing Grace an ice pack, but Jack barely saw them. He couldn't take his eyes off Grace, and he saw the playful gleam lingering in hers.

That might have been the moment he fell in love. Right then. That playful little prank that seemed so out of character. He scooped her right up off her feet, carried her to a chair, and then sat in the one beside her. She propped her injured ankle across his legs, and asked him to hold an ice pack on it for her.

Of course, he happily obliged.

Eventually, wounded-looking suitors faded away and

stopped with their wimpy questions. And when Jack could speak for her ears alone, he said, "So, you want to tell me what this was all about?"

"I didn't want to dance with any of them, Jack. What would have been the point?"

His throat went dry, and a little flame of panic—and something else—started licking at his belly.

Jack let the ice pack slide to the floor. The only thing on her cool wet skin now was his hand, rubbing slowly, massaging a nonexistent injury. He wanted to slide off her shoe and caress her foot, her toes. He wanted to run his hand further up her leg, feel the curve of her calf and the power of her thigh. And he thought she knew it. The way her eyes clung to his, and the dancing heat he saw in those blue depths—the little catch in her breathing told him as much.

He didn't know how long they'd been sitting there when she said, "We've got some awfully impressive gardens out back." And her voice was the barest whisper.

"I'd dearly love to go out there and see them," Jack said, his voice equally raspy.

She looked a little afraid but mostly excited as she lowered her foot to the floor, got to her feet and, taking Jack's hand, limped to the patio doors.

Chapter 4

Jack walked with her onto the patio, where some of the party guests milled around, sipping drinks from cut-crystal glasses. Grace leaned on him, but she was the one leading the way. They moved slowly to the farthest corner from the house, and down the steps to the ground below. The beautiful people glanced their way, but no one made comment. This was the golden child of Harrison Phelps and one of the men from his group of chosen ones. At least, that must be how it appeared to them. So what could they say?

They took a path lined in white gravel, and the moment they were out of sight, Grace's mysterious limp vanished. She stopped leaning on him and walked easily, sending him a mischievous smile.

"You never fooled me for a minute, you know," he said, his voice low, his body at odds with his mind. Hell, he knew she was too good for any kind of fling, and he also knew anything more was impossible. She wasn't cut out to be a cop's wife. Hell, they'd had seminars on this kind of stuff. The divorce rate, the depression rate, the suicide rate. But

Jack didn't need seminars. His father had been a cop. And he'd watched the stress and the strain of that reality slowly wear away at his mother, making her old, making her hard long before her time. And his mother had been tough. Strong, cut from burlap...not silk, like Grace Phelps.

Yet, here was Grace, looking up at him with eyes bluer than the sky...waiting for him to...kiss her.

Yeah. That was it, no doubt. She'd stopped walking, and was leaning now with her back against a flowering apple tree, all in blossom. The smell of the flowers was intoxicating and heavy and sweet. Little paper petals of white with a touch of pink tinting them at the edges. Growing in bunches, and raining down like confetti every time one of them moved.

And Jack thought for the thousandth time that he was only human. So he leaned in, and he kissed her. She slid her arms around his neck, and she kissed him back. And he fought with everything in him to keep it sweet and tender. No tongue, no grinding of hips, though damn, how he wanted to add those elements. She wasn't like that, though. She was crystal glasses and he was paper cups. She was as pristine and delicate as one of the petals that drifted to the ground around them. Still, her body pressed to his, and his to hers, and his arms held her tight, and he kissed her long and slow amid a shower of apple blossom petals.

And it was just like magic.

A month later Jack sat in the Five-Alarm Diner on Main, across from his partner of more than a decade, and he broke the news.

"What do you mean, you're quitting?" JW sat there looking at him as if he'd grown a second head.

"Look, I can't start out married life with a lie this big hanging between us. I just can't."

"No, you're right. You can't. So tell her, Einstein. Tell her you're a cop."

Jack shook his head slowly. "She couldn't handle it."

"I think you're underestimating her."

"Look, what makes you think I want to be a cop all my life, anyway? Huh?" He averted his eyes when he said it. "The way Harry Phelps has things set up, I can practically pick a job and name the salary."

JW sipped his coffee, then set the cup carefully in its saucer. He ran a hand over his widening bald spot and the thick dark hair that surrounded it like a horseshoe. He sighed. "You don't want to work for your father-in-law, Jack. Believe me, it's not—"

"I wouldn't be working for my father-in-law. He has friends. Tons of them. They like me."

"You mean, they like the guy they *think* is you. Jack McCain, security consultant, the guy with the expensive suits and shiny shoes that are costing you every bit of your paycheck. They don't even know the real Jack McCain, the cop who spends ten hours a day with the scum of the earth." JW shook his head. "And come to think of it, neither does your bride-to-be."

Jack faced him slowly. "That's right. And she never will."

"You're making a mistake, Jack."

"She's worth it, JW. I don't want this garbage touching her. I've seen what it can do. My mother—" He bit his lip, cut himself off. "I just don't. You understand?"

JW nodded. Sighed heavily, rolled his eyes, but nodded.

"I knew I could count on you."

"Yeah. You always could."

"I'll, uh, be needing a best man."

JW lifted his head. "Do I have to use a pseudonym?"

"Knock it off."

"So how long before I get the incomparable joy of breaking in a new partner, buddy?"

Jack licked his lips. This had been the toughest conversation of his life. But at least this part of it wasn't going to feel like a betrayal. "Not until we bag, tag and deliver that scurvy little dealer, JW. I won't bail on you in the middle of a case this big."

Jack could almost see his partner slump a little bit as the air left his lungs. Relief. But then JW frowned. "How the hell you gonna manage that? The wedding's in two weeks!"

"Doesn't matter. As much as I hate to lie to Grace…it would be worse to walk out in the middle of this. No. I'll stay on until we wrap it."

Jack had been having nightmares. Of course he hadn't told anyone. Who could he tell, anyway? Not Grace; she didn't know the truth. And certainly not JW, since he was the one getting blown away by some punk who thought himself a kingpin in the recurring dream that had been haunting Jack since he'd made this decision.

He didn't know if the dream meant anything. He only knew he couldn't walk out on his partner in the middle of a case this volatile, because it could happen. And Jack couldn't live with that.

"What do you mean, you're quitting?"

Charlie sat on the foot of Gracie's bed, gaping at her. Hope sat on the far edge, and Grace was curled at the head, pillows pulled around her as if she needed something to cling to.

"He is marrying a delicate, society miss, not a jock who spends way too much time at a smelly gym on the bad side of town, Charlie." Grace sighed, lowering her head. "Besides, all that stuff was…childish. I'm not a kid anymore. I'm a grown-up. I'm going to be a wife…and a mother, eventually. I mean, how many mothers do you know with black belts, anyway?"

"Not nearly enough," Charlie said.

"But…but Grace, what about basketball?" Hope asked.

Grace shrugged at her sister. "What about it? I played on a college team. College is over. It's not even an issue."

"Well, of course it's an issue. Grace, you're *good*. You love the sport too much to just…just let it go. What about those kids, huh?"

"What kids?" Then Grace's brows went up. "You mean, those girls from the gym? How the hell do you know about them, Hope?"

Hope looked guilty. "One of them called for you yesterday while you were out. And we…talked."

Grace got to her feet, taking a pillow with her and flinging it to the floor. "How did those kids get this number? Good grief, what if Mom had answered the phone?"

Charlie picked up the pillow, plumped it, and settled it back on the bed. "You need to stop being so afraid of what your mother might think, Grace. You gotta be honest. Those girls were starting to depend on you."

"I didn't ask for that," Grace said, battling a surge of guilt. "I was just trying to be nice, giving them some pointers when they showed up at the gym."

"Yeah, and then they started showing up three times a week, same as you, just like clockwork. And you started 'giving them pointers' for an hour before you went about your business every single time."

"So?"

"So, you were coaching them, Grace. Maybe it wasn't official, and maybe you were never asked, but that's what you were doing. And you know it, and I know it."

Lowering her head, Grace closed her eyes. "Maybe…I can keep going down there a couple of times a week…for the girls."

Hope smiled. "You should, Grace. I don't think those kids have much else to look forward to."

"Yeah, and I think you were enjoying it as much as they were," Charlie put in.

Grace nodded. "Yeah, I guess I was. Besides, Jack doesn't have to know about it."

Hope looked at Charlie and rolled her eyes.

"Stop it," Grace said. "You guys just aren't getting it, are you? I love this man. I *love him*."

"So you love him! So what? Does that mean you have to lie to him?" Charlie demanded.

"I am not lying to him!"

"You are so!" Charlie snapped.

"Grace, she's right," Hope whispered, putting her soft, perfectly manicured hand over Grace's. "You can't start out married life pretending to be something you're not."

"That's just it. I'm not pretending. I'm...I'm changing." Grace paced the room slowly, turned and paced back. "I can be the kind of woman Jack thinks I am. The kind he fell in love with. I know I can. And it'll be fine. I promise you guys, it'll be just fine."

Charlie sighed, lowering her head and shaking it slowly. "Where did I go wrong?" she muttered.

"I blame myself," Hope said.

"Knock it off, you two. We've got tons more to do than discuss my retirement from sports, at the moment. I'm getting married in two weeks."

Hope sighed, ignoring her sister's attempt to change the subject. "He'd love you, anyway, you know. That's what you're afraid of, isn't it? That he wouldn't?"

Grace stared at her sister for a long moment, struck by how hard she'd hit the mark. Their mother's love had always been conditional. Be what she wanted, act the way she wanted, do what she expected, and you would be showered in her love. Yet always, always, both girls had kept parts of themselves hidden away, secret, out of fear they would lose that love if they revealed themselves to be less than the image their mother demanded. Grace had led a double life, and she sensed Hope, too, was hiding more than anyone knew.

But understanding why she felt the way she did certainly did nothing to change the feeling or make it go away. Jack had fallen in love with the belle of the ball that night. With the elegance and grace she'd had to practice for hours to pull off with any degree of success. He was always telling her how sweet she was, how delicate, and pure. Those were the qualities he loved in her. And she loved him so much...he was the only man she'd ever felt this way about.

No. She couldn't risk everything, not now.

She wouldn't.

Two weeks later she stood near the swan pond on the grounds of her parents' home and vowed to love, honor and respect the man who'd stolen her heart. And he promised to do the same in return. When he kissed her, her heart melted and her blood warmed.

And it was all pretty much downhill from there.

Chapter 5

Grace had bought a naughty black teddy, all but transparent, with garters and lace and a built-in push-up bra—and a pair of high-heeled slippers with fuzzy tufts of black at the toes. She had even packed them.

But she couldn't wear them. Oh, she might fantasize about slinking across the hotel room while Jack's eyeballs popped. But he wasn't like that.

He was…above that kind of carnal decadence. It must have been bred out of him, or trained out of him, but either way, he was above it. A gentleman. His every touch, every kiss, had always been gentle, respectful, careful.

And he thought she was some kind of an angel.

So, with a sigh of reluctance and a nagging feeling in the pit of her stomach, Grace stuffed the black lace back into the very bottom of her suitcase, and she put on the long, white satin nightgown instead. It was sexy, too, but in a clean, virginal-bride sort of way.

She was no virgin bride. He was going to know that, but he would be too much of a gentleman to ask about it.

She almost wished he would. A spark of jealousy, a burst of anger, would reassure her somehow. Because though she loved him, and she knew he loved her, there seemed to have been something missing in their relationship so far.

Passion.

Jack tapped on the bathroom door. "Are you all right in there, Grace?"

Closing her eyes, she shook away her foolish notions. It was wedding-night jitters and nothing more. "Fine, darling. I'll be right out."

She looked one last time at the suitcase that held her hidden fantasies tucked away in the bottom. Then she closed the lid with a decisive click and, turning, opened the door.

Jack smiled gently when she did. His eyes skimmed lower, to her feet, and up again, and he said, "You look like an angel." With one hand, he stroked her outer arm, shoulder to wrist. "Almost too beautiful to touch."

Not exactly the reaction she'd been hoping for.

They had never made love before. Jack had never even suggested it, but Grace had seen fleeting, all-too-brief glimpses of the fire buried deep inside him once or twice. When their kisses had become heated, when she'd forgotten for an instant the role she was supposed to be playing. She'd told herself he was holding his passion inside because he was a gentleman and because he respected her enough to want to wait until they were married. She'd told herself it would be loosed tonight. That his restraint, so obvious she could feel it tugging at him every time they touched, would fall away. That he would take her to the very heights of ecstasy tonight.

He didn't.

Oh, it was tender, their lovemaking. Tender, and gentle, and slow. More like intimate snuggling, she thought, than actual sex. She felt him trembling as he moved on top of her, his shoulders virtually quivering like a volcano of passion bubbling beneath the surface, waiting to erupt. But it didn't. He held her as carefully as if she were a fragile porcelain treasure, and when he finally stopped, she was unsure whether he'd climaxed or not. She…hadn't even come close.

He kissed her cheek, rolled off her, and held her lightly. "I didn't hurt you, did I?" he asked.

Hurt her? He'd barely touched her. "No, of course not."

"Good. You're…okay, then?"

"I'm fine." If feeling like clawing her way up the wall to the ceiling and shrieking like a frustrated tomcat could be called fine, that is.

"Good." He rolled over, snagging a robe off the bed. "I'm gonna run you a nice hot bath, then. And then we'll go out. Do something special. Okay?"

"Sure." She had thought that what they had been doing was something special. But it hadn't turned out that way.

Maybe, Jack thought, this had been a mistake. Hell, their courtship had been torture, but the actual marriage turned out to be far worse. He tried his damnedest to be the man his beautiful young wife thought he was. All well-bred and gentle. When deep down, he'd wanted to throw her on the bed that night, tear that pristine dress off her and ravish her from her head to her toes. He'd been holding back for so long—because that was what a girl like Grace would expect. Restraint. Decency.

Not making love to her had been bad enough. But how could he have known that actually doing it would be so much worse? His desire for the woman had been building ever since he'd first set eyes on her. No, desire wasn't even the right word. It was more than that. So much more. It was carnal. It was hunger. It was pure undiluted lust. If he had let it loose…hell, she'd have packed up and gone home before morning. So Jack had bound himself up in chains of restraint. He'd held back. He'd vented the tiniest fragment of what had been building inside him. And all it had done was make him want her even more.

He thought that within six months, he would probably explode from the pressure within. Or go insane.

Ah, but looking at her, looking into those innocent eyes of hers that night after he'd made love to her for the first time, he'd realized that even though he'd held himself in fierce check, the sex act had traumatized her a bit. She'd looked confused, bewildered, upset. Just think how much worse it might have been.

He was an animal. He felt guilty for having touched her at all. God knew he wasn't worthy.

That night, their wedding night, had pretty much set the pattern of intimacy between them. They'd settled into a routine after the honeymoon. Sex was infrequent—because it was a hell of a lot easier for Jack to not have her at all, than to have her while fighting his own feelings and holding himself back.

And there was more, of course. There was Jack's work. He and JW were closing in on the cocaine supplier they had been after for so many months. But they still hadn't caught him. Jack couldn't leave his job to take one of the fabulous ones he'd been offered for five times the money. Not until he nailed this guy. But lying to Grace was wearing on him. Every day, she would ask him something about his work, and every day he would tell a half-truth or skirt the question.

The combination of not wanting to suffer the fiery temptation of being near her, of hating to have to look into her blue eyes and lie to her, and of wanting this damn case finished so he would no longer have to, resulted in a lot of late nights. Worked weekends. Missed dinners. And while Grace said she understood…Jack rather doubted it.

But she was all right. She had her family. She had the house—oh, hell, the house. A wedding gift from Harry and Mitsy. Jack had to give Harry credit, though. The old man had taken Jack's taste into account. It wasn't a sprawling mansion enclosed in a fence. Instead, it was a redwood-and-glass modified A-frame, sitting on its own fifty acres on the shore of Looking Glass Lake. Thirty minutes from the city, and perfect. Jack had loved it on sight, but he couldn't even think about the price tag without feeling like the world's biggest moocher. When he mentioned that to Harry in a rare private moment, his father-in-law's reply had been predictable, if not entirely accurate.

"You saved my life, son. All I gave you was a house. We're not even close to being square."

He was wrong, though. Dead wrong. Harry had given Jack his daughter, and that was one gem Jack knew he couldn't earn in a dozen lifetimes. Not if he saved a thousand lives.

Things should have been unbelievably good.

So why weren't they?

Jack began to suspect that maybe his precious Grace was beginning to see through him. To catch glimpses of the low-class fraud inside. He didn't know how. He'd been so careful. He'd been studying things like etiquette and wines. All his old clothes were at the apartment, which was still his for a year no matter what, according to the lease, but he hadn't told Gracie that. He didn't want her seeing the way he used to live.

Sometimes after work, Jack and JW would head over there for a couple of beers and a hand or two of poker. Watch some sports on TV. Then Jack would change into one of his new suits, and dust off his phony-baloney brief-case, and head home in the fancy new car that had cost a third of his retirement account. All his other savings had gone for the rings on his wife's finger, because nothing but the best was good enough for Grace.

After a very short while, though, it seemed to Jack that Grace would look at him real close when he came home late. As if she suspected the truth.

It was eating at him. Damn, if he could just nail that dealer and get it over with. Then he could move on with his new life, in a job he wouldn't have to lie to his wife about.

Maybe he should just tell her.

He loved her. And he knew she loved him, and the rational part of his mind really didn't believe she would stop loving him if he told her the truth. The irrational part did, but that was a whole other ball game. The reasons he gave himself for continuing this grand deception were that she was too good and too fragile. It would scare her to death, for one thing, and if she got too close, it would disgust her. Seeing her husband grilling an addict while he threw up on his shoes. Watching her husband don his homeless bum costume and sit between trash cans on surveillance. Seeing the kind of scum he had to deal with day in and day out. The stress. The worry. The constant fear.

Maybe part of it was selfishness, too. To Jack, Grace was like a haven. For so long he'd been immersed in filth. She had pulled him out of that. When he showered and put that suit on at the end of the day, it was just like washing away the slime. He never used to feel that way. He used to go home feeling as if it were clinging to him. Like a dark cloud or an oily film that he couldn't scrub off.

Not now. Now he washed it away, and went home to a clean, nice place, with an angel waiting for him. And from the minute he set foot there, he never thought about work again until he headed out the next morning. Never once. So in a way, he guessed he was enjoying the game he was playing with his wife.

He should have known better. He really should.

After all, he was practically living two lives at once. And the wounded, worried look in Grace's eyes seemed to be getting more and more pronounced all the time.

It had to end. Soon.

Late one night the phone rang, and for the first time Jack's real world, the dirty, smelly, low-down one in which he lived every day, invaded his make-believe world—the one in which he took refuge every night.

Jack rolled over in the king-size bed, glancing at the huge

window that overlooked the lake and seeing the stars dotting the sky beyond it. Frowning, he picked up the phone and when he heard JW's voice, he looked at Grace fast. She seemed to be sound asleep. He whispered, "God, why are you calling me here?"

"It's too big to wait, pal."

Jack sighed, glancing again at his sleeping wife. "I'll call you right back," he said, and hung up. Then he tiptoed out of the bedroom, closed the door quietly behind him, and went down the open stairway to return his partner's call from the living room below.

Chapter 6

"I knew it!" Gracie paced the length of her living room again and again, crossing in front of the huge fireplace she loved and barely looking at it. "I mean—I didn't know it. I knew there was...*something*. I just thought it would be something else." Her throat went tight, and her eyes burned. "Oh, God, anything else."

"Grace, honey, you aren't making any sense." Hope stepped into her path with a cup of tea in her hands, thrusting it under Grace's nose. "Settle down, sip this, and tell me again."

"She told you twice already, Hope." Charlie was on the sofa, sock feet propped on the coffee table, watching the proceedings with an I-told-you-so look on her face. "He got a midnight phone call from his lover and off he went to meet her."

Grace stopped pacing and glared at Charlie. "We can't be sure who was on the other end of that phone call!"

"Hey, I'm just repeating what you said!" Then she looked around. "You got any chips or anything?"

"Now do you see how foolish you sounded?" Hope asked.

Grace looked down at the cup of tea her sister still clasped. "It was just so odd. The way he sneaked away and called back. The way he whispered into the phone so I could barely hear what he was saying, even though I came halfway down the stairs to try to hear him."

"Yeah," Charlie said. "Trusting soul that you are. Why didn't you just pick up the phone upstairs?"

"Ah, the wiring is messed up. When you pick up an extension the call gets cut off. It's a pain in the..." Then she stopped speaking. "He wrote something down."

Charlie's brows arched, and she turned her head, glancing at the notepad beside the phone. Hope shook her head in disapproval as Grace went to snatch it up. She held the pad this way and that, squinting at it. "He took the top sheet, but I can almost—"

"Give me that," Charlie said, coming to her feet and taking the pad. She grabbed a pencil and went back to her seat to begin coloring the entire sheet.

"Grace, this is just silly. You love Jack. And you know he's crazy about you. Why would you be so suspicious of him the very first time anything the least bit odd happens?"

Grace lowered her gaze and her sister gasped. "You mean...it's not the first time?"

Grace shook her head. "He's...he's so secretive, Hope. He comes home late and...sometimes I can smell alchohol on his breath. He gets all...odd when I ask him about his work. And...and, well, there's more."

"What more?" Hope gripped Grace's shoulders, and pushed her gently into a rocking chair. "Tell me."

Grace shrugged, studying her fingernails, which she'd been chewing mercilessly. "Well...it's...the sex." She peeked up to see her sister's cheeks turning pink. "Nothing to blush about, Hope. Believe me. I mean, it hardly ever happens, and when it does, it's like...well...it's like it didn't.''

"I...don't follow," Hope said.

"I do," Charlie called. "No fireworks, no screaming of names. You getting the picture yet, Hope?"

Hope turned her head away from them both, clearly embarrassed. "That doesn't mean he's cheating."

"One way to find out," Charlie said. She held the notepad up, its front all colored in pencil gray, with white outlines standing out. An address. "You wanna put an end to this, Gracie? Find out what's really going on?"

"She can't!" Hope said. "She wouldn't!"

Grace stepped forward, taking the pad from Charlie's hand. "Yes, she would."

"Oh, Grace, don't do this. Just wait until Jack comes home and ask him to tell you what he's been keeping from you. And while you're at it, you might think about telling him all the things you've been keeping from him, too. The black belt, the college basketball, the M.V.P. awards, the tournament trophies, the W.N.B.A. scout... The fact that your entire wardrobe at college consisted of jeans, T-shirts, jerseys and that white pajama getup you wear for kickboxing.''

"It's called a *gi*, and you know it."

"Tell your husband the truth. He'll return the favor and all will be well," Hope went on. "Don't spy on him. He'll resent it."

"Well, maybe I resent having to!" Grace huffed.

Hope sent an exasperated look at Charlie, who only shrugged and said, "I'm in."

"I'm going alone," Grace said.

"In your dreams," Charlie replied. "Go get dressed. And forget the pretty designer skirts and jackets, honey. This is down-and-dirty time—and high time the real Gracie Phelps stepped out of the closet. Maybe if Jack knew his wife was fully capable of kicking his tail all the way home, he wouldn't be quite so...adventurous.''

Grace made a face, but obeyed, trotting up the stairs to the bedroom. She opened her closet and eyed the wardrobe that had become her daily costume—and *costume* was the right word for it.

Dammit, she'd tried. She'd tried to be everything she thought Jack wanted her to be. Why hadn't it been enough? Tears burned in her eyes as she recalled his conversation on the phone. First the part about not calling him here— God, could he have *been* more obvious? Then the bits and pieces she'd heard downstairs. Oh, she hadn't been able to make out much, but she'd seen his face, caught the edge to his voice. The passion in it. The excitement.

Why couldn't he be that way with her?

Swallowing hard, she slid the closet door closed, brushed the tears away. Charlie was right. It was time to stop pretending for him. It wasn't enough. If she were going to lose her husband...well, hell, at least she needed to have herself to fall back on. Not the make-believe Grace she'd tried to become. But the real Grace.

And if she were going to fight for her marriage...well, then she'd need her even more.

She dropped to her knees and hauled the box out from under the bed, where she kept the clothes she used to live in, and now only wore for those days when she slipped out of the house to spend time with a bunch of twelve-year-old girls who wanted to play basketball. Some of them had some real potential, too. Pawing through the box, Grace found her favorite warm-up suit, and threw it on, with a snug black tank top underneath. She left the jacket undone, and pulled on a pair of socks and Nikes. She was ready. No makeup, no hair-fussing. This was it.

She got her keys off the dresser and headed downstairs. "Let's go."

* * *

Jack was just so damned relieved that it would be over soon! After tonight, their up-and-coming friendly neighborhood drug supplier would be cooling his heels behind bars and Jack would be able to get on with his life.

When JW had called to tell him that their favorite snitch had given him the lowdown on a meeting between the nameless drug lord and his henchmen, Jack had damned near shouted for joy. He'd had to bite his lip to keep from doing just that, waking Grace, and ruining everything. Over. It would be over.

He could hardly believe it.

He'd left the house in the best mood he'd been in since the day he'd asked Grace to be his wife and heard her whispered "yes."

But by the time he got to the address JW had given him, he was losing that mood considerably. He didn't like it. Didn't like it at all.

He was unfamiliar with the area. It was outside the city. Way out. An exit off the thruway, that led to not much more than the biggest swamp in the State of New York, or at least, the biggest one Jack knew of. Montezuma was real picturesque if you liked cattails and rushes and the occasional wood duck, Canada goose or blue heron.

It was also a favorite dumping ground...and that wasn't referring to your typical garbage, either. Bodies were routinely found...more often *not* found...in the brackish muck of Montezuma.

Anyway, the address was that of a tumbledown house along the edge of the slime-bottomed wetlands. One story, drooping eaves, brown shingles for siding, and gaping places with none at all; a mouth with missing teeth.

Not a light from inside the place, either.

Jack drove on by the first time, nice and slow, but steady. Not to give himself away, although the unlikelihood of anyone just happening to be on a dirt road that skirted a swamp at midnight on a Tuesday was probably not going to be lost on anyone with anything to hide.

Hell.

He went a quarter mile farther, then pulled off onto a hard bit of ground along the roadside. And when he did, he spotted JW's car already there, waiting.

JW got out. Jack did, too. "Did you see the place?" he asked, looking about the way Jack felt. Jittery, not at ease. Something wasn't right here. It was chilly for early summer, and even so, JW had sweat beading on his upper lip. And his thick black hair looked as if he'd been running his hands through it too much. It was usually neat, unless he was playing an untidy role.

"I saw it," Jack said. "I didn't like it."

"Me neither." JW looked at the patch of solid ground on which they had parked and were now standing. It wasn't a natural occurrence. It had been built here. "What do you suppose this is for?"

Jack shrugged, looking at the dark water with its green foam border lapping at the edge. "A boat launch?"

"Illegal to put boats in. It's a wildlife refuge," JW pointed out.

"Hey, the DEC boys must have to patrol it now and then. Check on their duckies and what not." Jack shrugged. "And the real cops, when they're looking for bodies."

"I suppose."

"You think we're being set up?" Jack asked him point-blank.

JW took a deep breath, bit his lip. "One way to find out."

He took out his gun, checked it, put it back. "You wearing armor?"

Jack nodded, having taken the Kevlar vest out of hiding and putting it on before he'd left the house. "You bet I am. You?"

"Hell, I sleep in it." JW sent Jack a wink. "Let's go."

It was dark, and the walk back to the little house seemed

longer than it was. It always did. Jack could barely see the dirt road under his feet. They couldn't walk beyond the tree-line, because that would have put them in the muck up to their knees, so they had to walk the road. Right in plain sight. Except there was no moon and the night was as thick as tar. That might work to their advantage.

Or not.

After all, if the bad guys knew they were coming, they could be sitting still. Listening. Waiting. Ready to open fire the minute Jack or JW snapped a twig or rolled a pebble. Jack could almost feel their damned sights on him.

The house came into view.

It wasn't dark anymore, and it wasn't silent. There were voices floating from it now. And the light from the shack's open door spilled into the driveway to illuminate the car that sat there.

It was Grace's car.

"What in the—"

Then Jack saw her. And her sister, and that lunatic Charlie, whom Jack secretly thought the world of, all standing in the open doorway chatting casually with whatever underworld kingpin stood on the other side.

"I don't understand," he heard Grace say as he edged closer. "This was the address. I'm sure of it."

Jack bent low, and kept going, JW right behind him. Vaguely he thought Grace looked odd…different, and not her usual self. But he didn't follow that thought. He was more concerned with getting her the hell out of harm's way.

The form in the doorway—Jack couldn't see him well, with the light behind him—stepped aside. "Come on in, ladies. It's cold out there. Maybe we can figure this out."

Hope walked in. The rest all happened at once. Jack lunged forward. His foot hit a rock that went skittering. JW grabbed Jack's arm and jerked him downward. Charlie walked through the door behind Hope, and the jerk in the doorway snapped his head toward the sound Jack had inadvertently made. Looking.

"Wait," JW growled in Jack's ear.

"That's my wife, dammit—"

But the criminal was speaking again, placing himself squarely in front of Grace, not to block her entry as it appeared—but to shield himself, should Jack decide to blow him away. "You said your husband's name is…?"

"McCain," she told him. "Jack McCain."

"Well, let's find him for you, shall we?" And in the blink of an eye, he'd spun Grace around, pulled her back flat to his chest, and had a gun to her head. Jack heard a scream from inside—Hope, he thought, but she went silent fast. No doubt some other goon in there had his gun on her and Charlie, as well.

"Jack McCain!" the criminal called. "Your pretty wife is here. So, uh, if you're out there, and I'm assuming you are, I suggest you step into the light. Otherwise…" He looked at the gun, adjusted the barrel against her temple.

Jack moved.

JW jerked him back so hard he almost fell on top of him. "What the hell is the matter with you, Jack? You step out there, he's gonna blow your head off!"

"He's got Grace," Jack whispered. "My God, she's so fragile. She must be terrified. She's—"

"Mister," Grace said, interrupting his harsh whisper. She said it loudly. "I'd like to say something to my two companions before you pull that trigger, if that's okay."

God, she looked so…well, scared wasn't exactly the word. As a matter of fact, she looked worried, but more…calculating. And what the hell was she wearing? A warm-up suit? Where did she get that?

"You go ahead, darling. You're very brave, you know."

"Charlie, Hope? Can you hear me?"

She must have heard an answer. Jack didn't, but she went

on. "Don't panic, okay? I'll get you out of here in a minute or two."

Jack's brows pulled together. The man holding her looked down at her quickly. At that moment Jack's timid, quiet, fragile wife, drove her elbow backward into the man's rib cage, while at the same time knocking the gun away from her head with the other hand, gripping his arm as she did so and neatly flipping him right over her shoulders.

Jack ran forward, his gun in his hand. The jerk landed hard on his back, but he still had his gun, and he pointed it at Grace. Jack lifted his at the same time. But Grace scissor-kicked him, first one foot then the other, connecting with an impact that Jack couldn't believe. The first foot sent the gun sailing, and the second smashed into his chin so hard it should have broken his neck. He was out cold before Jack heard the splash of his gun landing in the swamp water.

Grace spun and headed back for the house. A gun barrel poked out a broken window, and Jack barely caught up to her in time to holster his gun and tackle her from behind. They hit the ground as the shot went off. Jack's wife flipped him off her like a dog flicking off a flea. He hit the ground beside her. She rolled onto her back and started to sit up, and Jack pounced on top of her again, grabbed her wrists, and held her flat. "Stay down, dammit!"

Grace's eyes went wide, and she stared at him. "Jack? My God, Jack, what are you doing here?"

"What *am I* doing here? Jeez, Grace, don't you think that's kind of a screwed-up question?"

Another shot exploded from inside the house, and Jack reached for his gun, pulled it out and fired one off over top of the house. The gun in the window withdrew.

"Stop!" Grace said. "Hope and Charlie are in there!"

"What do you think, I'm an idiot? That was cover fire."

"What the hell are you doing with a gun?" she demanded.

"Where the hell did you learn to beat the hell out of an armed felon?" Jack shot back.

They lay there, blinking at each other in the darkness. And Jack realized for the first time that she'd been keeping as much from him as he had from her. And it stung, dammit. It hurt. He wanted to be furious with her, but how the hell could he, when he'd done the same damned thing?

He gave his head a shake. None of it mattered at the moment. What mattered was getting her out of the line of fire, keeping her safe. Not the puzzles in his head or the sudden feeling that he'd just been harshly slapped out of a pleasant but nonsensical dream. And certainly not the way her body felt, long and firm, beneath his, or the way her heartbeat thudded steadily against his chest. Or how close her mouth was...

Dammit.

Jack kissed her. Suddenly, and without warning, quick and hard. And then he rolled off her, grabbed her hand and pulled her into a run.

She tugged back. "We can't leave them!"

He was ready for that, and holding on tight, pulled her onward. "We won't."

"Over here!" JW called, and they headed for the sound of his voice, ducking behind a clump of some bush or other that smelled like garbage.

Only when they were there, invisible to the guy in the house, did Jack start to breathe again.

"Hey there, Grace. Nice to see you again."

Grace eyed JW, the gun in his hand, and shook her head. "So I take it you're not in the professional security business, either," she quipped.

"Sure I am," JW told her. "I'm a cop. If that's not professional security, I don't know what is."

Grace lowered her head, lifted it again after a long moment. "You, too?" she asked.

Jack could only nod. He saw her eyes growing damp. "Jack, why? Why did you lie to me?"

"I didn't lie to you... Hell, Grace, I knew damn well you'd react this way."

"What way?"

"It's over. I'm quitting just as soon as JW and I wrap up this case, taking a job offer from one of Harry's friends, and then everything I ever told you will be the truth."

She bent her brows until they touched. "You can't make a lie into the truth! What kind of twisted logic are you—"

"Ah, don't be too hard on him, Grace," JW said. "Or...should I say, Amazing Grace?"

Grace's mouth slammed shut and her eyes widened. She swung her head around. "Where did you hear that?"

"Well, it was your nickname in college, wasn't it?"

Grace seemed to glare at JW, and JW just grinned and went silent.

Jack just sat there, hearing faint traces of *Twilight Zone* music in the hum of the swamp bugs. "Why did they call you 'Amazing Grace' in college, Grace?"

She waved a hand as if it were unimportant. "I...played a little bit of...basketball. It was just a team nickname."

Jack blinked. "You played college basketball."

"It was nothing. I mostly warmed the bench."

But it was so totally opposite to everything Jack knew— or thought he knew—about his wife. That she'd even want to be involved in sports, no matter how little playing time she'd had. "And you knew about all this?" Jack asked his alleged best friend.

"Well, yeah."

"Why the hell didn't you tell me?"

"Well, shoot, you wouldn't let me tell her you were a cop! I figured fair was fair. Figured she'd tell you herself when she was ready. Besides, it's not like she's been sneaking out every day to shoot hoops while telling you she's at the office, now is it, Jackie, my boy? Hmm?" Then JW looked at Grace, and so did Jack, and neither could have missed the guilty look on her face. "Or have you?" JW asked.

"This is ridiculous!" Grace said. "Listen, my sister and my best friend are in that…that hovel with guns to their heads. Don't you think we can save all this for later?"

Jack looked at JW and JW looked back at him. They both nodded.

"How many are in there, Grace?" Jack asked her. "Besides the leader," he added with a nod at the guy on the ground.

"That wasn't the leader," she said. "Someone inside was giving him orders. I heard at least two other voices, but there could have been more."

"Shh!" JW put his finger to his lips, tipped his head to one side. "What is that?"

Jack listened. There was watery noise. Lapping, a splash. Then suddenly a motor.

Swearing, Jack scrambled out of the bushes and raced around the house full-tilt. But he only got there in time to see the small boat's lights vanishing steadily in the distance.

"No!" Grace cried. She stared at the open door to the shack, even went toward it, calling for Hope and Charlie. But it was no good. It was obvious they'd been taken.

And before they ever found the note left inside the house, Jack knew what it would demand. But he read it, anyway.

"'If you want to see the women alive again, you will release Havilar—'" Jack looked up. "That must be the guy Grace kicked into oblivion." Then he read on. "'Release Havilar, and drop the investigation of Paulo K. Darius, officially.'"

Jack looked from the note to JW. He smiled, and Jack smiled back.

"What's so damned funny?" Grace demanded. "That maniac has Hope and Charlie."

"Yeah, but we have two bits of information that we didn't have before."

"Oh, well, in that case..." Grace tossed her head.

"First, we know our drug lord isn't any too bright. And second—" JW nodded at the note "—we know his name."

Chapter 7

Her husband—or, the stranger who looked like her husband—stared at Grace, sighed deeply, and took her hand. "We'll get them back, Grace."

She studied him, his tanned face, his square jaw, the gray of his eyes, and she realized she didn't know this man at all. She'd been married to him for all of two weeks, and she didn't know the first thing about who he really was. "How?" she asked, without thinking first.

Jack held her eyes. "It's what I do. I do it well."

Confident, his tone. Strong. As strong as his hand around hers. She believed him. And that simple reassurance made her feel slightly less afraid. As little sense as that made...and she knew it made damn little. Still, she sensed he was being completely honest with her for the first time since she'd met him. "Okay."

Jack started walking, still holding her hand, back down the dark path that passed for a road out here. "My car's right here," she said.

"I'll send someone back for your car. I think you ought to ride with me. We can...talk."

"Something we haven't done enough of." To her own ears, her voice was low, wary. And for a long time she searched his eyes, trying to see the man she'd seen before. The staid, reserved man who went to work every morning in a nice suit and carried a briefcase. But instead she saw only this stranger, his clothes rumpled, his hair uncombed, his strong jaw lined with stubble. And a big black gun that still smelled of hot sulphur clutched in his hand.

"JW?" Jack called.

Grace looked around, saw JW handcuffing the still-unconscious man, rolling him over. "We'll get the cars and toss him in on the way back. He ain't goin' anywhere."

Jack looked at her, and a grudging half smile tugged at one side of his mouth. "Where'd you learn all that, Grace?"

She shrugged, saying nothing. "Where's your car, Jack?"

"Back here." He led her onward, JW bringing up the rear. When she saw the two vehicles sitting on the little pull-off alongside the dirt road, she frowned. "That's not your car."

Jack sighed. "I couldn't drive the Lexus on the job," he said. "I'm supposed to be stopping crime, not volunteering to play the victim."

She nodded slowly, thinking as he spoke. "You, um, must work in some pretty rough neighborhoods."

He licked his lips, a little nervously, she thought. "Not for much longer, Grace." Then he looked right into her eyes. "I promise you that."

Tilting her head to one side, Grace asked, "Why?"

"Why what?"

She thought about that for a moment, but couldn't come up with a single answer. Instead there were a dozen pecking at her mind. Why was he going to quit? Why had he lied to her? Why had she never known about this old car of his? Where had he been keeping it? What else had he been hiding from her? She gave her head a shake, deciding there was no time for all of this now. Later, though, they were going to have to have some serious discussions. She yanked open the passenger side door of the car—a mid-seventies model Ford Mustang—and got in.

A second later Jack was behind the wheel, and the car roared to life. The stick shift was on the floor, in between the leather bucket seats. New carpet covered the floor—in fact the inside of the car had been totally renovated. Right down to the CD player in the dash.

"So...you've been...what? Restoring the car bit by bit?"

"Hmm?" He glanced her way, then nodded. "Yeah, for a couple of years. Most of the parts are original."

"Looks like it's almost done."

"Just need a set of white-wall tires and a paint job."

"What color?" she asked on impulse.

"Black," he said without hesitation.

Black. She swallowed hard. She'd have expected her husband to be more of a beige kind of a guy. Or maybe powder-bluc. But black?

She had a suspicion that this car was one of his passions. One he'd kept hidden from her. But it was reassuring to know that he did have some. Passions, that is.

"Where are we going?"

"JW's already called for search units to be sent out here. He'll head back to headquarters with his charge...maybe with a side trip to Memorial, depending on how hard you kicked the poor slob."

"Not *that* hard," she interjected.

"Here." Jack leaned over the back seat, brought out a huge contraption and set it in her lap. Upon closer inspection, she identified it as a spotlight. "Shine that out your window as we go. See if you can spot anything out there on the swamp."

She found the on button, aimed the thing, and hit it. It

sent a powerful, wide shaft of light out onto the swamp as the car rolled slowly onward.

"We'll drive around the perimeter, see if we can spot any sign of that boat, or a car waiting somewhere along the edges."

She strained her eyes to see, and realized she was hanging on his every word. "Will we find either of those things?"

Jack glanced sideways at her. "I doubt it. I imagine they had a car hidden somewhere on the far side, and are already heading back down the highway by now." He reached over, clasped her shoulder, closing his hand around it. "He won't kill them, Grace. He wants to use them. Obviously, he knows this guy we took can give us information on him. Testify against him. That's why he wants him back. Otherwise he would leave the poor bastard hanging out to dry. That's the way his kind work. But as long as it's a risk to him, he'll do what he has to in order to get his buddy back—and right now, that means taking good care of Charlie and Hope."

She turned to watch his face as he spoke. He looked at her, taking only quick fleeting glimpses of the road, but for the most part, looking her right in the eyes. As if he knew, somehow, that helped her to believe him. She could see in his eyes that he was saying what he honestly believed.

"Will you trade this...this witness to get them back?"

For the first time his gaze flickered. "It won't come to that."

"But if it does?"

"It won't be up to me, Grace. I would do it in a minute, but it won't be up to me."

He stopped the car and took the light from her, flicked it off and set it on the dash. Grace licked her lips, blinked at the tears that threatened, but Jack gripped both her shoulders now and stared straight into her eyes.

"Even now, they're punching this guy's name into a computer back at headquarters, Grace. Within the hour we'll know where he lives. We'll have the names and addresses of his friends, relatives, lovers, ex-lovers, enemies and casual acquaintances. We'll know where he eats, where he walks, what he drives, where he hangs out and how many times a day he goes to the bathroom. We'll have his driver's license number, his credit card numbers, his Social Security number and his shoe size. We'll get him, Grace. And we'll get your sister back safe and sound."

Swallowing hard, she nodded.

"Say it," he told her.

"We'll get Hope back safe and sound." Then she closed her eyes and the tears she'd been fighting all night long finally broke free. "God, we have to, Jack. I love her so much…"

His arms slid around her, and he pulled her close to him, held her gently. "I know, I know."

"No, you don't." Sniffling, she rested her head on his shoulder and twisted her arms around his waist. "I never told her. I've wasted my time being petty and jealous of her and teasing her for being all the things our mother wanted…things I thought were silly and foolish…until I met you."

Jack's hands stroked her hair. "You know I don't have a clue what you're talking about, don't you?"

Sniffling, she nodded against his shoulder.

"You never had any reason to be jealous of your sister. Never. But it doesn't matter, because she knows you love her. You hear me?" Another nod, as she burrowed closer. "But even if she has the least little doubt about it, Grace, it doesn't matter. You can tell her when we get her back. And we will. Understand?"

"Yes."

"Good." He squeezed her one last time, and set her away from him. "Now fasten your seat belt. I'm gonna take you to your parents', and then I'll—"

"No!"

Jack blinked and looked at her.

"I need to be looking for my sister, and for Charlie. God, Jack, I couldn't just sit by the phone and wait to hear."

He tapped his palm on the steering wheel, pursed his lips. "This is filth we're dealing with, Grace. I'm liable to be up to my elbows in it before I tug Charlie and Hope out again. This is no place for you."

She sat back, and buckled up. Then she grabbed up the light and resumed shining it on the murky swamp. Jack put the car into gear, and drove slowly.

"You don't have a clue what kind of place is for me, Jack. I'm not afraid of getting dirty. I'm not afraid of much of anything."

"No?"

"No."

He took a deep breath.

"Jack, if you take me home, I'll just come after you. Wouldn't you rather know where I was, than have me stumbling into situations the way I did tonight?"

He let his chin fall almost to his chest, then quickly brought it up again. "You're right, dammit."

"I know I am."

"Grace...you're going to see things...that might change the way you..."

"The way I what?"

His face, shadowed and lit in turns by the interior lights and the movements of the steering wheel, seemed tense, and taut with concentration. "The way you feel about me."

"It works both ways, you know." She kept her eyes on the water, the swamp, the creatures writhing around in the mud and slime. "Now that the masks are off...I suppose I'm going to be telling you a lot of things about me that you didn't know before. You thought you married a delicate socialite, Jack. But you're going to know, pretty soon, just how wrong you were. And maybe I'm not the wife you had in mind at all."

"That's not gonna happen."

"You can't be sure of that."

He lowered his head. "And I guess you can't either, can you, Grace?"

"I guess not."

"It's like starting over, isn't it?"

She glanced over her shoulder at him, nodded and attempted to smile. "Hi, there. I'm Grace Phelps. Pleasure to meet you."

He smiled back, but it was strained. "No, hon. You're Grace McCain. And the pleasure's all mine."

He *did* know her. Or…he thought he did. So she'd taken a few karate lessons or a self-defense course at college. So what? And according to Jack's know-it-all buddy, she'd played some team sports, as well. He could see why she might have wanted to keep all that to herself. Hell, her mother was intimidating at best, terror-inducing at worst, and she was pretty clear about what she saw as acceptable and what she did not. She would have thrown a fit if Grace had told her about the sports thing.

So it had been a secret, and Grace had carried that over to Jack—for some reason decided to keep it from him, as well. Maybe she thought he wouldn't approve or something. He didn't know. And yes, it was a revelation to him…but it didn't change what he already knew about his wife. That she was sensitive, well-bred, a lady through and through.

He had never wanted this kind of garbage to touch her. Now it was.

"I'm sorry, Grace."

She shook her head. "We messed up," she said. "Both of us."

But it was worse than that. Jack knew it was. Oh, she was dealing with it all well and good right now, but he knew.

He'd been born under this star. He'd been destined for police work. He'd always known that he would follow in his father's footsteps. But Grace hadn't been born to this. Nor had Jack's mother, and it had damn near destroyed her.

One day, after a particularly stressful week, Jack's mother had quietly suffered a breakdown. And it had scared Jack to death. His dad retired after that. He sat Jack down and told him that being a police officer's wife was too hard on a fragile woman. That it was his job that had driven Mom over the edge, and that he wouldn't let that happen again.

Jack's mother had spent a month in a hospital. His father had taken a job as a night watchman. But the trauma of that time had stayed with him.

Damn, he didn't want to see the same thing happen to Grace. But it wouldn't. Because this sham of a marriage wouldn't last that long. Maybe Jack had fooled her into thinking he was up to her standards for a little while, and it had been a beautiful fantasy. But it was over. She had seen the truth. There was no more to be said.

Once Jack got his wife's sister and her best friend back home, safe and sound, he would more than likely have to pack up his fake possessions and head back to his real life. His apartment over the bar. His crass friends, and their poker nights and football games and pizza and beer.

He wouldn't miss the spit polish all that much.

But *damn,* he was sure going to miss Grace.

They skirted the swamp as they headed back to the highway, but despite Grace's efforts with the light, they saw nothing. Then they waited in a turnaround for the troops to arrive. And they did, by the dozens. Carloads of them, with spotlights and motorboats. JW filled them in, and Jack was left without much to do but wait for the information to come in on their felon. That and...talk to his wife.

"We're going to need to tell your parents what's happened," he told her as men scurried around like ants, talked into radios, and leaned over maps.

She lowered her head at once. "They'll blame me." Then, shaking it slowly, "Hell, they should. It was all my fault."

Jack cupped her chin, made her look up at him. That face of hers, tilted up toward his like that, made him shiver. "You never told me," he said. "Why did you follow me out here tonight?"

She closed her eyes. "You got a phone call in the middle of the night," she said.

"So?"

"So…you whispered 'Why are you calling me here?' and then you sneaked downstairs to call them back. It was pretty obvious you didn't want me hearing that conversation."

"Well, I didn't. But I still don't see what…" Jack stopped there, and his stomach lurched. "You thought it was a woman, didn't you? My God, Grace, you thought I was sneaking off to meet some woman?"

She pulled away from him. "Well, what was I supposed to think? It was so obvious you were keeping secrets, Jack. And there were all those late nights. And the way you are with me when we…" She bit off the rest, but Jack saw it, saw it clear in her eyes.

"Damn," he whispered. "Baby, if you only knew." He shook his head slowly.

"McCain?" JW called.

Jack turned, hating like hell to leave things that way with Grace right now, but knowing he had no choice. Hell, it was starting to rain. A fine mist, coming down, gently coating them without them even noticing or feeling the drops. JW handed him a cell phone, and Jack snatched a notepad out of his pocket as the female officer on the other end read him off a list of names, addresses, and other pertinent information that might help in tracking Hope and Charlie's kidnapper. Jack wrote quickly, filling two pages, top to bottom.

Then he flipped the phone shut, and took his wife's hand. "Now we can get to work. We'll call your parents on the way."

She nodded, started to pull free of him, to head to her side of the car, but on impulse, Jack held on. When she turned to ask why, he pulled her close. "I never cheated on you, Grace. Never even thought about it."

The mist on her face made her skin shiny and moist. "Do you believe me?" he asked her.

She nodded.

"No, you don't. And I know why." Jack let his hands slip lower, cupping her rounded backside, and pulling her tight to him. Then he arched against her just a little, leaned down, and kissed her, briefly, quickly, and not nearly the way he wanted to. But even then, he tasted her lips, closing his around them, and suckling just a little. She went stiff with shock. He'd never kissed her like that. Not even on their wedding night. When Jack let her go, she just stood there, staring at him, blinking in the misty rain.

"It's my fault you felt neglected. I just...I thought I was being careful with you. Maybe I was too careful."

"Maybe you were," she said.

"Maybe you should have said something."

She shrugged. "I guess I should have."

He let his eyes roam her face, thinking of all the wasted time. Damn, damn, damn. Too late now, but he wished to God it wasn't. That he would have one more chance with her.

He let her go, because he had to. She walked around the car and got in, and Jack slid behind the wheel.

Chapter 8

"Daddy?" she said when she heard her father's voice on the other end of the cell phone.

"Gracie? For God's sake, what time is it, girl?" She heard the covers rustle as her father turned in bed to eye the clock's luminous dial. She could picture it clearly when his face paled and his eyes widened. "What's wrong?"

"Daddy...it's a long story, but...but it's Hope."

"It she all right?" her father demanded. "Are *you*?"

Grace could hear her mother now, sleepy and distant. "What's going on, Harry?"

"Daddy, Hope and Charlie are...they're missing."

"Missing? What do you mean, missing?"

A strong hand closed over Grace's on the cell phone and gently tugged it away. A second later she managed to brush enough of the tears from her eyes to see Jack's face, to watch him watching her as he drove and spoke calmly and clearly to her father, explaining what had happened. He didn't pull punches, but he didn't sound worried, either. His voice carried confidence and authority when he told Grace's father it was only a matter of time before he had both his daughters home again.

The rain smacked against the windshield, and the wipers slapped it back and forth. It would be light in a few hours. But right now it was black as pitch.

"Yes," Jack said. "She knows the truth now."

Grace glanced at him, met his eyes.

"No, she hasn't asked for a divorce yet. But your wife will probably demand one." He pretended to smile at whatever her father said. "Maybe it's time you told her, Harry. Mitsy would hate being the last to know. And don't worry. I'll take care of this."

When he disconnected, Grace said, "My father knew? The whole time, he knew you were a cop?"

"He knew."

She blinked, thinking back to the night she'd met Jack— the night her father had been mugged and nearly had a heart attack. The hero he'd made out of Jack. "What really happened that day?"

"Does it matter?"

She pressed her brows together. "You said you were going to tell me the truth from now on. It seems like as good a place to start as any."

Licking his lips, he said, "I suppose it does." He turned off the highway and headed back into the city. "The day I met your father, I was sitting across the street from a crack house, waiting for this Darius character to show up."

She blinked, and tipped her head sideways. "The same guy who just kidnapped my sister?"

"The same. I'd been watching the place for quite a while, but then your father came along. Some punks decided to roll him, and when one of them pulled a knife, I had to step in." He shrugged. "And that's about it."

"How many of them were there?" she asked, suppressing a shiver.

"Five."

"And they had a knife?"

Jack's mouth pulled into a crooked smile. "I had a gun."

"Oh." She looked at her hands in her lap, trying not to envision the scene. It was basically just the way her father had described it, except for Jack's gun. "What the hell was he doing in a neighborhood like that?"

Jack glanced at her. "He never did tell me that."

"He'll tell me."

"Don't be angry with him, Grace." Jack's hand covered hers. "If he hadn't been there…we might never have met. And…hell, no matter what happens now…I wouldn't have wanted to miss it."

"Jack," she said, then the lights caught her eye and she turned fast. "Jack, look out!"

He saw it at the same instant she did—a shiny wet car, tipped onto its side. Vehicles with flashing lights. Flares in the road, and yellow slickers with men underneath.

Jack hit the breaks and jerked the wheel, and the car skidded to a sideways stop in the road. He gave his head a shake. "You all right?" he asked.

"Yeah." She gave her seat belt a tug and a grateful look. "What the hell is this?"

Jack glanced again at the car, lying just off the edge of the road, tipped onto its side. She followed his gaze but didn't feel the cold breath of fear whisper over her nape until she heard Jack murmur, "Oh, no."

She blinked, looked at Jack, looked at the car again. It was deep blue. She'd thought black at first, but she saw now that it was dark blue. Four-door. She couldn't tell the make without seeing the little nameplate tacked on the tail end by the manufacturer, but she was betting Jack could. She was betting it was a Ford Fairlane. And she was betting the plates matched the numbers and letters Jack had scrawled down on his notepad. Grace strained to remember that plate number as she squinted through the rain at the rectangle on the front of that car. Blue letters and numbers on a white background.

Lady Liberty outlined in red, standing to the left. D-R-N-7-6-9.

"Jack…? Is that…?"

"Stay here." His voice was taut, tense. He opened the door and was halfway out of the car before she could move again. She got her seat belt off, opened her own door, and started to follow.

One of the troopers in his yellow slicker, with a matching plastic rain cover stretched over his wide-brimmed hat, stepped in front of Jack and held up a hand. But Jack already had his badge out of his pocket, and he held it up in front of him now. The trooper nodded, and stepped aside, and Jack hurried closer.

Grace tried to follow. The rain was coming down so hard by now that her hair was plastered to her head and streams kept flooding her eyes. The trooper caught her shoulders, and said, "Ma'am, it would be best if you stayed away."

She shook her head. "You don't understand. My *sister* was in that car!" She pulled free of him, but he didn't let her pass. He just calmly blocked her path again.

They were pulling someone out of the wreckage now: through the smashed windshield, all trussed up in a neck brace, coming out stiff as a board. Grace strained to see as they moved the victim onto a waiting stretcher and began moving toward the ambulance. Grace pushed against the trooper's arm, which had lowered like a railroad crossing barricade, but it didn't give. She could have forced the issue, but thought better of that. "Jack!" she yelled instead.

Jack turned, caught her eye, then nodded at the cop. "It's all right. Let her through."

The trooper nodded and let his arm fall to his side, and Grace rushed forward just as the men paused near the back of the waiting ambulance.

But it wasn't Hope lying there. It was Charlie. And she was trembling, and soaking wet.

Grace leaned over her, gently moving the hair off her

forehead, careful not to move her. "Charlie? Honey, are you okay?"

Wet eyes blinked open. "Hope," she whispered. "That bastard…took Hope." She swallowed, licked her lips, and it was plain that speaking was an effort. "He got out of the car…he took Hope."

Blinking in confusion, Grace looked up when a strong presence warmed her, just by standing close. Jack nodded to the men, who lifted the gurney into the ambulance. Then he reached past them, to yank a blanket off a shelf, and shoved it at one of them. "Cover her up, for crying out loud. She's freezing."

The guy nodded, even as Grace searched Jack's face. "Charlie's right," he said. "Hope isn't in the car, and neither is Paulo Darius."

"What about the other one?" Grace asked. "There were three men in that cabin…two of whom left on that boat with Hope and Charlie. So what happened to the other…" She stopped there, because she saw her answer. Another gurney was being carried from the overturned car even now. But the person on this one was covered in a white sheet, with dark stains already spreading. Grace looked away quickly.

"Gracie?" Charlie called, her voice raspy.

Grace stiffened her spine and climbed up into the ambulance. She crouched beside Charlie, reaching down to hold her hand. "You're going to the hospital now, Charlie, and you're going to be fine. I don't want you to worry. We'll get Hope back."

"Gracie…" Charlie licked her lips. "Hope…"

"Hope what?"

"She's hurt," Charlie blurted. "I don't know how badly, but she…she was hurt."

A cold steel rod seemed to slip between the discs of Grace's spine…one of fury, one of rage…it straightened her back and lifted her head. That animal had pulled her injured sister from the car he'd wrecked, and was making her walk, through the rain, in the dark. Her jaw set, her teeth clenched, she turned and stalked away from the ambulance.

Chapter 9

Jack had never seen her the way he saw her then. The way her face changed. The look— Yeah, that he recognized. He'd seen that look before—outrage, fury, righteous indignation. A man wrongly accused would get that look. A rape victim's father or husband would get it. But Jack had never in all his years seen that kind of rage cross the face of an angel.

It made him shiver, way down deep inside.

He leaned into the ambulance just long enough to tell Charlie everything was going to be fine, that he would take care of things, and then he went after his wife.

Her walk was even different. Stride, longer. Footfalls, almost stomping. She walked right up to a volunteer fireman and tugged the flashlight from his hand. The man swung his head around, mouth open, took one look at her face, and snapped it shut again.

Jack thought that was probably a wise decision on his part.

Grace went to the overturned car, to the muddy roadside

around it, and she shone that light on the ground. This way, that way, the light beam moved. But it only illuminated the tracks of a dozen rescue workers.

"Damn! How the hell are we supposed to find which way he took her!" She flung the light to the ground, arms raising outward in frustration.

Jack took her shoulders, held on hard. "Take a breath, Grace. Come on, do it."

She did, but he could see the tears of frustration and fury standing in her eyes. He bent to pick up the flashlight. "The rescuers were walking all around the car. They had no choice. So was Paulo, when he first got out with Hope. But he would have kept on going. Away from the car. Away from all these other tracks."

"If he kept to the pavement…"

"He didn't," Jack said.

"How can you be so sure?"

"Trust me, hmm? Come on." Jack took her hand and pulled her along the shoulder of the road, about ten feet from the car. "Now we just make a circle." He climbed over the guard rail, held out his hand, and helped her over it. Then he aimed the light's beam at the ground, and they walked, down the steep, muddy slope, and around the car at a distance of about ten feet, all the way.

Not a footprint in sight.

Jack shook his head. "Damn. He's smarter than I thought."

"I told you," Grace said. "He walked on the road."

"No. He just crossed it." Again, they climbed over the guard rail and crossed the street in the pouring rain. Grace looked at Jack with doubt in her eyes, but as soon as they got to the far side of the road and he began shining the light around, he found the tracks. Two sets of them, clear as hell, in the mud. Just until the spot where the grass grew thickly and the ground was harder.

Jack signaled the nearest body—a cop standing on the

yellow center line. The trooper came over and Jack pointed in the direction the tracks headed. "What's that way?" Jack asked him.

He bit his lower lip in thought. "Let's see…there used to be a trucking company off that way. Out of business now. Yeah, yeah, just beyond that hill there, and then there's a diner, I think, and maybe the animal shelter just past that."

Jack ignored him, flipping through the soggy pages of his notepad. "D & D Trucking?" he asked.

"Yeah—yeah, that's the name."

Jack nodded, looked at Grace. "Darius's father owned it. That's where he'll be holing up, and I wouldn't be surprised to find that he has help."

"He's gonna need it," Grace said, that look still in place.

"Grace." Jack caught her wrist when she would have walked past him into the darkness, across untended lots that ran between side streets and the urban area beyond. "We can get there faster by car. I'll call for backup and…"

She shook her head rapidly, her gaze flying to Jack's. Then she glanced at the cop and pulled Jack aside. "We have to slip in there unseen, and quietly."

"The place could be guarded."

"Right. And if the cops come charging in, sirens blaring, what's going to happen?" She shook her head. "She's hurt, Jack. We don't know how badly. We don't have time for a standoff."

"It won't turn into that."

"Are you sure? Can you promise me that? Can you stand there and say you know without a doubt that my sister isn't going to bleed to death while some negotiator plays psychological chess with this idiot?"

Jack licked his lips. She had a point, and a damned good one.

"At least let's try to get close enough to see her. To see how badly she's hurt. Then we can make a decision. With all the information. Okay?"

Jack nodded. Then he smiled just slightly. "You'd make a hell of a cop, Grace."

"Oh, hell, Jack, you probably say that to all the social-ites."

"Only the ones I'm married to."

There was a strength in her that Jack hadn't seen before. Should have, probably. But hadn't. Or if he had, he hadn't recognized it for what it was.

But she was something.

Little did he know, he was only beginning to know his wife.

As the ambulances rolled away, Jack left instructions to keep the scene secure, but do nothing more. He made the obligatory suggestion that Grace stay behind, and her response to that was a look that could have wilted lettuce. He'd known better.

And then he and Grace started off across a littered lot in the rain.

Grace lay on her belly on the rain-wet grass, Jack's hand on the center of her back to keep her there. Just ahead of them down a slight incline and beyond the veil of pouring rain, was a large, long building made of powder-blue, ribbed steel. The front of it was lined with giant-size white doors that looked as if they'd roll upward to let large vehicles inside. Five of them. And at the end, a normal-size door, also white, for a person to enter through.

"That must be the office down there," Jack whispered, pointing to the little door on the end. "I'll bet that's where they went inside."

"Why?"

He shrugged. "They were in a hurry. It's the easiest access. Lots faster than messing with one of the overhead doors—less noticeable too."

Gracie watched her husband for a moment, the way his eyes scanned the area below with hawklike focus. He didn't even blink. "How are we going to get down there?" she asked. "There's not so much as a bush on this slope…and it's going to be light soon."

"This way." He slid backward a few feet, before getting up and helping her to her feet, as well. Then he started off in another direction, walking a parallel line with the wall of the building they'd been studying. She assumed he knew what he was doing—so she didn't ask. But it seemed damned strange.

When they'd gone far beyond the point where the building ended, he turned right and walked this time in line with the rear of the building. She could glimpse it every now and then through the shrubs that were clustered back here. No windows that she could see. No back doors. Again, they kept going after the building ended, and Jack took them to the right again, all the way to the front, so they wound up directly opposite of where they had been before.

He crouched there, looking down at the door. "Only one way in," he said. "Let's hope they aren't right there waiting."

"So all that walking was a waste of time?"

He smiled slightly at her. "No. He'll be expecting us to come from the opposite direction, if he's expecting us at all. He won't likely be looking this way."

She nodded. "I like the way your mind works." Then, glancing down at the little white door, she shivered.

"Stay here," Jack told her. "I'll go in alone."

"Right."

He looked at her, surprise etched on his face.

"Well, I'm not going to let you go down there and get shot," she told him. "Suppose Darius is waiting on the other side of that door with a gun drawn?"

Jack licked his lips, averted his eyes. "He won't be."

"Maybe we can make sure of that." She'd been crouching low, but now she dropped to her knees and began patting the ground with her hands. She found one stone, then another, and a third. Gathering them up, she rose.

"What do you have in mind?" Jack asked.

"I'll chuck these at one of the other doors. It'll make noise. He'll go to check it out. And you'll be able to get inside without getting yourself killed."

Jack nodded. "Good plan."

"What if he has others in there with him?"

Jack shook his head. "I don't think he does. The place doesn't look like any kind of home base. Looks deserted. He may have called for some help by now, but I don't think any has arrived."

She nodded. "Okay, then. Let's get on with it."

Together, they crept closer to the large garage-like structure. Until Jack signaled her to stop.

Grace lifted the first rock. "I'll aim for the door on the far end," she said. "It'll take him longer to check it out and come back that way."

Jack looked at the door, then looked at her. "You'll never reach that far."

She lifted both brows and tipped her head to one side, then chucked her first stone. Jack's head moved to follow its flight path, and when the stone clattered against the far side of the farthest door, he muttered, "I'll be damned."

"Go." She gave him a shove, and even as he took off, she pegged the second rock. It hit louder than the first, and she reached for the third.

But before she could throw it, Jack was shouldering the little door open, vanishing inside. Swallowing hard, Grace pulled back to throw the third stone...but froze in place when a gunshot ripped through the gathering gray dawn and the sound of her sister's voice screaming her husband's name made Gracie's blood gel in her veins.

"That's real clever, isn't it now?" a voice said from just behind her, close to her ear. "You got a nice arm on you, you know that?"

Instinct told her to spin, knee his groin, twist his arm, and floor him. She bit the instinct back. She needed to get inside, find out what had happened to Jack, and to Hope. Maybe it was best to play the helpless victim for just a little while. At least she wouldn't get shot the second she walked through the door...

The way Jack just did....

No! She wouldn't let the thought linger. Stiffening her spine, she put up her hands. "Just tell me what you want me to do," she said. She tried to make her voice unsteady and tainted with fear.

"Walk." The gun barrel dug into her spine.

Gracie walked.

The rain had eased to a light but steady drizzle, and the clouds hung so low the air seemed to have turned gray, holding off the dawn. As she was prodded further, Grace's gaze fixed on the white door looming ever larger before her like some Pandora's box waiting to be opened. She was scared to death of what was waiting on the other side. What she would see.

The man behind her shoved her nose almost into the wood, and barked out, "It's Benny. Lemme in."

Grace half expected the maniac on the other side to blow a hole through the door and her belly. But he didn't. Instead the door opened, and Grace's worst nightmare revealed itself in an ever-widening arc as the door swung slowly back.

Jack was on the cement floor, back braced against the far wall, arm crossed over his middle...but not quite hiding the blood staining his shirt.

She slid her gaze higher, meeting his eyes. They looked back at her, sharp and clear. Not dulled with pain or delirium...not until the killer glanced his way, and then he seemed to deliberately lose focus, his eyes going droopy and dull.

Grace's brows knit as she watched him. But she was distracted by her sister's voice. "Oh, God, Gracie, they got you, too?"

Sliding her gaze sideways, Gracie saw Hope sitting much the same way Jack was. She looked as if her arm was broken, and there was a huge lump forming on the front of her head. She was pale and sweating despite the chill in the air.

"My sister needs a doctor," Grace said slowly, turning her gaze back to the leader of the group. He was sitting in a dusty old swivel chair that had been forest green once but was now faded. A desk stood to one side, big and wooden, and peeling. Across his lap, he held a shotgun, and he faced the door.

"Tough," was all he said.

"Letting her die isn't going to do you any good," Grace said, fighting to keep her voice calm.

"Neither is lettin' her live."

Grace tilted her head to one side. "A live hostage is a hundred times more valuable than a dead one, Mr. Darius."

He shrugged. "Lucky for me, I got a live one. Thanks for coming, by the way."

She blinked. "My goodness. You're dumber than I thought."

The guy behind her jerked her arm, twisting it behind her and sending a bolt of pain into her shoulder. "Watch your mouth, sweetie."

She ignored him, talking only to the leader—Paulo Darius. "You don't even know who we are, do you?" she asked.

"I don't really give a damn who you are, lady."

"Oh, you should. Because we are the daughters of the richest man in the state."

His eyebrows rose, twin arches of pale brown, just like his hair. He looked like a prep school grad, not a drug lord. "Right."

"My wallet's in my pocket," Grace said, hands at her sides again, Benny holding on to one wrist in case he felt like hurting her. "Take a look at the name on my driver's license. Hell, if you look, I think there's a photo of my father in there, as well. Harrison Phelps?"

"Bull."

She shrugged. But Paulo nodded to Benny, and Benny let go of her wrist, reached around her, slid his hand into the pocket of her warm-up jacket. She could have broken his arm, slammed him to the floor and had his gun. But maybe not fast enough to avoid the one in Paulo's lap. She glanced at Jack. He shook his head side to side so slightly it was barely a movement at all. But she got the message anyway. Not yet.

Benny had the wallet by then and, stepping back, he flipped it open. "Grace Phelps McCain." Then he flipped through the photos. "Shoot, she wasn't kidding. Harrison Phelps's picture *is* in here."

"Lemme see that," Paulo snapped, coming to his feet and snatching the wallet away. He stared at the photo, the one Grace knew was of her and her father arm-in-arm, on her wedding day.

"So who'd you marry?" Paulo asked, leering at her. "Donald Trump?"

"No. I married a cop." Both men swore, but Gracie rushed on. "So you can see you got yourself a solid-gold hostage in me. It wouldn't hurt you a bit to let these other two go."

He shook his head slowly. "Your father would pay more to get both of you back alive than he would for just one."

"My father would give every nickel he ever earned for either one of us," Grace said. "He'd also spend it all trying to hunt you down if you harmed either one of us…and make no mistake, Mr. Darius, if my sister doesn't make it, he'll blame you. He'll never give you a dime, and he'll die trying to make you pay."

The man flinched. It was subtle, but she saw it.

"On the other hand, if you let her go, she can tell our

father that I'm alive and unharmed, and that I'll be returned safely just as soon as your demands are met. Hell, he won't even tell the police he's been contacted if Hope tells him not to. Will he, Hope?''

Hope lifted her chin just a little, and seemed to try to focus. "Daddy…would do whatever he had to, to keep us safe.''

Grace nodded hard. "Including seeing to it you had money, a safe ride out of here and a private jet to take you to wherever the hell you want to go, and anything else you might ask for.''

Benny said, "Paulo, maybe it's not a bad idea—''

"Shut up.'' Paulo paced, shotgun clasped in his hands. "How the hell would I even contact him?'' He yanked his cell phone from the inside pocket of his battered suit. "You think I'm an idiot? You think I don't know the cops have already tapped his phones?''

"Just write him a note, Einstein. Give it to my sister, and let her go. I'm telling you, my father has the clout and the money to get you out of this mess. He might be the only person who can.''

Paulo scowled. "If I let her go, how do I know she won't just tell the cops right where we are?''

"I don't *know* where we are,'' Hope muttered.

"Listen, blindfold her, have Godzilla over here drive her around for a while, and drop her off at the nearest hospital. Just to be sure she lives long enough to deliver the message.''

His eyes narrowed on Grace in suspicion.

"What the hell have you got to lose?'' she demanded.

Licking his lips, he seemed to give the matter a lot of thought. Then, finally, he nodded at Benny. "There's a parts room in back. Put these two in there, and lock it.''

"And what about Hope?'' Grace demanded.

Paulo looked at Grace for a long moment, and she stared back at him. Then finally he went to Hope and crouched in front of her. "If you don't do this exactly the way your sister said, I'm gonna kill her. You understand me? The first sign I get that you screwed me over, she dies. And I'll *hurt* her, lady. And I'll *like* it."

Hope was sobbing softly. "I d-don't want to leave you, Grace…"

But Grace was already being nudged along again by that damned gun barrel. "You'll be okay," she told her sister. "Just do exactly what they tell you, and you'll be fine. I promise you that, Hope."

"But…but…"

"I can take care of myself. You *know* that."

Benny paused only long enough to kick Jack in the ribs and growl at him to get up. Jack did, doubled over and clutching his arm to his blood-soaked shirt. He walked slowly, grunting in pain with every step he took. Grace moved up beside him, and pulled his free arm around her shoulders. "Lean on me," she told him.

He did.

She was worried as hell about him. But, God, one thing at a time. At least Hope would be all right now. Please, please, let Hope be all right now.

At the back of the place, a smaller door stood open into a room that was pitch-black and tiny.

"In you go," Benny said.

"You're going to take her to a hospital, aren't you, Benny?" Grace asked. "If she dies, she'll never deliver your boss's note. And she's in bad shape, Benny, I can tell. I know her, and I can tell—"

"Yeah, yeah, enough already. I'll drop her across the street from Memorial. Now get in there, already, will you?"

She turned, looked him in the eye. "You keep her safe, and I'll repay you a hundred times over. That's a promise."

He held her eyes for a moment, and she thought maybe he believed her. "Sure you will," he said. "Don't worry. I'll see to it she's okay." Then he gave her a shove and she stumbled through the doorway behind Jack, into the pitch blackness. The door banged shut, and she heard the padlock snapping.

"Jack?"

She reached out a hand, only to feel his chest, strong and solid. And then he pulled her close to him, pressing her face to his neck, weaving his fingers in and out of her hair. "You're okay," he whispered. "My God, you're okay."

"But you're not." She felt tears threatening, and battled them for all she was worth. "Jack, you're wounded!"

"Not so you'd notice." Tipping her face up, he kissed her mouth, then backed up slightly. She could only see the darker outline of him, and bits of shape and shadow. But she sensed him removing his shirt and whatever he wore underneath it. "Still got that flashlight?"

"Yeah." She pulled it out of her pocket, flicked it on, and set it on a nearby shelf, so that it spotlighted her and Jack. Her gaze skimmed his unclothed chest now, damp with the rain, but not bloody. And no wounds marred his tight belly or his hard abs. "But...I saw it!"

"You saw the same thing they did—which was what I wanted them to see." He tipped his arm toward her, and she saw the nasty, bloody gash across the forearm. "Paulo's a lousy shot. He grazed my arm. I automatically clutched it to me, and it bled like hell. When I went down, he thought I was gut shot. I thought it was best to let him keep right on thinking it."

"Give me your shirt," Grace said, and when he did, she located a sleeve, used her teeth to tear it off, and then wrapped it around Jack's wounded arm, pulling it tight enough to stop the bleeding, and tying it in a knot. She sighed, not happy with the job. "It's going to have to do, for now."

"It's nothing, Grace."

Grace closed her eyes slowly, finally letting the relief warm her, ease her rigid spine. "My God, I thought I was going to lose you.'' Then she curled into her husband's arms, wrapped hers tight around him, and held him close. ''You scared the hell out of me.''

''Yeah, well you scared the hell out of me, too. When that goon reached for your wallet, I thought for sure you were gonna try something.''

''I was,'' she said. ''I would have, if you and Hope hadn't been in the line of fire.''

''Thank God, you didn't, Grace. Just because your self-defense moves worked on that one bastard, don't go getting overconfident. You got lucky. Okay? I don't want you getting yourself killed.''

She stared up at him for a full minute before the smile finally pulled her lips upward, and then she stroked his dark hair, and shook her head slowly. ''We're…going to be honest with each other from now on…right?''

''Right. But that's changing the subject.''

''Not really.'' She licked her lips, turned herself away from him and, looking down, said, ''Jack, I know you wanted a real…lady. Delicate and well-bred and classy. I—I basically tricked you into marrying me under false pretenses…but…the truth is…I'm none of those things.''

Catching her shoulder, he turned her slowly. ''Grace… hon, you are all those things. And then some. Don't you ever sell yourself short.''

She took a breath and blurted the truth. ''I'm a black belt in karate, and the current State kickboxing champion.''

Jack stared at her for what seemed like a long, drawn-out moment. Then he smiled. Then he laughed. Very softly, not at her, maybe, but still, it was a laugh. As if he thought it the cutest thing in the universe that his sweet delicate wife would make such a claim.

Grace rolled her eyes, and turned in a slow circle, looking around the tiny room as his chuckles continued. The shelves were made of two-by-six frames, with plywood surfaces. She eyed one of the thick boards holding them up…then, with a sigh, she heeled off her running shoe, centered herself, and kicked it. The board snapped neatly in two, and Jack's laughter stopped.

She looked at him. He looked back at her, all traces of amusement gone from his face. Only astonishment stood there now.

"I'll understand if...when this is over, if you decide you...well, you... I'm not gonna to hold you—"

"Gracie?"

"Hmm?"

He smiled slightly, came closer, and cupped her cheek in his hand. "Can you do that thing you just did...to the door?"

"Of course I can. And I can do it to Paulo's head, as well." She turned, focused on the door, began to move, but Jack's hands on her shoulders stopped her.

"Not just yet, hon. Let's wait until we know Hope is safe."

She nodded at him. "You're right. And even when we hear Benny leave with her, she won't be safe. Not really. Paulo could call Benny on that cell phone and order him to kill her the minute he suspects we're up to anything."

"Then we'll just wait for Benny to get back. Then we'll know Hope is out of range." Jack put out a hand, and when she took it, he tugged her to the back of the small room, and down to the floor to sit beside him. "Might as well get comfortable, hon. It could be a while."

Chapter 10

"Well, as long as we're here...with nothing to do but wait," Grace said softly, "maybe it's time we talked about...our marriage."

Jack didn't want to talk to her about their marriage. Hell, he was scared to death to talk to her about their marriage, because he didn't want to hear her tell him she was having second thoughts about continuing with it. But what choice did he have? Besides, maybe he didn't actually need to be as worried as he had been. His wife obviously wasn't the delicate flower Jack believed her to be.

"What about our marriage?" he managed to ask, sounding about as intelligent as day-old bread, he figured.

They had flicked off the flashlight to save the juice. And just a few moments ago they had heard Benny drive off with Hope. But they still had no idea when or if he'd be back. There was probably nothing to do *but* talk.

"I don't know." She sat beside Jack, her back against the wall, her shoulder pressed to his. "Tell me something, Jack, have you been...happy with the way this whole thing has been going so far? I mean...happy with me?''

"Of course I've been happy!" He answered too fast, he knew he did. And he felt Grace shaking her head.

"No, you're just giving me the automatic response, the answer you think I want to hear. But I don't. I want the truth. I want you to think about it first. Have you been happy, keeping so many secrets? Thinking I was so shallow and so arrogant that I'd stop loving you if I knew you weren't a rich prep-school grad with a six-figure income?"

He turned his head toward her. "I never thought that."

"No?"

She sounded so doubtful. "No. Not...not exactly. It was more I thought you were too delicate to handle the truth. That it would disgust you to know the kind of violent world I lived in. The filth I wallowed in every day."

Grace sighed deeply, reached forward to pick something up, and then placed it in his hand. A piece of the board she'd broken in two. Then she said, "Does this look delicate to you?"

"Depends," Jack said. "How's your foot?"

He could hear the slight smile in her voice when she replied, "Not even a twinge." Then she took the piece of wood from him and tossed it. "I suppose it's my fault you thought of me that way, though. At least partly."

"Partly? More like one hundred and ten percent."

"No way, Jack. I'm only half to blame for this mess. I may have been playing a role, but only because I thought that was the kind of woman you wanted. And I wasn't playing...not really. I was trying to *be* that woman."

Jack sighed softly. "And just how did you get the idea I wanted you to be anything but what you were? Hmm?"

She reached out to take his hand. "Mother made me dress the part, and act the part, and become the part the night of my party. She said no decent man would ever look at me twice in my jeans and T-shirts, my hair hanging loose and my face usually dirty.''

"But you didn't believe her?'' Jack said.

"Sure I did, I just didn't care. I'd never been looked at twice by the kind of men my mother wanted for me. I liked it that way.''

"So then why did you go along with her that night?''

She leaned a little closer. "It was a big night for her. It meant a lot to her. I thought it couldn't do any harm to do it her way. My mother's done a lot for me, and it wasn't so much to ask really.'' Her hand slid over the back of Jack's fingers, lacing from behind. "Then I met you, and all of a sudden…''

"All of a sudden…?''

"It mattered. I cared. I wanted to be the kind of woman a man like you could…care for. And I was glad I'd gone along with my mother's plan, because you…you responded.''

"And you naturally assumed that what I was responding to was the dress? The hair? The makeup?''

"What else?'' she asked softly. "You couldn't even see the real Gracie under all the gilt.''

"Maybe I could,'' he told her. "I don't even remember what you were wearing that night, Grace.''

"No?''

"No. I remember the sound of your laugh. The way you felt in my arms when I stole that kiss in the garden. I remember the way your smile made my heart spin in circles and fall over like a cartoon character who's just had an anvil dropped on his head.''

She lowered her head a little bit. "We kind of…got off the subject, didn't we?''

"I don't think so. You asked if I'd been happy. I have. Being with you, being able to come home to you every night…that made me happy.''

"Having to lie about where you'd been, living with the

constant fear that I'd find out and stop loving you? Did that make you happy? Planning to give up a career you obviously love so that you could be something you aren't, and being afraid to make love to your own wife? How could you sit there and say you were happy with that?''

Jack opened his mouth. Closed it again, and tried to swallow. But he couldn't.

''I'll tell you right now, Jack, I haven't been. I haven't been at all. I almost stopped going to the gym altogether, I quit my martial arts classes, and I tried to be the perfect little socialite wife, but it's not me. I'm tired of keeping all my trophies hidden under the bed, and I'm tired of these stupid dresses and suits all the time. I want my jeans. I want to pop open a beer and eat junk food and watch a New York Liberty game on TV in my sweats and a ponytail. And— well, I was afraid to say this before. Afraid you'd think it was…unladylike and crude…but we can't go on like we've been, Jack. We're going to fall apart if we try. So here it is, straight up and undiluted. I want sex.''

Jack didn't think he could talk, but for some reason his mouth was moving and words were coming out, anyway. ''But…we *have* sex.''

''We make love, Jack, and I'm not even sure there's enough feeling involved to call it that. You've been doling it out with an eye dropper, and so damned gently I barely know I've been touched when we finish. That's not sex. I don't know what the hell it is, but it's not sex.''

Jack sat there, cut to the bone. ''I—I'm sorry.''

''Don't be sorry,'' she said, and she turned toward him, laid her palm on his cheek. ''I thought you must have some wild lover who was leaving you too worn out for me, Jack, but it wasn't that, was it? It was that you were thinking I was too damned delicate to touch the way you wanted to. That you'd shock me or scare me or hurt me if you loved me the way you wanted to…. Unless…it was just that you didn't…want to…at all.''

Jack slid his good arm around her waist, and pulled her hard to his chest. "Don't think that, Gracie. Don't ever think that. Because it couldn't be further from the truth." And then he kissed her. And for the first time, he let himself forget who she was, and what she was…and to just feel the woman in his arms. Nothing else. Woman. And man. And good old-fashioned lust.

Her heart pounded hard as his tongue delved deep into her mouth, licking and tasting every bit of her, like an invasion, but one she wanted. One she'd asked for.

When he lifted his head, she lifted her hands, and Jack heard the zip of her warm-up slide down. Heard her take it off. Then there was more rustling, and he couldn't believe she was doing this…undressing, in this dark, dirty room… for him. He could feel soft skin, warm wherever she brushed against him now, and it drove him crazy. But then her hands were on him, sliding over his chest, curling around his shoulders. And her lips were on him, following the path her hands set on fire. Warm and wet, but doing not one damn thing to extinguish the flame.

His hands slid down the length of her spine, closed over her buttocks, and he almost exploded when he found them bare. She'd taken off every stitch. And the floor in here was dirty, and she didn't seem to care. She pulled him on top of her as they kissed, cradled him between her legs, and moved against him. He still had his jeans on, but she wasn't waiting. And slow, tender foreplay didn't seem to be what she had in mind, either. Not when her hands slid between them to tug at the button fly of his jeans. Not when she shoved them down over his hips, underwear and all, and dug her fingernails into his flanks as she pulled him to her.

He entered her, hard and fast, and she didn't flinch or pull away. Instead she arched against him, held him to her. There was no way to be gentle with her when she was like this. Each time he pulled back, she clamped her hot little hands hard on his backside and jerked him deep inside her again. And pretty soon she didn't have to, because he was gone, over the edge, thrusting into her with everything he had. She panted, whimpered, cried, moaned his name, kept saying "Yes, yes, oh, yes." Those sounds in his ear, breath on his skin…his mind spun out of control as he drove into her. He didn't think. He didn't plan. He just felt and acted on those feelings. His mouth captured her small breast, and he tugged and worried its distended peak as the pace of their frantic coupling increased. And he bit down when he finally spilled the essence of himself into her, and he felt her shuddering release, the way she pulled against his teeth, the fierce bite of her nails and the convulsing of her body milking his. One ecstatic moment that stretched out endlessly…until finally his body was spent and he melted into a puddle of sated, drained flesh. Sliding to the side, he pulled her with him, keeping her anchored tight and close. Sweat coated his skin, and hers, as well. And she was breathless, but limp as she burrowed closer to him.

"Better?" he asked after a long moment.

"Now *that's* what I call sex," she murmured, pressing her mouth to his chest one more time.

"If you only knew how hard it's been for me to hold back…but I thought…I thought I had to."

"You thought wrong. I think we both did, about a lot of things. But just so we're clear on this, Jack, I'm not gonna stop loving you because you're a cop."

"Yeah, well, I won't be a cop much longer. But just for the record, I'm not gonna stop loving you because you're a jock."

She sighed. "That remains to be seen," she said softly.

"Now what is that supposed to mean?"

"Shh! Listen!"

They both heard it. The sound of the engine, distant, but there. Benny had returned. Jack quickly righted his clothes, and made his way to the door, pressing his ear to it to listen. In a few moments he heard voices, but couldn't make out what they were saying. Still, they were clearly male voices. He didn't hear Hope at all.

"Benny's back. I don't think Hope is with him," Jack said.

"Then it's time." He could hear Grace putting on her clothes, tugging up the zipper.

"Yeah. It's time."

A second later she was beside him, running a hand along the surface of the door, probably deciding exactly where to plant her killer foot.

But before she could do much more, they heard the men approaching from outside, and then the snap of the padlock. They both moved back, away from the door as it opened and the slice of light widened. Benny and Paulo stood there, looking from one of them to the other. "What the hell happened to you two?"

Jack looked at Grace, and she looked at him. She had black smears on her cheeks, her neck, in her hair. He glanced down at his hands and saw that they, too, were stained dark. Glancing at the floor now he saw that it was stained black. Old grease, motor oil, and God knew what else had been soaking the concrete for years. It got on Jack's hands, and from there, pretty much all over his wife's body. He shuddered to think how many smears and streaks he'd painted across her skin. It was almost as if the fates were mocking him for thinking, even for a moment, that he could truly be with a woman such as Grace and not soil her with the filth that had already stained his soul. He was contaminating her. And she would realize that, too, and be repulsed....

Then he heard a soft sound, and dragged his gaze upward to meet hers. And he realized with a shock, that she was battling laughter. Looking down at her own hands, and forearms, and then at Jack's, she smiled and choked on a chortle.

* * *

"Wait a minute," Benny began. "Did you two—"

"Is my sister safe?" Grace cut in. "Did you get her to a hospital like you said you would?"

"Yeah. Dropped her at Memorial. Even stayed until she got through the doors. But back to this other thing..." He looked at them, looked at his boss. "I thought she said she was married."

"She did," Paulo said grimly. "To a cop."

"Man, he's not gonna like this, is he?"

"You freaking moron!" Paulo pointed his gun at Jack. "So, you're a cop. If you'd said so in the first place, it would have saved us all a lot of trouble." He shook his head slowly. "One hostage is all I wanted to deal with, anyway."

"Jeez, Paulo, you're gonna shoot him? A cop?" Benny asked, sounding nervous as hell.

"What do you think I'm gonna do, let him go? Or keep him here so he can pull something that gets you and me killed?"

"Oh, he's not gonna pull anything," Gracie said. "I'm the one you'd better worry about."

"Oh, yeah?" Benny smiled from ear to ear. "Isn't that cute, Paulo? She said—"

He stopped speaking when Grace's foot landed, knocking Paulo's gun flying across the room, and at the same instant, Jack's fist slammed into Benny's smiling face. Benny went down, but Paulo tried to hit back. Jack lunged forward, intending to protect his wife, but he couldn't get that close without risking his own hide. The woman was moving so damned fast, delivering rapid-fire kicks and a couple of blows with her hands, backing Paulo up across the floor until he was to the wall. He never landed a punch. Then she flipped him, and he hit the floor.

She looked up at Jack. "Will you stop gaping and grab their guns?" Paulo sat up. She kicked him right back down again.

Jack spotted his gun on the floor and grabbed it. He pointed it at Benny. ''Come on, toss the weapon out.''

Benny did. Jack glanced back at Paulo, but he wasn't getting up again. ''It's okay, Grace, let him up. We'll toss them in the parts room for safe-keeping.'' Grace lowered her boxer's stance hands and stepped back. Paulo got up, and she walked behind him, ready to strike. Jack just watched her, shaking his head. Kickboxing champion, Jack thought, smiling. Imagine that.

Chapter 11

"I can't believe it. I just freaking can't believe it." Jack sat on the sofa in his old apartment. One last time, and this time he'd told Grace where he was going. He and some of the guys from the department had gathered here to watch some sports and eat some junk food—sort of a going-away party. His retirement would be official at the end of next week.

Anyway, JW had somehow got his hands on a videotaped college basketball game—and Jack sat there watching his delicate little wife mop up the floor with most of the other players. "Bench warmer" was not *quite* the term he would have used. He watched her post up like a pro, watched her drive to the basket to sink a reverse layup without even looking, watched her sink a three at the buzzer to win the game. And he sat there and he shook his head.

"Oh, man, where did you get that?" her voice said.

Jack turned around, startled out of his wits. He'd never wanted Gracie to see this shabby little place. But there she was, big as life, two large white boxes balanced on one hand.

"Hi, hon," she said with a smile. "I brought the pizza."

"Pepperoni and mushroom?" JW asked.

"As per your request."

"All right!" one of the guys yelled, and he took the boxes from her to set them on the table, while JW popped the top on a can of Budweiser and handed it to Grace.

"How's your sister doing?" JW asked as Grace sipped from the can.

"They're letting her come home today. She's almost back to one hundred percent."

"Oh, man, that's great."

"Wait a minute...wait a minute," Jack said. "You guys knew she was coming?"

"Well sure. We invited her."

"But...but..."

"Jack, shut up and listen for a minute," JW said. He shoved Jack into a well-worn easy chair, and handed him a slice of pizza. "Now, I know you never wanted your wife to see the way you used to live. And I know why, but I think you've been selling her way short. So I called her and asked her to come. 'Cause she's got a few things she wants to say to you." Then he waved an arm. "Gracie?"

Smiling, Grace took another swig of the beer, set it down, and then came to take the seat beside Jack. "You love being a cop. Admit it."

Jack shook his head. "It's just a job, Grace. I'll be just as happy—"

"You're a liar. I want you doing what you love, not what you think is socially acceptable. JW and I had a long talk, Jack. I know all sorts of things about you that I didn't know before. I know about all the commendations, and about all the war stories, and the good you've done. And I'm not prepared to let you give that up for me."

"I'm not!" he protested.

"No? Listen, Jack, I know one thing for a fact. You can't be that good at something, unless you truly love it."

Jack's gaze slid from Gracie to the TV set behind her. Someone had hit the pause button and the frame, frozen on the screen with wavy lines breaking it in two, was Gracie's face, sweaty and red, hair plastered to it, smiling broadly, eyes sparkling as she walked off the court.

"You're right," he said finally. "No one's that good at something unless they love it."

"Will you guys…excuse us for a minute?" Grace asked.

JW chucked her under the chin, gave her a wink, and led the other guys to the door. "I think we need pretzels, guys. Let's go to the corner store and get some, hmm?"

When they were alone, Jack sat there and stared into his wife's eyes.

And she said, "JW told me about your mother, Jack."

Jack leaned back against the sofa. "Hell, Gracie…"

"Talk to me," she asked him. "Please?"

He sighed. "I was twelve," he finally said. "She went to take a shower, and she stayed in the bathroom for…too long. I got worried. She wouldn't answer the door. So I forced it open, and found her sitting there. Just sitting there in the shower, fully dressed, all her clothes soaking wet, with the water running down on her. She was all curled up, and staring at nothing." He shook his head. "It scared me, Grace."

"I know," she said. "But I'll tell you something, Jack. It's not going to happen to me."

He looked up at her, loving her with every cell in his body. "How can you be so sure?"

"Because if it starts to get to me, I'm going to tell you so. No more secrets. No more lies. I promise you that. I want you to be who you are, Jack, not who you think I want you to be. And who you are is one hell of a cop. And that's who you should stay."

Jack sighed. "What about your mother? Her friends? Your friends?"

"If they don't accept the man I love, they aren't friends at all," she said. "And as for my mother...well, there's a big family dinner at her house tomorrow. A welcome home celebration for Hope. And I think it would be a good time for me to learn to stand up to my mother. I love her, Jack, but her snobbishness is misguided. It has hurt me, and it has hurt you, and it's still hurting Hope. So I'm gonna tell her the truth about you, and tell her how very proud I am to be married to you, and that's the end of the discussion."

"So...you're saying...you honestly don't want me to quit the force?"

"I'm saying I won't let you quit the force."

Jack felt as if a heavy weight were suddenly lifted from his shoulders. "And what are you going to tell her about you?" he asked.

Grace averted her eyes, swallowed hard. "I'm...still thinking about that one."

"She's not going to stop loving you any more than I did, Grace. But you'll see. I'm gonna make things right for you, from now on. And it's going to be fine. You'll see."

Proudly, Grace sat beside her husband at the dinner table and said, "I have something to tell you, Mother."

Her mother lifted her head, glanced worriedly from her husband to Jack, and back to Grace again. "You sound so serious. Surely after all this family has recently come through, nothing can be that bad, can it, Gracie?"

Grace smiled. "It's nothing bad."

"Well, that's a relief. But before you go on with this, I have a few surprises planned for tonight. So, would you mind terribly, darling, letting me go first?"

Frowning, Grace shot Jack a look. He only shrugged. "Sure, Mom. Go ahead."

Mitsy smiled, took her napkin from her lap, and rose to her feet. "Good. I'm so glad to hear it." She walked to the sideboard, opened a drawer, and produced an envelope.

"Your surprise." She handed the envelope to Grace, who opened it and peered inside.

"These are airline tickets."

"Yes, dear. First-class to New York."

Gracie looked again at Jack, but he only shrugged. "You're sending us on a trip to New York?"

"Yes. And don't worry about work, Jack. I've already cleared this with your sergeant and your partner. Such a nice man, that JW. Why you haven't brought him by to visit is simply beyond me."

Grace practically felt her jaw drop open. "You...you... Mother, you knew?"

"I'm your mother, dear. Do you think I'm an idiot?"

"But...but..."

"Oh, do stop gaping, dear. Your husband and I had a long talk last night, and, well, I've realized that there is a whole side to you that you've been afraid to show me. That ends today. I won't tolerate any more such nonsense."

Grace blinked in shock, and looked at Jack. He smiled at her and shrugged innocently. She glanced back at the envelope she held, and frowned harder. "Mom, there are...a dozen tickets in here."

"Yes. For the girls you've been coaching at that gym. You all have floor seats for one of those basketball games. They're in there, too. The, um, oh..." She wiggled her fingers in the air as she sought for a word. "Freedom...or, um, independence or some such patriotic thing...."

Stunned, Grace dug, and found the tickets for the New York Liberty game at Madison Square Garden, about a month from then.

"Here's the thing, dear. One of the assistant coaches and I went to school together. And when I called him to make these arrangements for your girls, I was very surprised to hear that you'd actually turned down an opportunity to audition for this...club."

Now it was Jack's turn to look surprised. "You what?"

"I was being scouted...but Jack, that wasn't...what I wanted to do with my life."

"Gracie, if I find out you turned this down because of me—"

"It wasn't," she said. "It was before I'd even met you, Jack."

"Quite right," her mother said. "I believe she turned it down because of me. Isn't that right, Grace?"

Grace blinked in confusion.

"No matter. You have another chance, if you want it. Whether you take it, is up to you, but I want to make it clear, darling, that I'll be behind you...behind both of my daughters whatever they decide to do. As for your girls, well, your father and I have decided to sponsor their little team. I'm going to pick out some uniforms for them this afternoon. They'll be needing a coach, darling, so if this other thing isn't what you want, then perhaps you can do this. Otherwise, Charlie has agreed to help in that capacity."

Steepling her fingers together, her mother took a deep breath, and said, "And that's it. We can go ahead with dessert now." And she sat back down.

Grace blinked. "You...you got me...a try-out with the Liberty?"

"No, your skills did that. I just...facilitated."

"Oh...my...God." Tears stood in her eyes as she sat there, blinking them back, not believing what she was hearing. She got to her feet and went around the table, hugging her mother hard. Then she straightened again, shaking her head.

"I think she needs some air," Jack said, coming up beside her, slipping his arms around her. "Come on, Grace. A little walk will do you good."

He led her through the house, outside to the patio, and then down the path to the garden, right to the spot where they had first kissed.

"What are you going to do?" he asked her.

"I...oh, Jack, I couldn't...I'm a married woman now. It wouldn't be fair to you—"

"Come here," he whispered, and he pulled her close, kissed her gently. "Anything that makes you happy, is fair to me. If you want to do this, I'll be with you. My job is gonna be here waiting when I get back. And can you imagine the bragging rights I could rack up? Hmm?"

She smiled weakly. "I don't know."

He took both her hands in his. "I love you, Gracie. I love you for who you are, not for what you do. And you of all people ought to understand that. You just spent the past forty-eight hours drumming the same message into my head."

"Jack..."

"Take your time, Gracie. Just know that this isn't a decision between me and something else. I'm a given. I'm here until you toss my sorry butt out the door. You said you could handle being a cop's wife. You made me believe it. Now you better believe that I can handle being your husband— no matter what you decide to do with your life."

Her smile pulled at her lips, as tears ran down her cheeks. "You really mean that?"

"With everything in me, Grace. I love you. I love you, and I have from the second I set eyes on you, lady. That's not gonna change. Not ever. No matter what."

"Oh, Jack. You can't know what that means to me." Licking her lips, she kissed him gently. "I love you, too, you know. The same way. No matter what."

"I know." He smiled, and for the first time, they were looking beyond the masks, beyond the acts, beyond the make-believe. Grace liked what she saw in his eyes when he looked at the real her, and she looked at the real him.

The real thing.

Love.

* * * * *

Dear Reader,

Anniversaries are always special, whether you're celebrating one year or fifty, but those milestone anniversaries are extra special. My husband and I celebrated our twentieth wedding anniversary last year with a laugh for all the people who'd thought it would never last. I could understand their skepticism—one hardheaded, hot-tempered soul paired with another hardheaded, hot-tempered soul doesn't seem like a formula for happily-ever-after. But we've weathered the rough times, learned to compromise, to forgive and forget—which should definitely be a part of all wedding vows!—and we're happily looking forward to our fortieth anniversary and beyond.

This year Silhouette Books is celebrating its twentieth anniversary, too—no small accomplishment. Publishers come and go, and romance lines are launched and sunk, but Silhouette has endured. They've adapted to changing markets and shifting trends, and through it all, they've continued to provide us readers with satisfying stories and quality writing, with great escapes, needed laughs, a good cry and, of course, those happily-ever-afters.

Here's to the next twenty years!

Marilyn Pappano

A Little Bit Dangerous
Marilyn Pappano

To Monica Reynard, who brightens our Fridays.
Chance is all yours, darlin'. Enjoy him.

Books by Marilyn Pappano

Silhouette Intimate Moments

Within Reach #182
The Lights of Home #214
Guilt by Association #233
Cody Daniels' Return #258
Room at the Inn #268
Something of Heaven #294
Somebody's Baby #310
Not Without Honor #338
Safe Haven #363
A Dangerous Man #381
Probable Cause #405
Operation Homefront #424
Somebody's Lady #437
No Retreat #469
Memories of Laura #486
Sweet Annie's Pass #512
Finally a Father #542
*Michael's Gift #583
*Regarding Remy #609
*A Man Like Smith #626
Survive the Night #703
Discovered: Daddy #746
*Convincing Jamey #812
*The Taming of Reid Donovan #824
*Knight Errant #836
The Overnight Alibi #848
Murphy's Law #901
†Cattleman's Promise #925
†The Horseman's Bride #957
†Rogue's Reform #1003
Who Do You Love? #1033
 "A Little Bit Dangerous"

Silhouette Special Edition

Older, Wiser...Pregnant #1200

Silhouette Books

Silhouette Christmas Stories 1989
 "The Greatest Gift"

Silhouette Summer Sizzlers 1991
 "Loving Abby"

36 Hours
You Must Remember This

*Southern Knights
†Heartbreak Canyon

MARILYN PAPPANO

brings impeccable credentials to her writing career—a lifelong habit of gazing out windows, not paying attention in class and spinning tales for her own entertainment. The sale of her first book brought great relief to her family, proving that she wasn't crazy but was, instead, creative. Since that first book, she's sold more than forty others.

She writes in an office nestled among the oaks that surround her country home. In winter she stays inside with her husband and their four dogs, and in summer she spends her free time mowing the yard and daydreams about grass that never gets taller than two inches.

You can write to her at P.O. Box 643, Tulsa, OK 74067-0643.

Chapter 1

Moving quietly, Chance Reynard let himself into the small room that adjoined the personnel director's office, then closed the door behind him. His boss, Anthony Ianucci, was already in the room, an unlit cigar between his teeth, his intense gaze directed at the two-way mirror. On the other side of the thick wall, Sara Walker, whose official title was Wait Staff Supervisor—unofficially, head cocktail waitress—was interviewing for the last slots they needed to fill, the sooner, the better.

"What do you think?" Ianucci asked softly, sifting through a file folder to locate, then hand him the woman's application.

Chance leaned against the desk and skimmed the paper. Francyne Davis, twenty-five, single. Under "Occupation," she'd listed college student, and for "Position Sought," she'd been very specific—cocktail waitress, California Deck, Pacific Lounge. That was where all the high-rollers played their million-dollar games, where the girls could take home more in an evening's tips than most legitimate jobs paid in a week, where just like the players they had the chance of striking it rich.

Of course, no new hire started out on the California Deck. That was a reward reserved for months of loyal service. If Francyne Davis really was a college student, she probably wouldn't be around past the end of summer and wouldn't work her way higher than the Texas Deck—though there was nothing shabby about it, either.

And he suspected she really was a student. As references, she gave the name of a dean over at Ole Miss, as well as her career counselor and... Chance looked at Ianucci. "She's using the pastor of her church as a reference?"

"It's a nice touch. Different, at least. Remember the girl who listed her parole officer?" Ianucci shrugged. "Maybe she wants to impress upon us her honesty."

"Or her naiveté."

"Working on the *Queen* will take care of that."

"The honesty or the naiveté?" Chance asked dryly.

"I think the customers will like her. Sara seems to. Check her out. Sara will hire her on a temporary basis pending the outcome of your investigation." Ianucci tossed the folder to him, then slipped out the door, closing it quietly, leaving Chance alone.

Francyne Davis sat with her back to him, giving him a good view of thick, wavy hair and little else. It was brown, though the word didn't do it justice. It was deep, dark brown, the color rich and pure and liquid, and it fell halfway down her back. It looked heavy and hot, as if it would plaster itself to her skin when the temperatures started to rise, and was custom-made for a man to tangle his hands in when he started those temperatures rising.

Swallowing hard to clear such thoughts from his mind, Chance leaned forward and turned on the speaker that let him eavesdrop on the interview. Sara was explaining the *Queen*'s schedule—two cruises a night, each lasting four hours—and Francyne Davis was nodding. If she was like most of the students who found summer jobs on the riverboat casinos, working from 6:00 p.m. to 3:00 a.m. wouldn't present much of a problem. Neither would working in an environment where the men outnumbered the women twelve to one most nights.

Not that even one of those men was worth having, himself included. Of course, he wasn't looking to be had, either.

"So…do you have any questions?" Sara asked. The redhead sounded cheery, as if being out of bed at eleven in the morning wasn't a rarity in her life. She looked cheery, too, and, in her cotton dress with a matching jacket, about as wholesome as Little Miss College Girl.

"No, I don't believe so."

Nice voice. Damned nice voice, Chance thought. Soft, pure South, womanly and delicate and sexy as hell. All she would have do was talk to her customers and they would open their wallets so she could help herself to whatever she wanted. Hell, he'd developed an immunity to these girls over the past fourteen months, but if she talked nice to him, *he'd* probably give her whatever she wanted.

If she talked dirty, he for damn sure would.

"Good. Then we'll start you this evening—"

"You mean, I've got the job?"

"On a trial basis. We'll have to check out your references and such, but that's not a biggie. As long as they check out and you don't do something awful like run us aground on your first night, you'll be a regular employee by the beginning of next week. What size are you?"

"Size?"

"For your costume."

"Costume?"

Sara smiled. "Honey, this is a Mississippi riverboat. All of our employees wear uniforms of one sort or another. Our dealers and the security staff dress like old-time riverboat gamblers. Our waitresses wear—well, you'll see, just as soon as you tell me your size."

Francyne mumbled an answer that he couldn't catch, but Sara did. Whatever size she wore clearly was bigger than she wanted to be. Of course, he couldn't tell until she stood up, but with that hair and that sultry wicked-sweet voice, he'd wager most men couldn't care less what size she was.

Sara left the office, but he stayed where he was. Some new girls used these few minutes alone to check their makeup or their hair. One had rifled through the papers on the desk. Francyne Davis sat without moving, her head bent. Praying for a decent costume? he wondered with a grin.

She had just leaned forward, as if to get to her feet, when Sara returned. Chance was disappointed. He'd hoped she would come to the mirror so he could see if the front view was as nice as the back.

Sara, bless her heart, hung the white-plastic-encased hanger above the mirror, then maneuvered the bag up and off with a flourish. "Here you go."

Francyne stood and turned to look. With the costume blocking him, he had to step to the side...where the shock that turned her peaches-and-cream complexion all cream couldn't begin to compare to the one that sent him stumbling back against the desk for support. For one endless moment he stared at the purest example of beauty he'd ever seen. She lived up to the hair and the voice, all right. She was womanly and delicate and sexy as hell. Her eyes were chocolate brown, her lips full and delicately arched into a luscious cupid's bow. She was gorgeous. Stunningly, incredibly, unbelievably gorgeous.

And her name was *not* Francyne Davis.

Ianucci must have handed him the wrong application. Jerking up the folder, he flipped through the paperwork filled out by two new bartenders, three busboys and three cocktail waitresses before finding what he was looking for—the form filled out by Mary Katherine Monroe of Jubilee, Mississippi.

A strangled sound from the other side of the glass, matching his own strangled groan, drew his attention back that way. Mary Katherine's mouth worked for a moment before she got any words out. "That? I have to wear that?" she asked breathlessly. "It's too small— My breasts— My hips—" She turned to Sara with a pleading look. "It's not made for my body. Isn't there something else? Maybe one of those riverboat gambler outfits you were talking about?"

Her breasts and hips looked fine to Chance, and always had, but she was right. The costume wasn't made for her body. It was made for tall women, short women, slender, curvaceous women. It was made for desperate women, bold women, women in need of money, in need of morals, in need of a man. The costume was perfect for easy women, tough women, women who'd survived everything life had thrown at them, but it absolutely was *not* made for the body of Miss Small-town Princess, Perfect-in-every-way, Waaay-off-limits-to-everyone-else-to-even-look-at Mary Katherine Monroe.

It had been eight years since he'd seen her, and the years had been kind. She looked exactly as she had back then, only *more*. More gorgeous, more womanly, more desirable. She was five-nine, maybe five-ten, with the longest legs and the curviest curves he'd seen in…well, eight years. She was going to look incredible in feathers and sequins and very little else.

And he was going to have a hell of a time not looking.

Unless he could persuade her to turn down the job. The *Queen* was no place for Mary Katherine, and there was certainly no room for the distraction she would cause him. She'd always distracted him, every time she'd walked into a room, every time she'd walked out. It had been as if he had some sort of radar that alerted him whenever she was around, that had drawn him like a moth to a flame.

But how to persuade—he checked her application—yep, a schoolteacher who was looking for a little summer change of pace to turn away from the best change of pace Mississippi had to offer? Maybe he could convince Sara to renege on the offer…but that wasn't likely to work, either. The redhead wouldn't simply accept his say-so for it, not unless it was a security matter, and no way was he going to tell her the truth. That he'd known Mary Katherine before. Hell, that he'd been in love with her, and the mere sight of her still did funny things to his insides.

So Mary Katherine would have to quit.

Or he would have to learn to ignore her.

He was thirty-four years old, too old to kid himself about unlikely possibilities.

"Sorry, darlin'," Sara said. "The gambler outfits are for the men only. Our customers prefer the girls in something far more revealing."

Gingerly, as if it might hurt, Mary Katherine touched one of the feathers. "Well, you've certainly given them what they want. If I squeeze my body into this costume, there's not going to be anything left to reveal."

The expression that crossed Sara's face was sympathetic. "You'll look fine. Don't worry about your hips. Men like hips. And did I mention that you can usually take in quadruple your week's salary in tips?" After a moment, she prodded Mary Katherine. "You do still want the job, don't you?"

Mary Katherine smiled ruefully. "The library back home has already hired somebody to run the summer reading program. Yes, I still want the job."

"Good," Sara said. "Oh, hey, I forgot to ask what size shoes you wear. I guessed an eight, but if I'm wrong, we can trade 'em."

"An eight's fine—" Mary Katherine got a look at the shoes Sara was holding up, and rueful turned sickly. "It's…it's fine."

"Take these home. Try everything on, then be back here by six—earlier if something doesn't fit. That'll give me an hour to go over things with you before we sail. Eat before you come, because you won't get a dinner break until after eleven tonight. Have I forgotten anything? No?'' Sara smiled brightly. ''Then welcome to the *Queen of the Night,* Mary Katherine. You're gonna love it here.''

Mary Katherine didn't look at all convinced as she took the costume and the heels and left the office.

Chance stayed where he was until she'd had time to go up one flight of stairs to the main deck where the gangway was, then he went out and leaned against the railing. She looked dispirited as she stepped off the gangway and started across the gravel parking lot. He watched until she got into her car—a small green import that looked like a million other imports—and then he turned away.

As soon as he got to his office, he would call Jimbo at the gate and get the make, model and tag number. Then he would start doing what Mr. Ianucci paid him very well to do—something he'd already done quite well eight years ago.

He would check out Mary Katherine Monroe.

Holding the hanger at arm's length, as if the costume might coil around and sink fangs into her, Mary Katherine carried it into the motel room she'd chosen for its cheap price and not its luxurious accommodations. She took it to the sink, hung it on the bar that served as a closet, stepped back and made a small distressed sound.

She was twenty-nine years old. She didn't get enough exercise, but she watched her diet, and she weighed only six pounds more than she had in high school. But she'd never, ever dreamed of squeezing herself into a garment so revealing.

She touched the filmy, see-through fabric that made up most of the outfit, the sequined cups that would remove any hint of natural shape from her breasts, the manmade superfiber that would force her hips—where every ounce of the six pounds had gone—into exactly the shape it wanted, and she whimpered again.

The finishing touch—three-inch heels in emerald green

consisting of little more than sequin-studded straps—darn near made her cry.

"You owe me, Granddad," she muttered out loud in the musty room. "You owe me big-time."

At the thought of her reason for being in Natchez, she went to the phone beside the bed. After six rings, her grandfather answered in his customary overly loud voice. She pitched her own voice louder. "It's me, Granddad."

Immediately he lowered to a whisper—pointless, when he was always alone at this time of day so no one would interfere with the watching of his soap operas. She felt honored that he didn't ask her to call back during a commercial break. "Is that you, Mary Katherine? Are you in Natchez? Have you been to the *Queen?* What did you find out?"

"I got a job on the *Queen* as a cocktail waitress. I start tonight."

"Wonderful! I knew I could count on you!" If he weren't holding the phone, he would be rubbing his hands together with conspiratorial glee. "You'll get the proof I need to convince everyone else I'm innocent. I just know you will."

She wanted to ask him if he'd heard what she said, if he'd paid the least bit of attention to the cocktail waitresses on his one and only visit to the *Queen.* Did he really want his granddaughter, his favorite of all his grandchildren, running around in front of a shipload of strange men dressed the way they dressed? Was he really willing to sacrifice her dignity so he could regain his?

And how could she help him convince everyone else of his innocence when she wasn't convinced of it herself? She'd learned from experience that there were only two hard, cold, indisputable facts about Paddy O'Hara. One, he was a scoundrel. Nothing was ever his fault. He was the unwitting victim of every con artist, ill wind or stroke of bad luck that passed through Mississippi. He was a teller of tall tales, an expert avoider of blame, eternally innocent in a world turned wicked.

And two, she loved him dearly in spite of it.

And that was why she was in Natchez. Why she was going to put on that poor excuse for clothing and wear it in front of God and the world. Why she was going to do her best to help Paddy prove a tale that she didn't believe could be proved.

Well, honesty forced her to admit it was also because she could spend a summer away from Jubilee. A chance to talk to adults instead of smart-mouthed kids. A chance to make more money in a week than her teaching job paid in a month.

Maybe even a chance to have the sort of wicked, passionate, going-nowhere-but-having-great-fun affair that was impossible to have in Jubilee. If she could find a willing, wicked and passionate man who didn't scare her to death. The last one she'd come across, back when she was still in college, had done just that.

Feeling a bit guilty, she forced her attention to the phone. "Listen, Granddad, I've got to go. I've got to get ready for work. I'll call you in a few days, okay?"

"Okay. Until then, mum's the word." He hesitated, then his voice thickened. "Thank you, Mary Kat. You're a better granddaughter than this old man deserves."

"I know I am," she teased, "but you're the only grandfather I've got, so I have to make do. I love you."

"I love you, too. Whoops, commercial's over. Better get back to my show."

Mary Katherine made a face he wouldn't see even if she were standing between him and the TV, then hung up. She was hungry, she needed a newspaper and a map so she could start looking for an apartment, and she needed a pair of sheer-everywhere hose to wear with the costume. Preferably made of some super-industrial microfiber that would make her thighs appear a teensy bit firmer, her stomach a teensy bit flatter, her hips a whole lot smaller.

Between standing in line at a fast-food restaurant, getting

lost and searching three stores for miracle hosiery, her errands took about twice as long as expected. She returned to the motel in time to shower, cool down in front of the window air conditioner and wriggle into the silky, sheer, illusion-creating panty hose. Now it was time for the moment of truth.

She shimmied, struggled, shoved and tugged her way into the costume, keeping her back to the mirror, not wanting to see herself until she was done. Sitting on the bed—and a bit uncomfortably, she might add, on a rump of sequins—she put on the shoes, took a deep breath for courage, then stood.

And swayed. Tottered. Stumbled. She'd never worn three-inch heels in her life. In fact, after her first year of teaching, she'd cleaned her shoe rack of anything higher than an inch. Already she could tell her feet were going to kill her. Oh, the sacrifices she made for her granddad. And a summer away from kids. And great tips.

Feeling reasonably confident in the shoes after a few circuits of the room, she finally approached the mirror over the sink.

The costume was in the Mardi Gras colors of green, gold and purple. It left her shoulders bare, with gold-sequined cups fitting—loosely, she noted with some regret—over her breasts. Emerald-green feathers curved down and away over the sequins in front and curled up over her shoulders and across her back. Translucent purple fabric stretched tautly down across her midriff to within spittin' distance of her hips, where undulating stripes of green and gold sequins extended upward from the crotch to meet in the middle in back.

It was...different. With her hair done up and a heavier hand on the makeup, she would look like a totally different woman. A sexier woman. A woman who just naturally knew things about men, sex and life that Mary Katherine Monroe couldn't begin to guess at.

She could become that person—could make up a name

and a background, could give herself a past, could live a whole other life for two and a half months. And even though she would eventually have to go back to being Miss Monroe, seventh-grade English teacher, she would always have the memories. She would always know she was capable of being more.

Then she became aware of the ache already starting in the ball of her right foot. Who was she kidding? Clothes did not the man, or woman, make. She was who she was. Schoolteacher. Single, small-town girl. Sheltered from the world, innocent, even a bit naive. Wholesome. A summer on the *Queen* wearing a trampy outfit wasn't going to change that.

She traded the heels for her own sandals, maneuvered out of the costume and put on a sundress instead, piled her hair atop her head and did her makeup. Feeling queasy, she gathered the sequins and feathers and made the return trip to the *Queen.*

A security guard at the foot of the gangway checked his clipboard for her name, then directed her to the women's locker room two decks down. There she changed into the outfit once again, finishing just as Sara came in.

"Not bad," the redhead said, giving her the once-over-and-all-around. "Let me give you a few tips before I take you upstairs. First, don't tug at the costume. It's not going to cover anything that isn't already covered, so adjust it and leave it alone. And don't bend over. When you're serving drinks, bend at the knees." Pretending to hold a tray on one palm, she demonstrated on her own three-inch heels in a smooth movement that made Mary Katherine marvel.

"By the way, hon," Sara added candidly, "you might want to stuff something in your top. The tighter the fit, the less chance of flashing anyone."

Mary Katherine gave her chest a rueful look. The same Mother Nature that had seen fit to give her too lush hips had stinted just a bit on top, but she'd accepted it and given up stuffing her bra the first time she'd done it at the age of fifteen...or so she'd thought.

"Flirt with any customer who likes it, but don't try to wander off for a rendezvous onboard the *Queen*. The boss seriously frowns on that. Any private meetings take place on your own time. Oh, and the customer is always right. Always. No matter what. Are you ready?"

"Sure." *Never.*

Sara led her out a different door and back to the main, or Mississippi, deck. "Some of the crew gather in the lounge to play cards before we start boarding. They'll be your first customers. Introduce yourself, first name only, tell 'em you're their waitress for the evening. Memorize their drink orders, and work on matching drinks to faces. The more special you make your customers feel, the more generous they are with the tips."

On the next level, she paused outside double doors that led into a smoky lounge. "Last tips—smile a lot. Make eye contact. And keep moving." She guided Mary Katherine into the room, then, with a wink and a grin, gave a less-than-reassuring explanation for her last bit of advice.

"It's harder to fondle a moving target."

By his count, tonight was Chance's five hundred sixty-second cruise onboard the *Queen*. The first five times it had been interesting. The last five hundred had been rather boring. Uneventful—exactly the way the assistant head of security was supposed to like it.

Tonight he was anything but bored.

Mary Katherine had been assigned, with Sara, to the main deck lounge. It was strictly a bar, a place for their customers to stretch their legs, quench their thirst and prepare to return to the gaming tables. All new girls started there and eventually worked their way up, literally. The restaurant, the by-invitation-only Pacific Lounge and the games were all on the next two decks up. That was where the waitresses made the better tips. That was where he usually spent his evenings, except when he was making rounds or with Ianucci. So far no one had commented that this evening he hadn't left the main deck lounge.

He sat at a distant corner table, left alone by the waitresses and customers alike. A tepid bottle of water stood beside a cigar burned to ash, and a sheaf of papers was spread out before him. Presumably he was working on the next month's schedule for the security staff, but for all the attention he'd paid it, he might have scheduled himself to work all forty-eight cruises alone.

He'd been right this morning. Mary Katherine looked incredible in feathers and sequins. A few of their regulars had spent more time in the lounge than their routines usually allowed, and they'd spent it damn near drooling over her. She'd been clearly self-conscious at first, but unabashed admiration from every single customer had taken the edge off that. She still cast an occasional longing glance, though, at the bartender's gambler get-up.

With a few minor modifications, she would look incredible in it, too. Ditch the brocade vest, the starched white shirt, the string tie, and substitute a tiny, bright gold, green or purple brocade bra... Revealing and concealing, masculine and damnably feminine, tempting, tantalizing. Man, oh, man.

He'd made a few phone calls this afternoon and found that everything she'd put on her application had checked out. Just as her parents had planned before she'd even finished junior high, she had graduated from Ole Miss, moved back home to Jubilee and taken a job teaching at the middle school. But the biggest part of their plan—the perfect husband, perfect house, perfect children—hadn't materialized. He wondered why, wondered what had happened to the perfect fiancé behind whose back they'd met. Whenever he'd allowed himself to remember her, that was how—married to

Mr. Right, chauffeuring kids from soccer to Scouts to ballet, living her perfect life. It had helped him keep his distance.

But there was no Mr. Right. No kids. She lived alone. *Why?*

By all accounts, she was a model seventh-grade English teacher, a model neighbor, a model everything. No one had had anything but praise to offer. She was a dear girl, devoted to her family, beloved by her students, respected by all. She was damn near a saint, to hear them tell it.

And Chance was still too damn much a sinner.

But that didn't stop him from following when Sara, taking pity on her as she did all the newbies, gave her a break right at ten o'clock. If Red was running true to form, she'd also given her directions to the Texas Deck, the second-highest deck where the bow end was reserved for employees on break. Few of them used it in summer, though, preferring air-conditioning, television and food in their own lounge below.

He knew the *Queen* intimately and wasn't hampered by stiletto heels. That was how he reached the Texas Deck a full ninety seconds ahead of her, long enough to settle in the shadows of the overhang from the sundeck above and take a cigar from his pocket.

Her footsteps sounded peculiar, until he realized she'd taken off her heels. As she came into sight, she dropped the shoes into a deck chair, then continued to a point where she could see ahead and to the side. She dragged a chair close to the railing, sat, then squirmed. "Sheesh, I can't even sit comfortably," she mumbled. "Whose bright idea was it to put sequins on the butt of this thing?"

"It wasn't mine, but I'd be happy to remove them for you."

She jumped to her feet and whirled around, searching the shadows for him. He made it easier by lighting the cigar. As soon as he exhaled the first smoke, he belatedly asked, "Do you mind if I smoke?"

He wasn't sure if she'd seen enough in the match's flicker, or if she'd recognized his voice, but he *was* sure she knew him. It was in the shock that left her pale in spite of the heavier makeup she wore. It was in the utter stillness that claimed her for a moment, and it was definitely in the stunned, startled way she said, "Chance? Chance Reynard? Is that— Oh, my God. It *is* you, isn't it?"

"Hello, Mary Katherine." He started to rise from the chair, only to catch the full force of a blow to the jaw that knocked him back down again. By the time he scrambled to his feet, she was on her way to the stairs. He scooped up her shoes as he passed them, stuffed one into each pocket, then grabbed her arm when he caught up with her. "Hey—"

She swung around, her delicate hand clasped again in a fist. Instead of punching him, though, she settled for slapping his hand away. "No, no, no!" she wailed. "This is *not* happening! You are *not* here! This is *my* summer vacation, *my* summer job! You can't possibly be here!"

Backing away a few feet, he gingerly rubbed his jaw. "Gee, Mary Katherine, a greeting like that could almost make a man think you weren't happy to see him. And it's been so long."

"*Happy?* To see *you?*" she shrieked. "I'd hoped you were 'gator bait in a bayou somewhere. I'd hoped— Ohhh!" For a moment he thought she might hit him again—Miss Perfect Manners, Miss Impeccably-Bred Southern Angel, who had probably never been rude a day in her life, who had assuredly never resorted to physical violence in that privileged life. Instead, she squeaked out a choked, distressed sound, then retreated to the railing and crossed her arms over her chest, making an effort to regain control. "*What* are you doing here?"

With the cigar, he gestured toward the gambler's outfit she'd pleaded for with Sara. "I work here. Assistant head of security. Sorry to disappoint you about the 'gator bait, but I'm obviously alive and well." He let his gaze start at the incredible hair piled high on her head, slide all the way down to her feet, then back again, and let a seductive note slide into his voice. "And, obviously, so are you. Which leads to the more interesting question of what are *you* doing here. What is Jubilee, Mississippi's sweetest, most honorable, most virtuous princess doing in an outfit like that in a place like this?"

She wriggled uncomfortably, breaking Sara's first rule about not tugging at the costume. "It's a summer job," she said with a trying-for-careless shrug.

"There are all kinds of summer jobs, like running the library reading program, that don't require you to dress like that or to work in a casino."

"Been there, done that," she said flippantly. "Do you know how much the *Queen* pays its waitresses? Do you have any idea how that compares to what the library pays its summer reading coordinator? Besides—" she tugged again, then gave up, accepting Sara's decree that the costume covered what it would cover and nothing more "—what's wrong with the costume? The customers don't seem to mind."

They certainly didn't. There'd been a time or two down there in the lounge when he'd been tempted to remove his coat and wrap it around her to shield her from a few of the more lascivious looks. Not that he had any right to be shielding her, other than the fact that he'd seen her first.

And how much did that count for? Other men had seen her first eight years ago. One in particular had had quite a prior claim to her, but it hadn't made him keep his distance. Other than a brief twinge of conscience, it hadn't slowed him down at all in his pursuit of her.

He blew out a stream of smoke and watched it hang in the heavy, humid air. "I'd ask how you've been, but your application and background check tell it all—mostly. You still live in Jubilee. You teach school just like Mama and Daddy wanted. And everyone damn near worships the ground you walk on." Eight years ago he'd done a bit of worshiping of his own. For one long, sweet night, he'd worshiped at her body like an altar. He'd fulfilled her every fantasy, satisfied his own every desire, and then...

And then he'd never seen her again.

"And you've graduated from garage mechanic to security guard in a casino."

"Assistant head of security." He was much more than a lowly security guard. More than Mary Katherine had ever suspected, more than he'd ever had the chance to tell her. "What happened to Mr. Right?"

"Don't call him—" She broke off abruptly and turned to face the river, her fingers curling tightly around the railing. Eight years, and the automatic defense of her fiancé—former fiancé?—still came.

Eight years, and he still remembered his automatic response. "If you don't want jokes about Mr. Right, darlin', then don't get yourself engaged to a man named Wright." Jonathan Winslow Wright, as smug and obnoxious as any well-bred young Southern man Chance had known. He'd never understood what she'd seen in Jonathan, but had understood entirely too well what Jonathan had seen in her.

"Jonathan is married and living in Jackson," she said stiffly. "He's a lawyer and doing quite well for himself."

Chance leaned back against the railing, close enough to see her face, distant enough to avoid any unexpected punches. The heat from the day's sun seeped through his coat and warmed him—or was that just the natural heat he'd always felt around her? "Naturally. Arrogant, condescending Southern lawyers tend to do quite well. But why isn't he married to you?"

She opened her mouth as if to answer—such a polite young woman—then closed it again resolutely. After a moment she turned to face him. "Any chance that it's time for you to pull another of your disappearing acts?"

He shook his head slowly from side to side.

"Of course not," she murmured. "You only do that when someone's counting on you."

Guilt prickled the hairs on the back of his neck and made him swallow hard. Often in those eight years he'd fantasized about looking her up in Jubilee and telling her the truth about why he'd disappeared without so much as a goodbye. In his fantasies, she'd understood, forgave him completely and professed her undying love for him, and they'd ridden off into the future together. In reality, he'd thought he would find her happily married to Jonathan, raising children and living the perfect life, and more likely to call the cops on him than to listen to him.

Shaking off the thoughts, he asked the obvious question. "Any chance that you'll change your mind about this job and go back to Jubilee where you belong?"

Just as slowly, just as definitely, she shook her head.

For a moment they simply looked at each other. Even with the heavy makeup and the showgirl costume, she looked amazing. Elegant. Classy. And he felt lucky to be breathing the same air. Some things never changed.

"Okay." She took a deep breath, squared her shoulders and exhaled loudly. "Okay. We're adults. Whatever happened in the past is *in* the past. Over and done with. Forgotten. We're capable of working in the same place for a few months. We're certainly capable of running into each other from time to time and behaving appropriately, right?"

"You mean, now that you've got the urge to smack me out of your system?" he teased, rubbing his jaw again.

"It's not out of my system," she replied seriously. "Just under control. For the moment. So…you'll do your job, and I'll do mine, and we'll never really have to see each other again except in passing, right?"

Chance just looked at her. Oh, lady, he wanted to say, you are so far from *right* that it's not funny. Spend nine hours a day in the confines of the *Queen* and not see each other? Already, the old radar was working again. Already, his stomach was tied in knots from remembering, feeling, wanting again. But he didn't tell her any of that. He let her convince herself and even played his part. "Right. Sure."

"And when school starts again, I'll be out of here, and everything will be okay, and—" Looking up, she smiled brightly, the same sort of sunny, barely-hiding-the-panic smile she'd given the evening's first customer who'd gotten overly friendly. "And until then we can make this work, right?"

"Right."

If his *right* sounded halfhearted and as phony as her smile, she gave no sign of it. "It's time for me to get back to the lounge. My shoes—"

Pulling them from his pockets, he dangled them by thin straps and watched the sequins catch and reflect the light before she pulled them away. She sat in the nearest deck chair to put them on, then stood and swayed just a second. Then she smiled that smile again. "So...thanks for letting me know in private that you're here. I'll head back down to the lounge, and...I won't be seeing you around."

Chance watched her move, so graceful in spite of the pain the green-sequined torture devices were inflicting. He watched until she was out of sight, and even then he spoke in a voice too soft to carry more than a few feet. "Oh, you'll be seeing me, angel. I'm not that strong."

Turning to the rail once more, he flipped the cigar into the river, followed its glowing tip until the water extinguished it, then took a breath of warm, reasonably fresh air. The river scents of mud, decaying vegetation and lush growth filled his lungs but couldn't overwhelm the delicate, subtle fragrance Mary Katherine had left behind. It had only taken him...oh, a year or two to get rid of the scent before. How long would it take this time?

"Was that the new girl?"

Chance had become aware of Ianucci's presence just seconds before he spoke—soon enough that he wasn't startled but instead turned slowly to look at his boss in the shadows. "One of them. Mary Katherine Monroe." In the all-too-luscious flesh.

"How is she doing?"

"The usual complaints. The costume's too skimpy. The shoes hurt her feet. You were right. The customers like her. Hell, I think some of them plan on taking up permanent residence in the lounge as long as she's there."

"She's lovely," Ianucci said dispassionately, in the same way he might remark that a cool spring day was lovely, or a newly acquired antique from Japan, or a sleek, fresh-off-the-assembly-line Ferrari. Nothing excited him much besides money and danger.

Chance didn't give a damn about either of the above, but Mary Katherine... She'd excited him in a way no other woman ever had. Eight years ago he'd tried to kid himself that it was purely sexual, that he'd been celibate too long, that any beautiful woman would have affected him the same. Back then he'd been too smart to believe his own lies, and he was even smarter now. It was *her*. There was something different about her, something special. Something...dangerous. And for that reason, along with all the others, he really was going to keep his distance from her.

Honest to God.

"Did her background check out?" Ianucci asked.

"So far. She's never been arrested, never even had a parking ticket. She owns an old house in Jubilee, pays her bills on time, gives money to charity and invests twenty percent of her income in low-risk, low-yield mutual funds. She teaches seventh-grade English, does volunteer work and is a top contender for the title of Little Miss Perfect."

"So what is she doing on the *Queen?*"

Chance shrugged. "She's twenty-nine, beautiful, and should be having the time of her life. Instead she's living in Podunk, Mississippi, where high school football is the most exciting thing that ever happens. She spends her days trying to teach kids who don't want to learn and her evenings sitting home correcting their lousy papers. For a change of pace, she spends her summers at the library trying to motivate kids who don't want to read to read. If that were your life, wouldn't you rather be on the *Queen?*''

"If that were my life," Ianucci said dryly, "I'd shoot myself. So…do we give Sara the okay on her?''

"I see no reason not to." Except for the fact that he wanted nothing more than to strip her naked and make love to her until neither of them could remember the reasons they shouldn't.

Ianucci nodded, then walked to the railing. Chance joined him, watching the water curl away from the hull. Before long, the *Queen* would be putting into her berth in Natchez. Some customers would leave, and others would come aboard. Over the next four hours an obscene amount of money would change hands, and a few bold guests would strike deals with a few enterprising waitresses. They, at least, wouldn't go home alone tonight.

He wondered how long it would be before someone tried to make such a deal with Mary Katherine.

He wondered what he would do if she tried to accept such a deal.

Ianucci broke his silence with the point of his visit. "Our friends from San Francisco are arriving in the morning. They'll be dining aboard the *Queen* after our meeting. Can you be here by ten?''

"No problem."

"Good." His boss walked away as quietly as he'd come.

Chance leaned on the railing. Ianucci's San Francisco friends were, of course, nothing of the sort. They were coming on business that involved great sums of money and, as a result, great risks. In addition to the Sig Sauer .9 mm tucked at the small of his back, he would need something more compact, easier to keep handy and out of sight at the same time. Ianucci didn't go in for overt displays of fire-power. A .22 in his coat pocket should be fine.

He stared into the water once more with one curious question on his mind. What would Mary Katherine think if she knew his job required carrying a gun?

And using it?

Chapter 2

Mary Katherine drowned out the beeping of the alarm clock by smothering it under the extra pillow, then slowly forced her eyes open. Lord, it hadn't all been a bad dream. She really was living in a cheap Natchez motel and working on a gambling boat as a waitress with exhibitionist tendencies, and her body really was killing her.

And Chance Reynard really was back in her life. After eight years of hearing not one word from him, eight years of feeling like a fool, of loving him, hating him, wanting him, cursing him, he was back. With his dark blond hair and wicked green eyes, he was as handsome as ever, quite possibly sexier than ever, undoubtedly more lethal to her ego than ever.

A young woman was entitled to make a few mistakes in her life, Mary Katherine's mother had always counseled her. Chance Reynard had been her first mistake. Telling Jonathan and the world about him had been the second. Not screaming and running the other way last night just might be her third. How many mistakes? she wanted to ask her mother. How many chances could she take—she groaned at the bad pun—and still survive?

She should follow his advice and go back to Jubilee where she belonged. But how could she tell Granddad his one opportunity to prove his innocence was blown because she'd run into an old flame? How could she tell anyone that her summer adventure—fabulous pay, decadent work hours and freedom from kids—had ended before it even started? Besides, who was Chance Reynard to tell her where she belonged? Hadn't she listened to him once before, and hadn't it cost her a broken heart? They were mature adults. They could handle this situation. He would stay out of her way, and she would most definitely stay out of his way, and they would both be happy.

Uh-huh.

She'd left the *Queen* shortly after three this morning, driven to the motel and fallen into bed, clothes dropped on the floor, makeup still on her face. She couldn't remember the last time she'd been so tired. The last time she'd spent eight straight hours on her feet, and in heels, no less. The last time every single part of her body had radiated pain with the slightest movement.

And here it was barely eleven o'clock, and the clock wouldn't stop its infernal beeping. Digging it out from under the pillow, she focused long enough to find the off button and pressed it, then dropped it to the floor. She desperately needed more sleep—eight, ten hours should do it—but Sara was on her way over to take her to look at an apartment she swore would be perfect, which this dingy room certainly wasn't.

Sitting up, she groaned out loud. Every muscle protested, some viciously, but she didn't stop the movement until she was on her poor, aching, abused feet. Maybe a shower and some aspirin would help—better yet, a week-long, drug-induced coma. Or maybe she could go to work early and serve herself a few stiff drinks, or just throw herself in front of the first busload of tourists.

The aspirin helped a little, the shower a little more. By the time Sara knocked at the door, Mary Katherine was dressed in a sleeveless dress with a fitted bodice and a flared skirt, and she'd eased her feet into her most comfortable pair of shoes. She limped to the door, invited the woman in, then limped back to the sink to put on makeup and braid her hair.

Sara laughed. "Feeling a little sore today, are we? I've got just the cure for you. Eladio."

"Who or what is Eladio?"

"He's the boss's masseuse—or is that masseur? Whatever. There's a massage room off the gym on the *Queen*, and whenever Eladio's not working on Mr. Ianucci, he's available to the rest of the crew."

Mary Katherine met her gaze in the mirror. "The *Queen* has a gym? And a masseur?"

"Sure. Mostly the bodyguards use the gym, but any crew member can. Some of the girls do, trying to look better in their costumes."

Mary Katherine felt sluggish, as if the lack of sleep had dulled her brain. "Bodyguards?"

"You know, security."

There was a big difference between bodyguards and security guards, Mary Katherine wanted to point out. Innocuous places like schools and shopping malls had security guards, but only the wealthy, famous, powerful or dangerous required bodyguards. Exactly which did the *Queen* employ?

Seeing the opportunity to fish for information, she injected a casual tone into her voice as she fastened her earrings. "I met one of the security guys last night on my break. His name was Chance Reynard." Not that she was curious about him, or cared at all about his life in the years since he'd left her. But forewarned was forearmed, her mother always said. Know your enemy, Jonathan had long preached.

"O-oh, wouldn't you just like to take him home with you?

He's incredible. Oh, and, hon, he's not *just* one of the guys. Chance is assistant head of security. He's not quite Mr. Ianucci's right-hand man, but he's close.''

Mary Katherine kept her gaze to herself as she recalled the lazy, sexy, tantalizing way he'd looked her over when he'd made the comment about being alive and well. There'd been a time when she was foolish enough, naive enough, to think that he saved those looks for her, but she was older now, and wiser. No doubt, he turned the same charm on every woman he came across—and no doubt, with often the same results.

"But," Sara went on with a melodramatic sigh, "guys like him never look twice at girls like me."

Her, either, Mary Katherine acknowledged, with the obvious exception. Living down the twin scandals of her infidelity and breaking off her engagement had required a lifestyle that was above reproach. By the time she'd finally gotten over that and the heartache, and decided it was safe to have a man in her life again, she'd acquired a reputation for being so proper that the only attention she'd attracted had come from the serious types like Dennis Mills, the principal at her school, not the handsome bad boys.

Not that Dennis wasn't perfectly nice. He was smart, liked his job and was good at it. Everyone in Jubilee knew he was in line to be the next principal of Jubilee High, and would probably go on to head the school board someday. It didn't matter one bit that he had a receding hairline, an expanding waistline, a poor sense of humor and no sense of adventure.

But it did matter that he'd never, not once, looked at her the way Chance had. It mattered a lot that she'd never, not once, considered risking anything, much less everything, to be with him.

"I take it Chance isn't married."

"Oh, no. He's available, if you're interested."

"I'm not interested."

Sara's snort was most inelegant. "Oh, come on. You're breathing, aren't you?"

Unable to dawdle a moment longer, Mary Katherine turned away from the mirror. "I'm ready."

"Good." Sara bounced to her feet with an energy Mary Katherine might never feel again. "I'll show you the apartment, then we'll have lunch, and then I'll take you to the *Queen* and introduce you to Eladio. Believe me, he'll fix whatever's broke. You'll feel like a million bucks for tonight's shift."

As she followed Sara less than gracefully to her car outside, Mary Katherine sincerely hoped she was right.

The apartment was on the first floor of an older house in an older neighborhood. It was a short drive to the *Queen*, the rent was easily manageable on her regular salary, and the tall ceilings and spacious rooms reminded her of her own house back in Jubilee. Mary Katherine signed the lease, took the keys and considered reneging on lunch and Eladio so she could move in immediately. But when the grumbling of her empty stomach was enough to send an ache through her, she decided to stick to the original plan.

Two hours later, with Eladio working his charm everywhere he touched, she was glad she had. The room was dimly lit, the table surprisingly comfortable. She lay on her stomach, wearing nothing but a sheet that was modestly draped, and she drowsily thought she might have gone to heaven as Eladio's strong fingers worked the kinks out of tight muscles down her legs. When he reached her left calf, she gave a great, satisfied moan.

"Now that sounded almost erotic."

Instantly her newly relaxed muscles tensed again. She opened one eye and saw a pair of running shoes, two nicely muscled legs and a pair of well-worn jogging shorts. She couldn't look higher without moving, but she didn't need to. She knew only one man with a voice like that, only one man who could send tension streaking through her with no more than a well-worded tease. "We had a deal," she murmured. "Go away."

Instead he crouched in front of her, where she could see that shoes, socks and shorts were all he wore. His chest was broad, smooth, golden-brown, damp with sweat and, like his legs, impressively muscled. His dark blond hair was damp, too, and slicked back from his face. He looked powerful. Purely male. Purely sexual.

And she felt like an inexperienced little virgin who just might melt into a puddle at his feet.

"You don't really want me to go away, angel. I have a message for you from Sara. She said to tell you she forgot she had a fitting for her wedding dress this afternoon."

"She's getting married?"

"In two weeks."

And just this morning she'd been bemoaning the fact that Chance had never looked twice at her. Not an auspicious beginning for a marriage, Mary Katherine thought. "Fine. You've delivered Sara's message. Now go away."

"That's not all of it. I'm giving you a ride home."

Home being a sleazy motel with a rumpled bed not four feet inside the door. This time she couldn't swallow, couldn't blink away the image of the two of them making good use of that bed, couldn't put the words together to tell him she'd rather walk all the way back on her poor, aching feet.

He didn't wait for a response, though. He unfolded to his feet with great ease and actually had the nerve to muss her hair as he walked past. "I'm going to take a shower and meet you outside. Don't take too long."

She delayed as long as she could, but her time with Eladio was up too soon, and he had another client waiting. Dragging excess sheet behind her, she padded barefoot into the dressing room, luxuriating in the miracles the masseur had wrought. Her body felt light, fluid, formless, though her feet still ached.

But once she stepped out into the hall—the passageway, the crew called it—and saw Chance waiting, the stiffness returned. ''I really don't need a ride home.''

He subjected her to another of those lazy appraisals that made her feel vastly underdressed, which was ridiculous. Except for her arms and a bit of her throat, the dress covered her from shoulder to ankle. She was appropriately dressed for anything from school to church to a casual dinner out.

For anything but Chance Reynard's lazy green gaze.

Folding her arms across her chest, she stumbled on. ''I— I can call a cab if you'll point me to a pay phone.''

Once again he leaned toward her and lowered his voice correspondingly. ''I've seen you in a lot less, angel.''

Giving him a narrowed scowl, she started for the stairs. He certainly had seen her in less, and long before last night. In fact, he'd seen her wearing nothing but moonlight on the banks of a lazy creek that meandered through somebody's property. He'd told her she was beautiful, told her he loved her, told her he wanted her more desperately than words could say, and then he'd shown her, time after time, all night long, until sunrise forced them back into their clothing. It had been the most incredible night of her life…followed by the most horrific day.

No matter how hard she'd tried, she'd never forgotten walking into the garage that afternoon, both emotionally jazzed from their lovemaking and wiped out from telling Jonathan and her parents about it. She'd gone to tell Chance that she'd ended the engagement, that she was free to be with him, that nothing stood between them. She'd expected to see joy in his eyes, to be swept up into his arms and thoroughly kissed, to hear once more those words of love that had wrapped themselves around her heart and her very soul.

Instead she'd been met by Jake, another mechanic at the garage. Chance was gone, Jake had told her. He'd packed up and moved on that morning. He hadn't known where he was going, hadn't known if he would ever be back. He'd only known it was time to go.

She'd thrown away her safe, secure future for him, and he'd left her.

God, just the memory of it made her want to smack him again!

She'd gone up two flights of stairs and halfway down the gangway, with Chance on her heels, before she stopped abruptly. "Which part of 'I don't want a ride' did you not understand?"

"I understand all of it." His shrug was pure innocence. "But I haven't heard you say it yet."

Mary Katherine closed her eyes and tilted her face to the sky. It was three o'clock, and she had plenty to do before coming to work at six, starting with checking out of Motel le Dump and moving into her apartment. It was a hundred and eighty degrees, the humidity made the air so thick she could barely breathe, and all the magic Eladio had worked was slowly seeping away into the hot nonskid surface beneath her feet.

And Chance was right. She hadn't actually said she didn't want a ride from him.

"I should think, after last night's conversation, I wouldn't have to bluntly spell it out for you. You remember. When we agreed to keep our distance."

"Aw, come on, angel," he said, his voice the essence of a lazy, sexy Southern drawl. "We tried that before, remember? And it didn't work. What makes you think it'll be any different this time?"

"Because we're older. More mature. Less naive."

"Sugar, I was *never* naive." He grinned as he covered his eyes with a pair of dark glasses. She wondered where they'd come from. After his shower, he'd changed into jeans worn to body-hugging softness and a snug-fitting white T-shirt. She would swear there wasn't room to hide a credit card, much less glasses...if she was looking that closely at him. Of course, she wasn't, she insisted as she forced her gaze back to his eyes, now hidden. She wished for her own sunglasses but couldn't remember where they should be, couldn't think where she might look.

The breath she took was superheated and spread through her with the searing force of a wildfire. She wasn't sure her voice would work, was surprised that it didn't come out a hoarse, husky rasp. "*I* was naive. I didn't know back then what a man like you could do."

He trailed one finger down her bare arm and sent a shiver racing through her. "And what can a man like me do?" But this time there was no drawl, no natural arrogance or sex appeal. Just a soft, serious question, as if he really wanted to know.

He could make a woman forget common sense, good intentions, her own name. He could make her throw twenty-one years of proper upbringing out the window. Could make her stretch out and purr, beg, lose herself and her dignity and her pride. He could make her become a whole other person, a special person to be wanted—at least, temporarily—by him, and he could just as easily turn her into a fool.

His finger curved around the crook of her elbow, glided down her forearm, then loosely encircled her wrist. Such a simple touch, so innocent and so wicked. Hypnotizing, mesmerizing, promising everything…and delivering nothing. Nothing but heartache, hurt, tears, guilt.

Mary Katherine forced herself to step away, to move resolutely down the gangway to the gravel parking lot. The *Queen*'s berth was at the end of a narrow street that led noplace else—to keep the common tourists away, according to Granddad. Regular tourists, he'd stated with some conceit, weren't really welcome on the *Queen*. She catered to a higher class of player.

Even now, remembering the self-importance in his voice made her eyes roll. Maybe he'd been fleeced, as he claimed, or maybe he was just a bad gambler. Either way, at least he'd found some satisfaction in the knowledge he'd lost his life savings in a place that didn't deign to rip off the common tourist.

In the middle of a hot June afternoon, hours before the *Queen*'s first evening cruise, there was no traffic at all on the street, but surely it wasn't far to the nearest pay phone. Not that Chance was going to let her walk to a pay phone, or honor the agreement they'd made last night, or do anything at all that wasn't exactly what *he* wanted. The sooner she gave in and accepted that, the sooner she could get to the motel and start packing.

When she'd come to a stop in the parking lot, so had he. She glanced at the dozen cars parked in a haphazard pattern, from the elegant silver Mercedes closest to the gangway to a cherry-red Cuda in the corner with enough power under the hood to leave all comers in its dust. With its sleek, mint-condition body and the powerful rumble of its finely tuned engine, it was enough to make any man with the slightest appreciation for things mechanical stop for a lingering, longing look. She and it had been the loves of Chance's life eight years ago, or so he'd claimed.

But when he'd left her behind without even a goodbye, he'd taken the Cuda with him. While he'd forgotten she even existed in the years since, he'd pampered the Cuda into impeccable condition. Of course, he'd still had a use for the Cuda. Sex, he could get with any woman anywhere merely by crooking his finger or grinning that brash, wicked, lust-inspiring grin. But when the sex was over, he'd always needed the Cuda to get away.

When she turned in the car's direction, Chance fell into step beside her, feeling a hint of unexpected relief that she wasn't going to be difficult. Until that moment he hadn't realized how important it was that she go along with him, that she give up this stupid notion of keeping their distance. He wasn't much interested in wasting his time on futile exercises.

He opened the passenger door for her, and a blast of heat billowed out. By the time they'd rolled down the windows and left the parking lot, sweat was trickling down his spine and his face was damp with it. "You know, I love this baby," he commented, patting the blistering dash, "but there are times when I find myself looking longingly at a newer model with dual climate control."

She smiled faintly. "But think of all you'd have to give up just to get a decent air conditioner. Newer models have no personality."

"Air cooled to seventy degrees can be personality enough." Reaching State Street, he asked, "Where to?"

She gave him the names of the intersection nearest her motel. When he pulled into the parking lot and followed her directions to her room at the back, he gave a low whistle. "Oh, angel, I wasn't just a once-in-a-lifetime aberrance, was I? You like living dangerously."

She glanced around the parking lot and at the bar next door. "This place is all right."

"All right? If Natchez has a crime central, this is it. You're probably the only law-abiding citizen anywhere on this street." He deliberately left himself out of the "law-abiding" part.

"I wasn't sure how long it would take me to find an apartment, so I wanted someplace cheap. But I'm moving out today."

"I'll wait while you do," he said, giving the parking lot another look while she unlocked the flimsiest of dead bolts, then led the way into a dingy room. The carpet's original color was indistinguishable, and its primary characteristic was the way it stuck to the soles of his shoes. The walls were dark brown, the light bulbs insufficient, and the window air conditioner provided more noise than cooling.

Leaving the door open, he stopped beside the bed and watched as she hefted a suitcase onto the rumpled covers. She packed quickly and efficiently, folding sundresses still on hangers into the suitcase, stuffing cosmetics and toiletries into a large zippered bag. Within five minutes, with the showgirl costume tossed on top, she was done.

He carried her bags to her car, stowing them while she went inside the motel office to check out. When she returned, he was leaning against the driver's door, blocking her way, watching as she struggled with her perfect-Southern-belle upbringing to find a way to politely send him on his way. Grinning, he said, "You're welcome."

That earned him the faintest hint of a smile. "Thank you. Since we've had this little…visit this afternoon, there's really no need for me to see you at work tonight, is there?" Though she phrased it as a question, she was clearly too hopeful by half that his answer was going to be no. He almost hated to disappoint her.

"I've always got a need, darlin'." Ever since the day she'd walked into the garage where he was working, wrapped in an aura of untapped sensuality, trailing subtle fragrances that snared him more thoroughly than the most addictive drug, rousing the most incredible sense of possessiveness he'd ever known. "I'm having trouble with my car," she'd said in a delicate-Southern-flower way, and he'd been a goner.

Jake had warned him away from her. So had the two-carat diamond rock on her ring finger. Hell, he'd given himself the sternest warnings of all. For all the good they'd done.

"Well…" Clearly she *was* disappointed with his answer. "Goodbye."

He grinned at the deliberate finality of her farewell and purposely made his own goodbye equally tentative. "See you around, sugar."

Moving aside, he let her climb into her car. The engine started right up, and he could see by the faint stirring of her hair that the air conditioner was turned on full-blast with all vents pointed her way. He could also see her lips moving as she backed out of the parking space, and he'd even give good odds that he'd understood what she'd said. *Not if I can help it.*

If she could help it, she was stronger than he was, or maybe more immune. He didn't think so, though. He'd felt her shiver when he'd touched her arm there on the gangway. He'd seen the look that had come into her eyes before she'd chased it away—the lazy, hazy, turned-on look that was damn near enough to make a man weak.

She wasn't immune. Neither of them was.

Giving the motel one last, disbelieving look, he got into his car and peeled out of the parking lot. Usually he reported to work around five o'clock. Today he wanted to make a phone call first.

His apartment was located in an older building a few miles from the *Queen*. It was pretty standard—living and dining room, galley kitchen, bedroom and bath. Like newer-model cars, it lacked personality, but the air-conditioning worked just fine, and he didn't spend enough time there to care that it was an exact cookie-cutter replica of literally tens of thousands of apartments across the country. It was a place to store his belongings and to sleep—usually alone. Nothing more.

He took a bottle of water from the mostly empty refrigerator, sat at the dining table and dialed the number he'd committed to memory fourteen months ago. He'd committed the usual answer to memory, too.

"Jake's Classic Cars. You need a part, we'll find it."

"Hey, Jake."

"Chance. One of my best customers. How's the Cuda?"

"Hot."

Jake put a different spin on the word than Chance had intended. "It's always been hot, son. That's what attracted you to it in the first place."

"Yeah, well, I gotta tell you, something with a really cold A.C. system is looking good about now."

"You say that every summer."

"This summer I mean it."

"You say *that* every summer, too," Jake replied, making Chance laugh. "You decide to trade it in on some little plastic-and-chrome four-wheel-drive sport-utility vehicle, let me know. I could come up with about a hundred buyers in an afternoon."

"I'm not talking about trading it in. Just maybe giving it a rest on some of these hundred-degree afternoons." He took a long drink of water, then said, "We've got a bunch of new hires. You ready?"

"Go ahead."

Aware that the tape recorder was running, Chance rattled off the list from memory, not hesitating until he got to the last name. Mary Katherine.

There was a moment's silence on the line, then Jake said, "*The* Mary Katherine Monroe?"

"The one and only."

The curse his boss muttered was low and indistinct. The sigh that followed it wasn't. "Your daddy named you right, son. You got some luck."

Chance lifted the water bottle to his forehead, letting the condensation help the cooling job the air conditioner had started. Jake was one of the few people in the state who knew much about Chance's family—that his father was a gambler, that he'd named his first son Chance because it was French for luck, that Chance's family nickname was, in fact, Lucky.

"She still turn you inside out?"

"And upside down."

"What in sweet hell is she doing on the *Queen?*"

"Summer job. Make some money. Get away from the kids she teaches the other nine months of the year."

"Does she know you're there?"

"We've had a few run-ins."

"She get over eight years ago?"

"Not so you'd notice."

After a moment Jake pointed out, "You've got the say-so to get her fired."

Chance was well aware of that, but what would it accomplish? All the old feelings—the need, the desire, the possessiveness—had already come back to life. Getting her removed from the *Queen* wouldn't make them go away. It wouldn't get her out of his mind, and it would be pretty damned unfair to her. Hell, being the determined person she was, she would probably just go on down the river to the next casino, where he couldn't see her every day, where he couldn't watch out for her and make certain she was all right.

"Let her keep the job," he said decisively. "It's just for ten weeks, and then she'll go back to school." And everything would be okay.

If you can let her go, a tiny voice whispered.

He'd walked away from her once. Was he strong enough to do it again? Did he even *want* to do it again?

"It's your decision," Jake said. "What do your other sources say about these new folks?"

"They all seem to be exactly what they say. Bartenders, bus boys and cocktail waitresses." Mr. Ianucci paid him well to do background checks on all the *Queen*'s employees, and had even provided him with the means—a credit bureau membership to gain access to financial records, a cop on the take to provide access to criminal records—but Chance liked to double-check everybody. After all, the FBI was often able to find out things that other people couldn't.

"Anything in particular you want to know about Mary Katherine Monroe?"

Chance stared at the painting that hung above the dining table. It had come with the apartment and consisted of blobs of primary colors in geometric shapes. Some joker of an artist had titled it *Country Flowers in Bloom* and persuaded some other joker to make prints and distribute it. It was true what they said—there was a sucker born every minute.

And he was the sucker born for Mary Katherine. Yes, there were plenty of things in particular he wanted to know about her. Such as every detail of the last eight years of her life. Why wasn't she married to Mr. Right? Why hadn't some guy swept her off her feet and claimed her for his own? Had there been many men in her life since him, and exactly how much a part of her life had they been? What did she do, think, say? How did she live? What had her life been like a week ago, and a week before that, and a week before that?

"No," he replied. He had a million questions, but he intended to get every one of the answers from the source.

"Okay. I'll run these people through our computers and see what comes up. How did this morning's meeting go with the San Francisco partners?"

Chance related the details of the meeting—who was there, what was discussed, what was agreed upon. He had a great memory for details, so great that he could discuss business without missing a single point and still have at least half of his mind focused on something—someone—else. He could recite percentages and cuts on Ianucci's latest money-laundering scheme while wondering where Mary Katherine's new apartment was, and if she'd chosen a better neighborhood than the one where she'd spent last night, and when she was going to acknowledge the futility of trying to avoid him. There was something between them—always had been and, he would wager, always would be.

The trick was figuring out exactly what it was, and making it work. With his secrets between them, that last might be damn near impossible.

"Okay," Jake said when he finished talking. "I'll see what I can find out about these new people and give you a call. And, Chance? Watch out for yourself."

It was Jake's standard farewell. Chance offered his standard, too. "Will do."

He always watched out for himself. When he lived a lie,

when he worked with dangerous people and deceived them
with everything he said, everything he did, if he didn't watch
out for himself, he could easily wind up dead. But somehow
that Wednesday afternoon, it seemed there had been an extra
measure of concern in Jake's voice.

Because of Mary Katherine.

There was no need for Jake to worry. Chance was going
to watch out for her, too. They were both going to come out
of this in one piece—maybe together, maybe not. Either
way, though, they would both survive. He was counting on
it.

Hell, he was betting his life on it.

Chapter 3

It was a quarter after eleven, and Mary Katherine was fifteen minutes into her hour-long dinner break. She'd filled a plate from the buffet that lined one long wall of the employee lounge four decks down, snagged a bottle of cold water, then made her way to the bow end of the Texas Deck to eat in blissful solitude.

Now only a few bites remained on her plate. Her green-sequined heels stood next to her chair side by side on the deck, and her feet were propped on the seat of a second chair as she gazed into the darkness. Other than the paddle wheel, the quiet was broken only by distant sounds—an occasional raucous laugh from below, a train whistle somewhere off to the east, a whippoorwill calling in the night. A faint breeze cooled the air, making the muggy heat bearable if not quite comfortable.

She'd had a busy evening, though the *Queen* always had busy evenings, according to Sara. Given the chance, she could probably doze off right there, at least until some other waitress in need of a dinner break came looking for her.

If *anyone* came looking for her, she hoped it was Chance, she thought, then felt a rush of guilt. No, no, she did *not* want him seeking her out...though she couldn't deny she'd been keeping an eye open for him all evening, wondering when he would put in an appearance, curious whether he'd believed her insistence this afternoon that she didn't want to see him tonight. Maybe so. The first cruise had come and gone with no sign of him.

Or maybe not.

The breeze brought a whiff of cigar smoke, pleasant in an outdoors-in-fresh-air sort of way. When she turned, her gaze went automatically to the shadows where he stood, as if drawn there by some power she didn't understand. She studied him for a moment, though she really couldn't see anything but shapes, and felt him returning the look. After a time, she gestured to the empty chair at the table. "Would you like to join me?"

For a long moment he didn't move except to lower the cigar from his mouth. She idly wondered if it could be someone else standing there—one of the three dozen security guards, perhaps, or one of the countless customers onboard for the *Queen*'s late cruise, but she didn't give the possibility any credence. Not one of the three dozen security guards or the countless customers could affect her the way Chance did. In fact, not one other man in her entire life had ever affected her the way he did. It was him. She recognized him as surely as if a spotlight shone on his face.

Finally he moved from the shadows, approaching her with his easy, lethal grace, sliding lazily into the chair. "Considering the extremes you've gone to, I thought you might want to be alone."

She shrugged. She was alone a lot. In the cosmic sense, she'd been alone for eight years. Ever since that warm April day when he'd disappeared without a trace.

"How's it going?"

"My feet are killing me, but not quite so badly as last

night. My back hurts, as well as every muscle in my legs, and sequins are still not the most comfortable thing to sit on, but...I've made a small fortune in tips, I've had two marriage proposals, and I've remembered to keep moving.''

''Because it's harder to fondle a moving target,'' he said dryly. ''Just be prepared, angel—some men can manage anyway.''

''So I've learned. It's definitely my most interesting summer job ever—not that that's saying a lot,'' she said with a laugh. ''I wouldn't want to waitress full-time, but it's fun for a change.''

He shifted to prop one foot on the chair beside hers. ''You look pretty sitting out here. Like some exotic bird.''

Her mouth curved in a rueful smile. ''I don't believe I've ever been called exotic before.''

''What's exotic but different and special? You're definitely that, sugar. At least, in my world.''

The smile slowly faded as a twinge of hurt whispered through her. ''Please don't say things like that.''

''Why not?''

''Because I might believe them, and they're not true.''

''They're true, angel. Every word of them.''

''Mary Katherine,'' she said sharply. ''My name is Mary Katherine.''

He gave her a long, steady look that made her feel warm and cold at the same time. Anticipating and dreading. Wanting and needing. ''I've never forgotten your name, Mary Katherine. I've never forgotten anything about you.''

Some traitorous part of her wanted to believe him— wanted it more than she'd imagined she was capable of wanting. Maybe because he'd been her first love, her only love, or maybe because she wanted to believe she hadn't been a complete fool all those years ago, that she wasn't about to prove the depths of her foolishness again. Whatever the reason, deep inside she *wanted* to believe him.

But she couldn't. Shouldn't. Wouldn't.

With an uneasy smile and no finesse whatsoever, she changed the subject. "Do you really smoke those things, or is it part of the costume?"

It took him forever to pull his gaze from her face, to shift his attention to the cigar he held. He studied the burning tip as if it might hold some great secret before flipping it with practiced ease over the railing and into the river. "I go through about one a night. Sometimes they just burn to ash. Sometimes I don't even light them. And sometimes I do smoke them. But I don't inhale."

She smiled faintly at his last dry remark. "How did you make the jump from garage mechanic to assistant head of security on a riverboat casino?"

"Is that your way of asking what I've done the last eight years?"

Mary Katherine considered it a moment, then shrugged. "I guess so."

"I've worked. Different places, different towns. A year or so ago, I met Mr. Ianucci in New Orleans—saved him from getting arrested. To show his gratitude, he offered me a job. I'd never worked security before, but it turned out I was good at it. I got promoted quickly. And so here I am."

"Arrested for what?"

He tilted his head to one side to study her. "Do you know anything at all about the man you're working for?"

She shook her head. She hadn't actually thought of herself as working for anyone in particular, but rather for a company—the *Queen of the Night*. Of course, somebody owned companies, usually lots of somebodies, but she hadn't given even a moment's thought to who owned the *Queen*.

"Anthony Ianucci is a very wealthy, very powerful businessman who's usually under the scrutiny of one or more federal agencies."

"You mean, he's a criminal," she said flatly. Which explained why Sara had called the security staff bodyguards this morning.

"I didn't say that."

"If the government is trying to arrest him—"

"The government is suspicious of his activities. If they could make a case against him, don't you think they would?"

"But—"

"He's a businessman, sugar—a very successful businessman whose business happens to be gambling. Because of the history of organized crime involvement in gambling, the feds tend to be overly suspicious of everyone in the industry." He grinned lazily. "So keep tabs on that small fortune in tips you're making and be sure you report every penny on your taxes next year. Otherwise, the IRS might come knocking at your door."

She studied him for a minute, not nearly as amused as he was, then turned her gaze to the riverbank, watching the occasional lights in the distance. The *Queen* routinely cruised an hour upriver from Natchez, then two hours down, with the final hour back up to its berth. A four-hour ride to nowhere, for the sole purpose of entertaining well-heeled gamblers—or players, as Granddad preferred—and lining the pockets of Anthony Ianucci. "Does it bother you— working for a criminal?"

Chance laughed. "You're not big on the concept of innocent until proven guilty, are you?" With the same exaggerated patience she sometimes found herself using with her students, he explained, "Mr. Ianucci has never been arrested. He has no convictions. The feds have no proof of wrongdoing. You want to know a little more about him before you judge and condemn him? He's a devoted husband and father, or so say his wife and kids. He employs a lot of people, and he offers better wages and benefits than anyone else in the business. He runs clean games, and he gives a big chunk of his profits to charity."

Interesting contradictions, Mary Katherine thought. But if she were a crook in a business that attracted lots of crooks—

and federal scrutiny—she'd be fair to employees, run clean games and give away a lot of money, too. She'd present an image so squeaky clean that no one would ever suspect she could possibly be crooked.

"You said you saved him from getting arrested. Why?" The Chance she'd known was a little wild, a bit of a bad boy, but he'd had a healthy respect for the law and hadn't shown the slightest inclination toward breaking it.

A distinctly uncomfortable look came over him. With a scowl and a shrug, he said, "I've had a few run-ins with cops over the years. I'm not particularly impressed with how a lot of them do their jobs."

What kind of run-ins? What exactly had happened to him after he'd left her and Oxford behind? She'd thought of him living a carefree life, traveling from town to town, seducing vulnerable, naive women who believed his sweet lies, then packing up and moving on whenever the urge hit. She'd imagined him living the good life, while she'd nursed her broken heart, repaired her sullied reputation and put her life back together into some semblance of *normal*.

Maybe she'd been wrong.

Moving carefully, she got to her feet, then padded to the railing. Below she could hear the sound of water against the hull, and the music from one of the lounges was a decibel or two louder. For a time she stared into the river's shadows before breaking the quiet with an unexpected question. "Did you ever regret it?"

Utter stillness settled around her. All she could hear was the sound of her own breathing, magnified a dozen times in her ears, and the rapid thud of her heartbeat. The paddle wheel, the river, the sounds of life both below decks and onshore all disappeared in an instant of pure anxiety that she'd asked such a question, and pure remorse that she wouldn't call it back if she could.

Somehow he moved without breaking the stillness. One moment he'd been seated at the table. The next, without a sound, he was standing behind her, so close she could feel his heat, so near she could feel the very essence of him drifting around her, enveloping her. "Did I regret making love to you?" His voice was quiet, hard, empty of emotion—because he felt too much emotion. She knew. *She* felt it. "Never, Mary Katherine. But have I ever regretted leaving you? Yes. Hell, yes. Every minute of every day."

She knew she should keep her back to him, knew that if she turned to face him, she just might fall so hard and fast that she would never recover. But she turned anyway in the narrow space between his body and the railing. Turned because she had no choice. Because she needed to see his eyes. Needed to see the truth there.

The look on his handsome face was intense. Powerful. He'd looked at her that way once before, that warm spring night when she'd told him she wanted him. Forget all the reasons they shouldn't be together, forget their differences, forget her fiancé. She'd wanted *him,* Chance Reynard, more than she'd ever wanted anyone or anything in her life. And he had looked at her, and with that one look she'd known she'd made the right decision. Whatever happened in their relationship or in their lives, making love with him that night hadn't merely been the right thing to do. It had been the *only* thing she could have done.

He raised his hand slowly, touched his fingertips to her hair so lightly that she might have imagined it, then stroked one finger along her jaw to her lips. "I'm sorry you were hurt," he said hoarsely. "I swear on my life, I never meant for that to happen."

She breathed through her mouth, a short, pain-filled breath that dislodged his finger. "You could have prevented it so easily. All you had to do was stay."

"Don't you think I wanted to?" he whispered, bringing his other hand up, too, his touches tentative, feather-light, sending fluttery sensations through her.

"Nothing was stopping you."

"Everything was stopping me. I was in so much trouble…I had to go."

"Then you could have taken me with you."

What he'd intended as a laugh, she suspected, came out a low groan. "Don't tell me you would have gone. You were only weeks from graduating. They were expecting you back home in Jubilee. You were marrying Mr. Right. Don't tell me you would have given all that up to go on the run with me."

"I would have," she whispered. She would have been scared spitless. She would have agonized over disappointing her parents and Granddad and hurting Jonathan, but she would have given up everything—*everything*—if only she could have had Chance instead.

With a raw groan, he cupped her face in his palms, then claimed her mouth with his, sliding his tongue inside as if it hadn't been eight years since their last kiss, as if he hadn't broken her heart and wounded her spirit and maybe done a bit of damage to his own spirit in the process. He kissed her as if he had every right, as if her mouth had been made for his alone, as if he might go mad without the taste of her, and she kissed him back as if she *had* gone mad without the taste of him.

The heat was incredible, the passion instantaneous, the need consuming. So much for keeping their distance, Mary Katherine thought in some small, still-functioning part of her brain. So it was wrong. Foolish. Dangerous. She *needed* this kiss. Just this one amazing, life-giving, sanity-stealing, incredible kiss. Just this one reminder that once she'd been wanted, needed, loved, in ways most women never knew. Just this one brief reliving, and then she would come to her senses again. Then she'd be ready for the next eight years alone.

One kiss was on the verge of becoming one steamy, intimate act. Chance's arm was around her waist, holding her tight against his arousal, and his free hand was sending tantalizing shivers everywhere he touched her—her jaw, her throat, the swell of her breasts—when running footsteps sounded on the deck.

"Chance, we've been looking all over— Oh, hell."

As Chance lifted his mouth from hers, Mary Katherine clung to him—*clung,* like a weak-willed, emotion-ruled, vulnerable, naive girl. He slid his hands along her bare arms to her wrists, pulled her hands back, gave her a sexy wink and a kiss on each palm, then turned to face the interloper. "What's up, Dunigan?"

A burly security guard built like a tank stood a half dozen feet away, looking as if he didn't know whether to be put out or amused. "Can't you hear your damn beeper going off? We've been looking all over for you. There's trouble in the Pacific Lounge. Mr. Ianucci wants you there on the double."

Vaguely Mary Katherine became aware of the incessant beeping coming from inside Chance's coat. He pulled out the pager and pressed whatever button was necessary to stop the noise. "I'll be there in a minute."

The guard returned the way he'd come, grumbling as he went. All she heard clearly was one complaint. "Jeez, next time get a room, will you?"

As Chance turned back to her, he was tucking the beeper inside his coat again, and the dim light glinting off something there caught her attention. Taking hold of the fine black fabric, she pulled his coat open wider...to reveal a pistol tucked in a shoulder holster. She stared at the gun with a mix of revulsion and fascination, but before she could summon even one word, he gently pulled her hand away and closed his coat again.

"Mary Katherine, I..." With a rueful smile, he touched her jaw. "I've got to go. I'll see you when the *Queen* docks."

Not if she saw him first, she thought as he walked away, his long legs rapidly widening the distance between them.

She was going back to work, and she was going to regain her sanity, and she was going to learn how to keep him at arm's length.

She swore on her heart she was.

Thursday morning was hot and muggy, with heavy dark clouds hanging low over the city and the sweet scent of rain in the air. Chance parked in front of the house Sara had given him directions to, rolled up the Cuda's windows, then climbed out, pausing for a moment to look.

Mary Katherine's second choice for lodging was a definite improvement over the cheap motel. The house looked about ninety years old—dusty red brick with arches over the windows and doors, a concrete-floored porch and a neatly kept yard. The neighborhood was a big step up, too. Instead of taverns, tattoo parlors and strip joints, her neighbors here were mostly young families, if the toys in the yards were anything to judge by, and mostly conscientious about maintaining their property.

It still wasn't too late to turn around and leave, he reminded himself as he started up the sidewalk to the porch. He could go back to his apartment and wait for Jake to check in, or head over to the *Queen* and spend an hour—or three or four—working off his excess energy in the gym. Hell, he could jump in the Cuda and go cruising down the Great River Road toward Baton Rouge and New Orleans.

Or he could climb those five steps, open the screen door, walk inside and knock at Mary Katherine's door.

And Lucky Reynard makes the sucker's choice, he thought cynically as he climbed the steps. The dangerous choice. The one that could leave him in even sorrier condition than he'd been eight years ago.

Or maybe in the best shape he'd ever been.

The screen door creaked when he opened it, and the floorboard protested his third step inside. She was renting 1-A, according to Sara, the only door on the left side of the long hallway. He raised his hand, hesitated, then knocked sharply.

The sound of a television inside was abruptly muted, then he imagined he could hear the faint slap of bare feet on bare wood approaching the door. When Mary Katherine opened the door, he was looking as careless and casual as he knew how, but inside he felt like a spring wound too tightly and about to pop.

The mere sight of her was enough to ease the tension—and create tension of another sort. She wore another of those innocent/sexy dresses, the kind that hugged every curve above her waist and concealed every one below. It reached practically to the floor but couldn't hide her feet, bare as he'd imagined, with the toenails painted deep pink. Her gorgeous brown hair was pulled back in a ponytail, and the expression in her gorgeous brown eyes—eyes that could make a man forget himself—was carefully guarded.

"Hi," he greeted.

"Hi."

She'd opened the door only halfway and blocked it partly with her body. Did she think he would force his way in uninvited? he wondered with some scorn before admitting that he just might, if she made it necessary. And did she think she could stop him if he felt force was necessary? Probably not. But like any good Southern belle, at least she would make a show of putting up a fight.

"I missed you last night." The incident in the Pacific Lounge had kept him occupied briefly after the *Queen* had docked. By the time he'd gotten off the boat, the parking lot was mostly empty, and Mary Katherine's car had definitely not been one of the few that remained. In truth, he hadn't expected her to wait for him, not after that kiss.

But he'd still been disappointed.

She had the courtesy to blush. "I—I was really tired, so I came on home."

"You couldn't have waited ten minutes so we could talk?"

"There...there wasn't anything to talk about."

"What about that kiss?" He watched her blush deepen, watched her gaze flutter helplessly before settling somewhere around his feet. "Or that look on your face when you saw my gun?"

Behind him, the door to 1-B opened and a man about his age came out. He gave Chance a curious look, smiled at Mary Katherine, then went outside, letting the screen door bang behind him. He took a magazine from one of the mailboxes, pulled a rocker from the corner of the porch and sat to read.

Chance scowled at the back of the guy's head before turning back to Mary Katherine. Before he could ask to go inside, she stepped back and opened the door wide in silent invitation. Feeling some stupid macho satisfaction, he went inside and closed the door behind him.

The apartment was filled with period furnishings, which translated, in his opinion, to ugly upholstered pieces and good woods. In the rooms in sight—the living room, the dining room, a small part of the kitchen—he couldn't see anything that he thought might actually belong to Mary Katherine. But that would change now that she was settled, he suspected. After all, Jubilee was only an hour away. Surely over the next ten weeks, she would want to visit her family or check on her house and pick up a few candles or flower vases or whatever sort of thing women tended to decorate with.

"Much better place," he remarked when he realized she was watching him.

"I like it." She clasped her hands together, then folded her arms across her chest. "Would you like a glass of tea?"

"Yes, ma'am." While she went to the kitchen, he wandered through the French doors that opened off the dining room onto a small covered porch. Strips of lattice at either end supported confederate jasmine that filled the air with its scent, and a gate blocked the steps that led into the side yard.

From the porch he had a good view of an angry sky. In the past few minutes the clouds had turned bluish-black, and the rest of the sky had taken on a purple-blue-gray tinge. An occasional flash of lightning etched across the sky, followed by rumbles of thunder so distant and muted that they were practically lost in the hum of the ions in the atmosphere.

"Does business on the *Queen* suffer in weather like this?" Mary Katherine asked as she came to stand a few safe feet away. She set two tall glasses of tea on the flat rail cap, then backed away a little farther.

"Not at all. People come from all over the world with money to spend on the *Queen*, and a little lightning and rain aren't going to keep them from doing just that. If the weather gets really bad, we don't leave port, but nobody seems to care." He picked up the glass nearest him and took a long drink. The tea was flavored with mint and sweetened just right.

As he returned the glass to the rail, the wind picked up, showering a few jasmine blooms across the ground. It sent a strand of Mary Katherine's hair across her cheek, which she impatiently brushed back. He was glad she did, because if she hadn't, he would have, and there would have been no impatience. In fact, it probably would have taken him forever, and they might have wound up naked in bed before he was done.

Needing space and air cool enough to squeeze into his tight lungs, he took his tea, moved a few feet away and leaned against the rail. "Is there anything you want to ask?"

A tight, troubled look came across her face. "What's to ask? You work security in a casino where hundreds of thousands of dollars change hands every night. It's only reasonable that you would carry a gun."

"But you don't like it."

"No."

"Because you're convinced that Mr. Ianucci is a bad guy, and I work closely with him, and so I must be one of the bad guys, too."

She gazed out across the yard. "I don't believe you're a criminal." But she didn't sound too sure of it. "I just don't understand... I assume he pays his security people even better than his wait staff. Is that it? The money? Is that why you're willing to take a job that requires you to carry a gun?"

"It's a job, angel. Nothing more, nothing less. A lot of people carry guns. Cops. Security guards. Couriers. Even some lawyers and cabdrivers. Hell, these days even some teachers are packing, Miz Monroe."

"But they don't work for people the government is trying to put in jail."

"It has nothing to do with that," he said with exaggerated patience. "I'm not armed at work because the feds believe Mr. Ianucci is a criminal. We don't shoot people, Mary Katherine. We don't rub out the competition, or shake down the local businessmen, or intimidate innocent townspeople into looking the other way while we conduct our nefarious business. It's *security,* sweetheart. The *Queen*'s never had a serious incident—no attempted robbery, no assaults, no nothing. How long do you think that record would stand if word got out that no one onboard was armed?"

Grudgingly she shrugged.

"You're right. We do have hundreds of thousands of dollars onboard—sometimes millions. If the *real* bad guys out there knew the most dangerous weapon we had was a steak knife, why in hell would they stay away?"

She smiled ruefully. "I understand the logic of what you're saying. It just doesn't balance the surprise of seeing you with a gun. In my world, people don't carry guns."

"In my world, they do," he said flatly. After an awkward moment he went on. "So you're convinced Mr. Ianucci's a crook. Does it bother you enough to make you quit the job?'' Say yes, the reasonable part of him silently wished while the realistic part just as fervently wished the opposite. He had enough to occupy his time without adding hour-long drives to Jubilee, and he had enough obstacles between him and Mary Katherine without adding her family. Surely they wouldn't want him around her, and surely they exerted the influence to keep them apart. Hadn't she planned her entire life according to their wishes?

And hadn't she upset that plan eight years ago to be with him?

Again came the rueful smile. ''Here comes the hypocrisy,'' she warned. ''No, I'm not going to quit.''

''Why not? If Mr. Ianucci's dirty, then the money he's paying you is dirty.''

''But I'm not doing anything wrong. I'm a waitress. I wear a skimpy costume and three-inch heels for nine hours a night, and I'm on my feet eight of them. I *earn* the money he's paying me.''

''And the tips are so damn good. You're right, sugar. You are a hypocrite.'' He smelled the first drops of rain and turned to watch them. They were big, fat, and landed with plops in the dirt, the grass. They brought a sweetness to the air that made him inhale deeply and think for the first time in years about playing in the rain with his brothers.

He wouldn't mind doing it now with Mary Katherine.

After a moment he put the image of her, with soaking-wet clothes plastered to her skin, out of his mind and looked at her again. ''So that pretty much exhausts the subject of the gun. That only leaves the kiss.''

A gust of wind came out of the north and slammed into the side of the house, bringing raindrops with it. They cooled his arms, splashed across her shoulders, left interesting shapes across the red cotton of her dress. He didn't think to move away from the rail where he might stay dry. Neither did she.

"It was just a kiss," she murmured, her voice soft and sweet and curling around him like a need he couldn't escape.

"Uh-huh. Just a kiss to make your blood run hot. To make your knees weak and your lungs tight and your skin quiver. To make you remember how good we were together, to make you want it like that again, to need me like that again."

Dazedly, without breaking from his gaze, she shook her head side to side. "It was just a kiss. I've had dozens of them. You've probably had hundreds."

Lightning struck nearby, followed by a crash of thunder that seemed to rumble through Chance's body as he pushed away from the railing. "No one's ever kissed you like that but me," he insisted as he took one step, then another, toward her.

She took a step back, but the railing was there, blocking her retreat. Instead of trying to sidestep him, she wrapped one arm around the slender column there and hugged it tight. "You are so arrogant."

He rested his right hand alongside her head on the column and placed his left on the railing, effectively trapping her without touching her. "It's not arrogance, darlin'. It's fact."

"And how do you figure that?"

"Because if any other man had ever kissed you like that, you would be with him right now, not me. If Mr. Right had ever kissed you like that, you never would have risked it all with me."

Though she clung to the column as if it might somehow protect her, she raised her free hand to touch his cheek gently, sadly. "There's a flaw in your reasoning, Chance. *You* kissed me like that...but where have you been the last eight years?"

He wanted to tell her everything—why he'd left, why he hadn't contacted her, how much he'd missed her. But telling her why meant telling her the truth, and telling the truth at this point could put his life, as well as this case he'd devoted the past fourteen months to, in danger. Telling the truth could put *her* in danger, because if there was one thing Mary Katherine Monroe wasn't, it was a liar. If she knew the truth about him, he wasn't sure he could trust her to hide it.

Grimly he moved away, turning to grip the rail with both hands. The windblown rain continued to slant under the porch roof, spotting his T-shirt, dampening his jeans, wetting her dress. There was a part of him that wanted to open the gate and go out to stand in the middle of the yard, eyes closed, face tilted up to the rain, arms open wide to embrace it. There was another part that wanted to stomp through the puddles, throw his head back and curse the unfairness of life.

Of course, he ignored both impulses and, instead, moved back to lean against the house, where only the hardest-blown raindrops reached.

After a time she moved, too, taking up a position on the opposite side of the door and facing him. "What was the problem in the Pacific Lounge last night?" Her voice sounded almost normal, and helped him to make his almost normal, too.

"One of the customers who'd had a bit too much to drink blamed his hundred-and-seventy-five-thousand-dollar loss on the dealer rather than bad luck. It took us a while to calm him down. Mr. Ianucci wound up giving him back his money." At the surprised look she gave him, Chance shrugged. "He'll be back tonight or tomorrow to drop that much and more."

"Was the dealer cheating?"

"I doubt it. We tape all our games—it keeps everyone honest. We'll check the tapes from his particular table and find out, but... Truth is, a lot of customers just don't want to accept responsibility for their bad decisions."

She remained silent for a moment, thoughtful, before asking, "Why did your Mr. Ianucci choose to set up business in Natchez? It seems if he's looking for high-rollers, he'd have better luck finding them in someplace like New Orleans or Las Vegas.''

He grinned, grateful to have a subject that was easy to talk about. "He's not *my* Mr. Ianucci, darlin', and he doesn't go out looking for high-rollers. They come looking for him. You may not have noticed, but the *Queen*'s clientele isn't exactly your average tourist. These people don't come to Natchez for the history or the sight-seeing. They come for the *Queen*. If she were berthed at Vicksburg, they'd go there. If she pulled in to Timbuktu, so would they, and if she found a way to dock in downtown Jubilee, darlin', they'd find a way there, too.''

"So why Natchez?"

"It's a nice town. It's not difficult to get to, and it's not too big, but it has everything a business like the *Queen* needs. There's decent shopping, some good restaurants and hotels and a population sufficient to staff the boat, without all the hassles of a big city.'' Of course, there were a few other reasons. Being small, Natchez lacked the federal law enforcement presence of a bigger city. There wasn't much of a crime problem, meaning there wasn't much of a scru- tiny-of-cops problem. Its size also allowed Ianucci's security to more or less keep an eye on new people in town.

"What were you doing in New Orleans when you saved Mr. Ianucci from getting arrested?"

"Working. Tending bar at a little place down on Deca- tur.''

"What happened to your plans to open your own ga- rage?"

They'd been part of his cover eight years ago, nothing more. He'd been playing a role that wasn't much play— brash, bold, a hot-shot mechanic with ambitions of the sort a mechanic would have. Much as he enjoyed tinkering with engines, and as good as he was, he'd never had any desire to make a living at it. The only engine he wanted to tinker with these days was the Cuda's, and even that as little as possible.

Since he couldn't tell her the truth, he shrugged and gave what he hoped was a close enough substitute. "Give me an old engine, and I can not only make it run, I can make it purr for you. But these engines today...hell, you need a computer just to find out what's wrong with them. They're not nearly as much fun as the old ones."

"So you tended bar, and now you work security. What else did you do?"

Once he'd been yanked off the auto-theft assignment that had put him undercover at the Oxford garage, he'd worked a number of cases, some as mundane as health-care fraud, some as dangerous as racketeering and organized crime. Obviously, he couldn't tell her about any of those. What he could tell her was the standard cover story meant to satisfy anyone who asked, but that would be lying, and he didn't want to lie to her any more than necessary.

So he told her another version of the truth. "I missed you."

His reply had the expected response—a brief softening of her chocolate-brown eyes, followed by a scowl and the assuming of a defensive posture. "Sure, you did."

"I did. Every day."

"If you missed me so much, you knew where to find me."

"I knew where to find you and Mr. Right. How could I come looking for you when I thought you were married to him?"

His question made her bristle with an energy that exceeded the storm blowing around them. "How could you think I would marry him after what happened between us? Did it matter so little to you?"

"It was damn important to me!"

"So important that you ran away when it was done."

"I told you last night, I had no choice!"

"And I told you, you had at least one choice. You could have taken me with you."

"I didn't know that," he protested.

"You made love to me. You told me you loved me more than anything. And you honestly didn't know I would go away with you?" She studied him for a long time, then gave a disgusted shake of her head. "You didn't know me at all, did you?"

"I knew you," he disagreed. "I knew you deserved better than me. I knew I wasn't worth giving up your education, your perfect fiancé, your perfect future, your perfect family. I knew—I thought—you'd be happier in the long run with Mr. Right and your parents' approval."

"Did you know that I went to see Jonathan first thing that morning? That I told him all about you and me and I ended our engagement?" she challenged. "Did you know that next I told my parents I couldn't marry the man they'd had their hearts set on because *my* heart was set on you?" Her voice grew thick with unshed tears, and her eyes glistened with them. "I gave up everything for you, Chance, and you left without even telling me goodbye."

Before he could speak, think, react, she opened the door, then paused. "No need to break old habits. Wait out the storm, finish your tea, whatever, and then go. And don't bother telling me when you do." Then she went inside, locked the door and disappeared from sight.

Chance stood where he was a long time, feeling numb and more than a little sick. When he finally moved, he didn't head for the gate, but braced one hand on the porch rail and leaped to the ground below. By the time he reached the car, he was soaked. By the time he pulled out of the parking space, he was steaming.

Why isn't Jonathan married to you? he'd asked her on her first night on the *Queen,* and she had refused to answer. Now he knew. He should have known all along. Her fiancé had been a moral barrier to their relationship from the day they'd met—one of the few things that had helped them to stay apart as long as they'd managed. He should have known that once desire had overcome honor, the first thing she would do was confess her sins and call off the engagement.

He should have known. And if he had…?

He for damn sure wouldn't have stayed away from her these past eight years.

And now that he did know…

"I'll make it up to you, angel," he murmured. Somehow. Some way.

Even though the odds were damnably against him.

Chapter 4

Sunday was Mary Katherine's first day off, and it arrived not one moment too soon. She slept until noon, took a leisurely bubble bath, dressed in shorts and a T-shirt and gathered her laundry. Balancing the basket on one hip, she locked up her apartment, then pushed open the screen door...and came to a sudden stop.

Chance was kicked back in one of the rockers, feet planted far apart, the Sunday paper scattered around him. She hadn't seen much of him the past couple of days. Friday and Saturday were, by far, the *Queen*'s busiest times. Both nights her dinner break had been cut from an hour to half that, and the customers had kept her jumping—literally, with those whose hands had a tendency to roam. She'd barely even noticed the other waitresses and had caught only a couple of glimpses of Chance as he accompanied Mr. Ianucci from one place to the next. She'd gone home both nights exhausted—and with enough in tips to make it worthwhile.

Though she hadn't let herself think about it before, now that he was here, she could admit that she'd missed him.

Missed his grins and his arrogance. Missed the way he looked at her and the way those looks made her feel.

She missed that kiss.

Not certain whether he was aware of her, she let the screen door close with a bang. He was aware. He didn't react to the noise, other than to take his sweet time closing the newspaper and gathering the sections back into some order. "It's about time you got up," he remarked lazily as he got to his feet, slid a rubber band around the paper, then returned it to 1-B's box.

"It's my day off. I'm entitled to sleep in." She set the basket down and leaned against one of the four brick pillars that supported the roof.

"It's everyone's day off. Mr. Ianucci believes any employee of the *Queen* who wants to attend church or spend the day with his or her family should have that option, so the *Queen* never sails on Sunday."

"Why, he's just a paragon of virtue and generosity, isn't he?"

"More so than most."

"He's certainly—bought? earned? otherwise acquired?—your loyalty."

"My loyalty's not for sale," he said stiffly.

"I'm sorry. That was uncalled for."

"Yes, it was." But he blew it off as if it didn't matter. "I came to see if I could tempt you into spending the day with me."

"What did you have in mind?" And if it involved bed, getting naked or making love, she was going to smack him and go take a cold shower and pray for the strength that had failed her eight years ago.

"Well, knowing you're such a good girl that you can't have fun until the chores are finished, I thought we'd start with doing laundry, then we could get groceries. After that, maybe we could have lunch somewhere—or dinner—and see a movie or talk or something."

She didn't allow herself to dwell on the "something." It well might lead to thoughts she couldn't handle. "Start with laundry and groceries, huh?" She glanced at her basket, where her shopping list was clearly visible, anchored under a bottle of fabric softener. "You are so full of it. Do you really expect me to believe you came here to ask me to do laundry and buy groceries with you?"

With a grin, he reached into his hip pocket and pulled out a folded piece of paper. She accepted it, unfolded it and scanned the list. *Water, beer, chips, cereal, shampoo, shaving cream, detergent.* When she looked back at him, the grin had broadened to almost unbearably smug. "And my laundry's in the car. So…now that you've misjudged me—again—what do you say?"

She returned the shopping list to him, then bent to pick up her basket. He took it from her and carried it easily braced against one hip, putting it in the trunk of the Cuda, where, indeed, another basket filled with his own clothes waited. "Hmm…Chance Reynard doing laundry. That's something I've never quite imagined."

"My clothes get dirty, too, darlin'."

"I guess I figured they magically cleaned themselves…or some starry-eyed, lovesick angel scrubbed them over rocks in the river in a vain effort to win your approval."

He gave her a chastising look across the roof of the car before she got in. "You're the only angel I've ever met," he remarked as he slid in beside her.

"Uh-huh. So all the other women you call that… They're not *really* angels."

He gave her another steady look. "You're the only one I've ever called that. Sweetheart, sugar, darlin'—I use those words a lot. Hell, most women expect them from me. But you're my only angel."

Careful, Mary Katherine. Don't go tumbling yet. She gave him an innocent look. "Funny. And you're the only man I've ever called bastard."

"You're not alone in that, sugar," he said in an easy careless manner, but underneath it Mary Katherine saw—or thought she saw—a twinge of hurt that passed through his green eyes. It made her ashamed, made her reach out and lightly touch his arm.

"I'm sorry," she murmured.

He shrugged off both her apology and her hand.

The Laundromat he chose was ancient, tiny, and had apparently stood in the middle of its neighborhood for decades. Miniature mountains of gray lint had built up on the ground where each dryer vented, and every window—the old-fashioned crank type—was open, along with each door. There were six washers, six dryers, two wheeled baskets and one folding table, and this hot afternoon, they were the only customers.

Mary Katherine had only enough clothes for three small loads. She eyed them, then Chance's sorting piles, then cleared her throat and asked, "Why don't we combine our clothes? It seems silly to use six machines for what can surely fit in three or four."

Leaning across, he hooked one of her bras with his index finger and let it dangle in the air. It wasn't particularly large, anyway, because *she* wasn't particularly large there, but hanging by one narrow strap from his big, powerful hand, it looked even more delicate than it was. "You want to wash your unmentionables with mine? Let them get all up close and personal while you're still keeping me at arm's length?"

He hadn't been at arm's length when he'd kissed her on the *Queen* Wednesday night. Not even so much as a breath could have fit between them, and still she'd strained to get closer. She'd wanted to curl around him, to crawl inside him, and stay forever.

He hadn't been at arm's length Thursday morning on her porch, either, when they'd talked about kisses. She'd wanted him to kiss her again, had wanted to pray that he *never* kissed her again. When he'd moved away without even touching her, she'd told herself she should be relieved, but inside all she'd really been was disappointed. Bereft.

She reached for the bra, but he pulled it back and dropped it onto a pile of his clothes. "Pretty little thing," he commented as he picked up the next one, then the next. "Nothing but lace and ribbons and this see-through gauzy stuff. Sexy as hell. But, darlin', if you're sleeping alone, why do you bother?" His gaze drifted down to her bust, and grew so intense that she swore she could feel it. Her body was pretty darn sure it could feel it, too, because her nipples began to swell. "Even if you aren't sleeping alone," he asked in a hoarse voice, "why do you bother?"

It was all too apparent that, this afternoon, she hadn't bothered. Resisting the urge to fold both arms across her chest, she forced her attention to the washer in front of her, plopping in quarters, measuring detergent, changing settings. She reached for the pile of clothes, but he had hold of the same garments and didn't let them go.

"Do you remember undressing for me that night?" His voice was low, dark, fierce. "I wanted to strip you naked like that—" the snap of his fingers was a small explosion in the room "—but you wanted to undress at your own pace. I was so damn hard, and I wanted you so damn desperately, and you..." He inhaled a ragged breath. "You took off your shoes and lined them up neatly side by side. Then you unbuttoned that jacket you were wearing and you slid it off one arm, then the other, and you laid it off to the side, too. Your skirt had a zipper in back, and you undid it and slid it over your hips and there was nothing but skin until finally, a pair of those lacy little panties. I'd never realized how long your legs were until I watched you slide that skirt all the way off and you were standing there in those panties and that little top with a million buttons and I thought I was going to die before you were finished."

Mary Katherine's hands were shaking with the memory. She'd folded her skirt and set it with her cardigan, then knelt in front of him on the quilt. Her top had been a fitted cotton camisole, nipped and pleated, sleeveless with lace and pale pink ribbons and an even dozen small buttons.

"You started at the top," Chance murmured, his words barely audible for the rushing that filled her ears and tightened her chest. "You undid the first button, then the second, and the third, and you looked so serious, and so sweet, and so innocent. And finally you finished, and you just sat there, with your hands on your thighs, and I pushed the material back and you weren't wearing anything under it. It was the most erotic sight I'd ever seen. Ever since then, watching a woman undress, knowing she's not wearing a bra, knowing I can slide my hands under her shirt and touch her breasts..."

His words ended in a choked groan. She was about to groan, too—to beg, plead, offer him anything he wanted if just once she could have him again.

And could she trust him this time? Would he break her heart again? Would she survive?

Desperately she breathed. Darn near frantically she tugged the clothes away from him and concentrated on sorting them into appropriate piles with her own. It wasn't easy when her brain was addled, when her body was about to spontaneously combust, when her hands were trembling too badly to overlook.

Finally, when the clothes were in the washers, when the temperature had dropped to bearable, she dared a look at him and forced an uneasy smile. "Has anyone ever told you you have a way with words?"

It took him a minute to summon his own brash smile. Nice to know he was as affected as she. "My mama once told me I could sweet-talk a 'gator into a frying pan."

"Your mama," she repeated. Just as she'd never imagined him doing something as mundane as laundry, she'd never imagined him with a family, either. Except for the one she'd fantasized about having with him in those few sweet hours before she'd learned of his betrayal.

"I do have a mother," he said dryly. "And a father and three brothers and a sister."

"Where are they?"

"At home, mostly. Little town down in south Mississippi that makes Jubilee look like a bustling city. Except my youngest brother. He's living over in Jackson."

"A family. Do you see them often?"

"Not as much as I'd like."

"Do they know what you're doing?"

For an instant his expression went blank, then he grinned again. "If you're asking whether they'd approve of my working security in a casino and carrying a gun, sorry to disappoint you, darlin', but they would. My daddy's a gambler from way back, and out where they live, everyone's got guns. Besides, they figure an honest job is a good job." Taking her arm in a surprisingly un-intense way, he pulled her outside the door, where an awning overhead provided shade and a slight breeze added its own cooling. "Do *your* parents know what *you're* doing?"

"They know," she admitted cautiously.

"They know you're wearing feathers and sequins and not much more than your birthday suit and parading around in front of strange men, smiling at them and flirting with them and sometimes letting them touch you, all for a paycheck and tips?"

Her face flushed crimson. "They know I'm a waitress on a riverboat casino." And they knew she was trying to prove Granddad's innocence, and they most certainly didn't approve. As did everyone else in the family, her folks loved Paddy dearly, but, like everyone else, they knew he was a scoundrel. Beyond that, they had no clue what she was doing to get that proof.

"A waitress," Chance repeated, managing to sound as prim as she did at times. "And maybe they think this waitress job is in an upscale restaurant, with a uniform of…oh, black pants, white shirt and brocade vest, or maybe even an old-time covered-from-neck-to-toe Southern belle gown.''

Her flush heated a few degrees. ''Okay. My parents aren't aware of exactly where I'm working, what I'm doing or what I'm wearing, and no, they wouldn't approve. But I'm a grown woman, Chance, and I've proven before that I don't always need their approval.''

Such as with him.

He looked her over head to toe and, like that, the temperature began rising again. ''You won't get any argument from me about the grown woman part, angel.'' Before she could enjoy her reaction—or worry over it—too much, he gestured toward the wood bench that stood along one wall. She sat at one end, and he sat at the other. The uneven legs wobbled, then settled in the dirt. ''Now that you've survived your first week on the job and the embarrassment and the shoes haven't killed you, what do you think?''

''It beats the library reading program job by a country mile,'' she said with a smile. ''I like teaching—really, I do. But when you spend your entire life surrounded by kids…''

''Surely there are men in your life.''

She glanced at him. He was leaning forward on the bench, elbows resting on his knees, his attention riveted on an ant making its way across sandy dirt to the cover of a tuft of grass. He looked ill at ease, and he sounded almost jealous. The combination was sweet enough to make her smile. If she were a wicked woman, she'd let him stew in that jealousy for a while, but being wicked was outside her abilities. About all she could manage to be was honest. ''I date occasionally,'' she admitted. ''There are some nice guys in Jubilee. But…that's all they are. Nice. They don't—'' She broke off with a shrug.

Chance twisted to look at her. ''They don't turn you on. They don't make you hot. They don't tempt you.''

They don't compare to you. Instead of admitting that,

though, she fell back on what seemed an appropriately teacher-like response. "There's no chemistry."

"There wasn't any chemistry between you and Mr. Right, either, but you were going to marry him, anyway."

"Yes," she agreed thoughtfully. "I was." It had been a long time before she'd gotten enough over her hurt at being abandoned to realize that Chance had done her at least one favor in unwittingly convincing her to break off her engagement. She'd never loved Jonathan, not in the way necessary to make a marriage work. She'd grown up with him, dated him all through high school and had simply fallen in with everyone else's assumption—his, her parents', their friends'—that she would marry him.

In her worst times, she'd wanted to turn back the clock to that April morning, to never confess her sins to Jonathan, to take back his ring and the words that had called off their wedding. She'd lost so much more than just Chance—her fiancé, her upcoming marriage, her parents' support, her reputation, her nice, secure future—and she'd been hurting so bad. She'd wanted part of it back, even if it was the wrong part.

"I would have married him," she acknowledged, "and it would have been a mistake. Do you know how long it took him to replace me? He was dating another woman by the end of the week. They were engaged within a month, and they got married at the end of his first year of law school. He sent my whole family an invitation to the wedding. And we all went." She gave a wondering shake of her head.

"Eight years and counting," Chance said quietly. When she glanced at him, a flush of color had darkened the skin stretched taut over his high cheekbones. "That's how long it's been. I've dated a few women, and had sex with a few more, but...you're irreplaceable, Mary Katherine. Any man who doesn't realize that is a fool."

A lump formed in her throat, forcing her to look away before the emotion turned to tears in her eyes. When she thought she could speak normally, she laughed—low, husky, unsteady. "You do have a way with words, Chance. You could sweep a woman off her feet with nothing more than your sweet lies. The only problem is, getting swept off your feet is generally followed by a mighty hard fall. I barely survived the last one. I'm older this time, less resilient, less likely to get the pieces back together the way they go."

He looked at her, his green eyes hard with conviction. "It's not a lie, Mary Katherine," he said flatly. "One of these days you'll know that for yourself."

Wouldn't she love to believe him? But she'd thought *one of these days* had arrived eight years ago. She'd thought she could trust him with her love, her heart, her life. And she'd been wrong.

She couldn't afford to be wrong again.

She might not survive it.

The *Queen* hadn't even left port for its early cruise on Wednesday evening before Chance's first problem arose. Clyde Ebert, Ianucci's chief of security, called him to the Pacific Lounge, where Chance found him in conversation with the casino manager, an intense, dark-haired woman named Casey. While she talked, Clyde handed him a piece of paper with a name and address on it. The name was only vaguely familiar—Paul Baker, Paulie to his friends—but the address, a block or so from Mary Katherine's cheap motel— was more so.

"That's the dealer involved in the incident last week," Clyde said quietly when the woman moved away. "He hasn't shown up for work the last two nights. Casey— " he nodded toward the manager "—went by this afternoon. Car's in the driveway, no answer at the door or on the phone."

"Want me to send someone over or to call Bubba?" Bubba, of course, wasn't the guy's name—wasn't even his nickname except among the few onboard the *Queen* who knew of his existence. He was a local cop who didn't take the laws regarding improper use of authority or violations of the privacy act too seriously. He was Ianucci's link to law enforcement and could be counted on to handle any problems that arose appropriately.

Chance was looking forward to seeing him in jail.

"Let's not bring him unless it's necessary. For all we know, this guy could have left town or might be too hungover to work," Clyde said. "It's too late to send anyone over there now, but when we get back, why don't you have one of the boys go by?"

"Not a problem." Chance slid the paper into his pocket, then called after his boss. "Hey, what did the tapes show?"

Clyde's smile reminded Chance of a shark—cold-blooded with lots of deadly teeth. "He wasn't cheating, just as we knew. Who in this business would make the mistake of trying to cheat Mr. Ianucci?"

Who, indeed. Certainly not a dealer who'd been around the business long enough to qualify for a job on the *Queen*. Some of the waitresses and the kitchen staff might be naive enough to believe the *Queen* and Ianucci were exactly what they appeared to be, but the dealers knew better.

As Casey hurried past again, Chance stopped her. "You have someone to fill in for Paulie?"

"Yeah, Keith Adams is on his way over now. Don't let the boat leave without him, or you'll be parking your carcass in here behind a table tonight."

"I'll notify Jimbo," he replied with a grin. Though he could easily call down to the guard shack, he walked instead. The instant he stepped out of the air-conditioned lounge, the heat hit him with the force of a sucker punch. By the time he reached the guard shack at the bottom of the gangway, he was sweating.

"How's it going?" Jimbo—really James Gomez—asked. He was about Chance's age, about Chance's size, but there the similarities ended. Jimbo watched his diet, worked out religiously and could bench press Chance without breaking a sweat. He was also the best damn shot in the entire bureau and the best backup Chance could ask for.

Except for the small detail that when the *Queen* left port with Chance onboard, Jimbo usually stayed behind.

"Next job I get had better be something where I can wear shorts and a T-shirt, or maybe no shirt at all. Maybe a pool boy or a landscaper. Or, hell, how about this for fun—a job in an office with a view and air-conditioning and—"

"A secretary with a great body in tight clothes."

"Son, the bodies don't get any greater, or the clothes any tighter, than they are here."

"So I hear. Of course, I work out here where I only see them in their street clothes, unlike some lucky bastard who's on the boat and sees them in all their feathered finery."

With a grin, Chance jerked a paper towel from the roll on the counter and wiped the sweat that beaded across his forehead. "We've got a late one coming in this evening—Keith Adams. Let the captain know as soon as he's onboard."

"He replacing Paulie?"

"Yeah. What did you hear?"

"Just that no one's seen him since the second cruise Saturday night. What about you?"

"The same. Clyde says he wasn't dealing dirty."

Jimbo waved through a couple of waitresses before fixing his gaze on Chance. "Might not have mattered."

"How so?"

"In a business like this, the implication of wrong-doing can be as damaging as an admission."

So at worst, Paulie was guilty of cheating. At best, he was guilty of making someone claim he'd cheated. Either way, he was guilty.

Chance copied the address and gave it to Jimbo. "Have someone check this out. And tell 'em to be out by ten. Clyde wants me to send one of our people over between cruises."

"Will do."

Chance started back up the gangway, but had taken only a couple of steps before curiosity got the best of him and made him turn back. "Hey, turn to your list of employees. I want to see if one's checked in yet."

Jimbo didn't bother checking the clipboard, where he recorded every soul to set foot onboard the *Queen* each evening. Instead he offered a smug grin. "Mary Katherine Monroe? Man, that one looks so damn good *in* her clothes that I don't bother fantasizing about her *out* of them. I think it's those big brown eyes, or all that heavy long hair. Or maybe it's the contradictions—so innocent and sexy, so sweet and wicked, so—"

"Watch your mouth," Chance growled.

Jimbo laughed. "She went aboard about fifteen minutes ago. Give her my best when you see her."

Chance gave a nod as he headed back onto the *Queen*. He'd been trying to give Mary Katherine *his* best, but she wasn't making it easy. It was because she didn't trust him, he knew. He just didn't know what to do about it. The only way to gain her trust was to tell her everything...but telling her everything was too dangerous. And, gee, novel idea, wouldn't it be something if she would just trust him, anyway—if he didn't have to earn it with reasons and explanations and proof that he wasn't a coldhearted bastard who'd used, then discarded her? Wasn't that what trust was—faith without proof?

He hadn't seen her since Sunday. Things had changed subtly after their little conversation at the Laundromat, when she'd accused him of telling sweet lies. They'd continued to talk while they finished their laundry, had a late lunch and shopped for groceries, but there had been some barrier between them that he couldn't talk, tease or charm his way around. When he'd taken her home, he'd suggested a movie. She'd countered with goodbye. She hadn't let him carry her grocery bags into the kitchen—hadn't even let him in the front door, a fact which had amused 1-B, on his way out again. Though he'd never been a violent man, Chance would have given a lot to wipe that smug smile off the guy's face.

On the one hand, it was good that she was afraid, because it meant she still cared. She might try to pretend otherwise, might keep hopefully suggesting that they not see each other, but she cared. On the other hand, he didn't want her to be afraid, because it meant she didn't trust him, and because it was a measure of how badly he'd hurt her.

God, he'd never meant to hurt her!

At the top of the gangway, he nodded to the two security guards stationed there until their guests were onboard and the *Queen* was ready to leave her berth, then headed for the main deck lounge. The evening was already off to a good start, with plenty of customers to keep the girls busy. Mary Katherine wasn't among those girls.

Spying Sara with a tray of drinks, he asked, "Hey, where's—?"

She didn't even slow down. "She's been moved up. Try the Memphis Saloon."

Jeez, that made twice. Was his interest in Mary Katherine so obvious that he didn't even need to say her name? Jimbo, he could overlook. It was entirely possible that Jake had told him all about their relationship back in Oxford. But Sara, too?

The Memphis Saloon was one level up and, its name aside, wasn't a bar but a gaming room. The stakes were lower there than elsewhere on the *Queen,* though still well above the limits of the average tourist/gambler. Liquor flowed just as heavily as in the Mississippi Deck lounge, but the focus was on the gambling.

He was barely five feet inside the door when he saw her, awaiting an order at the bar, and the sight literally stopped him in his tracks. She was wearing scarlet tonight, a dazzling little outfit with a neckline that plunged below the waist and not much of a back—hell, not much of anything. Basically, the costume was strips of body-hugging spandex artfully arranged with strips of see-through scarlet something or other, with a sprinkling of matching sequins to catch the light and make her sparkle.

By the time he reached the bar, he was too aroused to move without discomfort, unless he was moving inside her. He stopped immediately behind her, bent close and murmured, "I'll pay you whatever you'd make tonight in tips if you'd come to my office and just let me look."

She glanced at him over her shoulder, just a quick look with a hint of amusement in her eyes, then she looked away again.

"In this outfit, I don't have to wonder whether you're wearing a bra. You're obviously not." There was too much skin showing—creamy, soft, kissable skin—to allow for even the most remote of possibilities. "And at least you can sit comfortably in this one. There're no sequins on the butt."

"Because they couldn't find enough fabric to attach them to," she said snidely.

Because she was right, he couldn't resist letting his gaze slide down for one brief look before he realized she was scowling at him. "Keep your eyes to yourself, buddy," she warned before turning her attention back to the bartender. "Hey, on the Bloody Mary, the guy wants extra pickled green beans."

"So Mr. Atkinson is onboard tonight." Chance eased onto the nearest bar stool to keep from pulling her close and rubbing—*hard*—against her scantily clad bottom. "Be nice to him. He's known to be generous with his winnings."

"I'm nice to everyone."

"Except me. I went by your apartment Monday."

"I had some errands to run."

"I looked for you on your dinner break last night."

"I decided to eat in the employee lounge."

"I looked for you when we got off."

"I must have slipped right by."

"If I were a gambling man, I'd say you were avoiding me."

"If you were a gambling man, you would have hit the jackpot."

The bartender set the last two drinks on her tray, but before she could leave, Chance blocked her way. "Why?"

"I have to get to work."

"A simple answer. Why are you avoiding me?"

Her mouth thinned, and her eyes darkened with impatience. "It's not a simple answer, Chance, and I've got six customers waiting for their drinks, and they tend to get a little rowdy if they wait too long."

Because she was right, and because he couldn't interfere with business, he relented—but not without another effort. "Meet me on the Texas Deck on your dinner break."

Though she looked as if she wanted to refuse, after a moment she sighed. "Okay."

He let her go, watching until he realized the bartender was watching him watch her. With a scowl, he ordered a bottle of water and pulled a cigar from his pocket. It was a long time until eleven. Even then, he wouldn't be surprised if she didn't show.

Not surprised...but incredibly disappointed.

It was an uneventful evening. He made his rounds, checked in with the staff, sat in on a conference call between Ianucci and his San Francisco partners and watched from the Texas Deck as the departing passengers disembarked. He left briefly to find out from Jimbo that Jake had sent a couple of men to Paul Baker's house and they'd found nothing out of the ordinary, and he sent two of Ianucci's men to the same address to bring back the same report.

Maybe Paulie really had left town. People did it all the time, especially those with few ties to the community. Maybe he'd met some woman and hadn't come up for air yet, or had followed her back to wherever she'd come from.

Maybe his absence was a perfectly innocent annoyance, no more.

Eleven o'clock came and, with a blast from its whistle, the *Queen* headed out into the river again. The minutes crawled by, one after the other, with no sign of Mary Katherine. He'd been stood up, which was only fair under the circumstances. Hadn't she made it clear from the beginning that she didn't want him back in her life? And hadn't he deliberately ignored her?

But hadn't she kissed him as though she wanted him? Looked at him as though she needed him?

At eleven-twenty, he decided to give up. He could track her down—they were under way on a riverboat, for God's sake, and more than half the boat was off limits to her—but what good would it do, forcing her to see him when she clearly didn't want to? He had a job to do—several of them, in fact—and would be better off concentrating on that. With a surge of restless energy, he turned away from the rail...and stopped.

She stood, heels in hand, right on the line between shadow and light. One step forward, and the deck lights would gleam on her pale skin and sequins. One step back, and the shadows would swallow her up, except for the telltale glint of light that penetrated the darkness. "I wasn't going to come."

"So I figured." He leaned against the rail behind him, gripping it tightly with both hands to keep from reaching for her. "I'm glad you did."

She came forward a few steps, detouring to leave her shoes on a nearby chair. With them out of the way, she went to the next section of railing, near enough that he could reach her with one long stride, distant enough that he might never reach her. She gazed into the night for a moment before facing him. "You were right. I have been avoiding you."

"Why?"

"In the interest of self-preservation," she replied with a wry smile. "You're a dangerous man, Chance."

"I'm not—"

"I'm not talking about your job or the fact that you carry a gun. I'm talking about *you*. You're too handsome, too charming, too confident, too arrogant. You're sexy as hell, and just that grin of yours is enough to make most women melt at your feet."

He wasn't sure he'd ever received so many compliments in such an unflattering way. "You're a little bit dangerous yourself, darlin'. You can make a man forget his name."

"And you can make a woman lose her soul." She turned her face into the breeze, eyes closed, for a moment before looking at him again. "Ever since I saw you up here that first night, I've been torn. I was shocked, angry, upset…and pleased. All those years I spent getting over you…it was as if they'd never happened. One minute I was recovered—I was strong, in control, rational and reasonable—and the next…I was falling again." She smiled faintly, regretfully. "I can't afford to fall again, Chance. I wasn't kidding the other day. I'm not as resilient as I used to be. I don't want to spend the next few years putting myself back together again."

"You're making the assumption that putting yourself back together will be necessary."

"It's the only assumption I can make, based on my experience with you."

He shook his head. "You could assume that this time will be different."

"How could it be different? We're the same people. We're feeling the same attraction, and we're starting out the same way as before. With everything else the same, you want me to gamble that the outcome will be different?"

"Would that be so hard?"

Her laugh was edgy. "Oh, no. Of course not. It would just mean trusting you. Unfortunately…I have no reason to trust you."

"So take a chance. Trust me anyway."

"Give me a reason—one reason. Tell me the truth about why you broke my heart the last time."

Tension tightened the muscles in Chance's jaw, his neck, his hands. "I told you. I had no choice. I was in trouble. I had to leave."

"What kind of trouble? With whom? Had you done something wrong? Were the cops after you? Were there bad guys out looking for you? Where did you go? What did you do? And why didn't you take five minutes—*five minutes,* Chance—to call me and tell me you were leaving?"

He couldn't answer even one of her questions—couldn't tell her that he'd been working undercover to break up an interstate auto-theft ring that was distributing hundreds of thousands of dollars in stolen cars and parts throughout the entire South from the Oxford garage. He couldn't tell her that the case agent had had reason to believe that his cover had been blown, that, yes, they'd thought the bad guys were on to him, that they'd snatched him out before the suspicion around him could extend to Jake—and before it could get Chance killed. Take five minutes to call her and say goodbye? They'd rousted him from his bed, and within five minutes he'd been on his way out of the state. The best he'd been able to manage was a few words to Jake. *Tell her I meant what I said. Tell her I love her and...I'm sorry.*

She waited expectantly, but he said nothing. The expectation disappeared from her expression, to be replaced by resignation. "Do you know there's nothing in my life I couldn't tell you? But it appears there's an awful lot that you can't tell me. Simple things. Honest things. Things that two people in a relationship should be able to share."

"What about trust?" he challenged. "Isn't that something two people in a relationship should share? And yet you don't trust me."

"I did, eight years ago, and you betrayed my trust. Once you've done that, you can't expect it to come as easily the next time. Maybe not even at all." There was a sadness in her eyes that made him want to hold her tight and protect her, but what good would that do when she felt *he* was the one she needed protecting from?

Then she took a breath, and the sadness disappeared. "As long as we're on the subject of trust, I'm not the only one holding back."

"I'd trust you with my life," he said flatly, but it wasn't exactly true. He *did* trust her. He just didn't trust her to lie well enough to protect them both.

"But not with the answers to the questions I just asked you." She sat, put her shoes on, then gracefully stood again. "Avoiding each other isn't easy. Believe me, I know. But for my sake, as well as your own, we need to do it."

"I don't want to," he said, feeling and sounding like a spoiled little kid. "I want to be with you."

"And I want you to be honest with me." She shrugged. "We can't always get what we want, can we?"

She'd taken a few steps away before he spoke again. "Mary Katherine? I'm not going to make this easy for you."

The look that stole across her face was exquisite in its hopelessness and said too clearly what she didn't—*I don't expect you to.* With a soft sigh, she said, "You do what you have to do, Chance. And I'll do what I have to."

This time she made it as far as the stairs before he spoke her name again. "Mary Katherine?"

And this time she didn't stop, didn't turn, didn't reply. She just kept walking away from him.

"Aw, hell," he muttered, turning to face the river again. Maybe she was right. Maybe, until this case was over, staying away was the best thing he could do for her. Maybe, until he could tell her the truth, it was the only thing he could do.

And when the case was over? What if it was too late? What if she'd found someone else? What if the truth no longer mattered?

Thinking about what-ifs would make him crazy. All he

could do was concentrate on the here and now. He would do his work, avoid Mary Katherine and pretend it wasn't killing him inside. He was strong. He'd walked away from her once before and survived. He could do it again—at least, in the short term. He would be all right. And when all of this was over, he would tell her everything. Even if it was too late, if she'd found someone else, even if the truth no longer mattered, he would tell her.

He owed her that much.

Chapter 5

Forty-five minutes after the *Queen* pulled into her berth Saturday morning, Mary Katherine wearily headed for the locker room below. She'd been more than ready to leave with everyone else at three o'clock, but several of her regular customers had been engaged in the millionth hand, or so it seemed, of a never-ending poker game, and she'd been told to stick around until the end. Five minutes ago, the end had come—with a five-hundred-dollar tip to her—and she fully intended to be home, in bed and asleep in another five minutes. Well, maybe ten.

The past week had been a good one as far as work went, she thought as she let herself into the empty locker room. She'd made a lot of money, had a minimum of overly friendly customers and had spent a good deal of time watching the games and talking discreetly with other waitresses and the bartenders who regularly worked in the Memphis Saloon. What little she'd learned was making Granddad's excuse that he'd been snookered look like just that. Granted, she was no gambler, but everything seemed legitimate to her. She wasn't quite sure how a dealer could cheat, or why. After all, Chance had said the games were taped; it kept everyone honest. The dealers were aware of the cameras and knew they would surely get caught if they tried anything underhanded.

Unless the *Queen*'s games weren't as clean as Chance insisted. Unless they were cheating on behalf of the house, with Mr. Ianucci's knowledge. Unless Chance was lying to her.

He was the only dark spot on her week. She'd missed him. Despite his promise Wednesday night that he wouldn't make things easy for her, he had. She hadn't caught so much as a glimpse of him since then. When the security staff made its usual between-cruises rounds, he was nowhere in sight. Each time she hesitantly made her way to the Texas Deck for a break, she found it empty. She knew he was working—the Cuda was in the parking lot each evening when she arrived and each morning when she left—but he was doing a good job of staying out of sight.

Unfortunately, whoever had coined the phrase "out of sight, out of mind" hadn't been referring to Chance. He was in her mind, in her dreams—everywhere except in her life—and she missed him. Wanted him. Sometimes thought about going to him and asking, pleading, for his attention again.

Thankfully she came to her senses first.

Or was it a pity?

Though she normally changed clothes in one of the curtained dressing rooms that lined one wall, tonight she undressed where she was. After all, unless the games were also running late on the California Deck, she was the only waitress onboard at the moment. Most of the girls didn't think twice about stripping down naked right in front of everyone. Of course, most of the girls didn't have her years or her hips, she thought ruefully as she hung her outfit over the open locker door.

Quickly she dressed in her own clothes, then shoved the

costume into the locker, grabbed her purse and left again. The *Queen* was unnaturally quiet, virtually abandoned, with the customers and most of the staff long gone. She assumed there were security guards onboard all night, but she saw no sign of them as she approached the gangway, and the guard shack where Jimbo always flirted with her was locked up for the night. But there were cars in the parking lot—she counted six besides her own, one of them a cherry-red Cuda—so someone was still around.

Chance was still around.

She didn't find much comfort in that, though, when all those people were somewhere inside and she was alone in the dimly lit parking lot. Inside, with the windows and doors closed, the air conditioner running and the conversation that was surely flowing, if anything went wrong outside, they'd never know.

Feeling just the slightest bit cowardly, she hurried to her car, unlocked the door and slid inside. She tossed her purse onto the passenger seat, locked the door again and started the engine—or, at least, tried. It choked. It coughed. It sputtered. It did everything except start. "Come on, baby," she pleaded. "You can't do this. It's practically four o'clock in the morning, and I'm tired, and I want to get home, and you just had a tune-up two weeks ago, and everything was *fine!* Please start!"

The sound of a motor more finely tuned than hers was even capable of interrupted her begging. She felt the deep rumble of the engine as it pulled alongside, like a dangerous, hungry cat ready to pounce, and knew without looking that it was Chance.

His window was down, and he was watching her impassively. He must have been waiting in his car—to make sure she made it safely to her car?—because there was no way he could have walked past without her seeing him. He'd removed his coat and tie, and the gold brocade vest hung open underneath the shoulder holster he wore. He looked dangerous and hungry, too, and ready to pounce on *her.*

Her throat went dry and her palms got damp. She felt about thirteen years old, face to face with a high-school crush who was going to teach the little girl a lesson. The smart, sensible adult in her told her to run away and hide. The sensual, once-mad-about-him woman wanted to learn the lesson.

Again and again.

With trembling hands, she turned the key, then pressed the button that rolled down her window.

"Want a ride?"

Yes. No. "Please." She rolled up the window, grabbed her keys and purse and climbed out. The muggy air enveloped her, making her too aware of her clothes sticking to her, of her hair curling damply away from her face. As she opened the Cuda's passenger door, he picked up his jacket from the seat and hung it over the back. The mixed fragrances of cigar smoke, aftershave and pure sexy Mississippi male drifted around her as she settled in.

Once they started moving, the wind coming through the windows ruffled her hair and lowered her body heat a degree or so, though she was all too aware that it would take only one look from him to make her hot again. Maybe he wouldn't give her that look. Maybe he would drop her off at her apartment without ever glancing her way, and she would get out of the car and go inside without begging for it. For him.

Her house came into view ahead. Chance pulled into the empty space in front of it and, for a moment, simply sat there, the engine idling.

Mary Katherine swallowed hard and wrapped her fingers around the door handle. "I—I— Thanks for the ride." When he offered no response, she opened the door and slid her feet to the ground.

Then he shut off the engine.

A Little Bit Dangerous

Though she heard noises—a car horn, a dog barking, the hum of a window air conditioner next door—it seemed the silence surrounded them. Thick, breath-stealing, ominous... or was that auspicious? Without looking at him, she stood, closed the door and started up the sidewalk to the porch. By the time she reached the top step, he was mere inches behind her.

Barely able to breathe, she unlocked the front door, then locked it again behind them. When she missed the lock on her own door twice, he steadied her hand with his bigger, darker, stronger grip. He inserted the key and turned it, pulled it out and twined his fingers around hers. Such promise in that small touch. Such need.

By the time they moved through the door, he was kissing her, and she was kissing him back, greedily, crazily. The smart, sensible adult disappeared, leaving only the still-mad-about-him woman. She pulled frantically at his clothes, at her own, touching him intimately, burning alive with the shameless need to have him inside her. When he thrust his tongue into her mouth, she welcomed it. When he shoved his hands beneath her top and rubbed his palms hard over her swollen breasts, she reveled in the sensations.

Still feeding on her mouth, he opened his trousers. She pulled up her skirt, helped him remove her panties, then wrapped her legs around his hips as he lifted her, bringing her down hard on his arousal. Turning so that she was braced against the door, he stretched her, filled her, took her hard and deep and so thoroughly that she felt consumed. She couldn't tell where she stopped and he began, couldn't separate his harsh breathing from her own ragged moans. He was touching her everywhere, claiming her, ravishing her, ravaging her.

When she came, it was sudden, intense, killing. With her eyes squeezed shut, everything went dark. Her body shook, clenching hard on his, and she clung to him desperately, gasping, pleading, whimpering. And when he came an in-stant later, all she could do was hold on for the ride.

As quickly as it had begun, it ended. Her skin was damp. His was slick. Her breathing was strangled, his raspy and loud. For long, shuddering moments, he simply held her against the door, then slowly he began to unbutton her shirt. Forcing her numbed fingers back to life, she did the same for him, working each pearl button free.

When he reached the last button, he pushed the sides of her shirt away and gazed at her as if...as if she were beau-tiful. "Look," she murmured, feeling as dazed as he looked. "No bra." Deep inside she felt him swell again, and as he ducked his head to kiss her breast, she felt herself growing needy again.

Somehow she got her feet on the floor, shrugged out of her shirt and dropped her skirt, too. While Chance struggled with his boots, she removed his shoulder holster, vest and shirt, then slid her hands over his rib cage to his waist, fol-lowing caresses with kisses, making him groan when she dragged her tongue across his nipple, making him curse when she reached inside his trousers to stroke him.

One boot hit the wood floor with a resounding echo. "Oh, angel, don't..." The second boot thudded, too, and the next thing she knew she was on her back on the Oriental rug and he was leaning over her, his weight braced on his hands and his knees, his thick arousal sliding home. "Do you know how many times I've dreamed of being inside you like this?" he demanded, his voice low, intense.

Probably nowhere near as many times as *she'd* dreamed it.

"Damn, Mary Katherine..." He kissed her tenderly, greedily, as he began moving inside her, filling her so snugly, withdrawing, filling her again. She matched his easy rhythm perfectly, met him stroke for stroke and felt those incredible sensations building again, curling her toes, heat-ing her breath beyond bearable, twisting and curling in her belly. They peaked with a low, ragged sob, exploding through her body into his, tightening her muscles and shuddering through her with an intensity just slightly less than brutal.

Slowly the tremors eased, the shivering faded, and awareness returned. Chance was still on top of her, still inside her, nuzzling her jaw, murmuring soft comforting words in her ear. She felt…fabulous. Sated. And, somehow, still greedy. She wanted to curl up beside him and go to sleep, to sit astride him and find the pleasure again, to take him deep and snug and give him the pleasure again. Instead, she opened her eyes and found him watching her so seriously.

"A million," he said as if their conversation hadn't been interrupted for fantastic sex. "A million times I've dreamed of being with you like this."

She knew better than to believe him. His lies had broken her heart once before, and even his own mama said he could sweet-talk a 'gator into a frying pan. But they were such sweet lies. As long as she reminded herself of the truth tomorrow, where was the harm in believing them tonight?

"I know," she whispered, gently touching his cheek. "It's been a million times for me, too. So let's go to the bedroom and make this one dream come true."

Chance lay on his back, one arm flung over his forehead to shade his eyes from the morning sun. The ceiling fan and the slow, steady sound of breathing were the only noises in the room. Noticeable by their absence were the creaking of the bedsprings and the sounds of incredible passion, now spent. At least, temporarily.

Mary Katherine lay asleep beside him, a corner of sheet tucked modestly over her body, her arms and long legs uncovered. Her hair tumbled across the pillow and his shoulder, tickling as it fluttered in the breeze from the fan. He thought about stretching out behind her and decided he didn't have to energy to move. They'd made love four times

last night—or was it five?—working their way from the door
to the floor and finally the bed. He had aches in parts of his
body that he hadn't known could ache.

But the big one was gone. The one that had been driving
him crazy from the moment Mary Katherine had set foot on
the *Queen*—hell, since she'd set foot in the garage all those
years ago. The one that had tormented his waking hours and
haunted his sleep. He'd never wanted anything so much—
had never enjoyed the having of it so much. He just might
never let her go.

And she just might not give him a say in the matter.

Unwilling to consider that possibility, he turned onto his
side, folded the pillow under his head in two and watched
her. Considering that she'd had no more sleep than him, she
looked amazingly well rested. There weren't any shadows
under her eyes or lines around her mouth. No, those would
come when she was awake, when the shadows would be *in*
her eyes once she realized what she'd done and with whom.

He thought about being gone when she woke up, so he
could at least be spared that, but it seemed the coward's way
out. Besides, running away wasn't likely to go far toward
making him seem more trustworthy. It sure as hell hadn't
done him any good eight years ago.

If he could go back in time, he would do it differently.
He would insist on seeing her, on telling her the truth. He
wouldn't let anyone hustle him out of town without telling
her goodbye, without asking her to go with him, without
making definite plans to meet again. Hell, maybe he would
have refused to leave, quit his job, taken his chances—whatever it took to keep the two of them together.

But he hadn't done any of that. And because of it, they
might never be able to stay together. *You betrayed my trust,*
she'd said Wednesday night. *Once you've done that, you
can't expect it to come as easily the next time. Maybe not
even at all.*

Even if he'd had a good reason? he wanted to ask. Even

if his life had been at stake? But of course, he couldn't ask her that, not yet. Even if he could, he was afraid of her answer. A lot of people had good reasons for things they did, but that didn't make their actions any more acceptable to the people they let down. Mary Katherine well might understand why he'd left the way he did, but it might not change a thing, beyond maybe giving her some small satisfaction that he hadn't *wanted* to go.

He was about to touch her, to brush her hair back from her ear to see what response a whisper and a kiss or two might bring when, from somewhere outside the bedroom, came the annoying beep-beep-beep of his pager. At home he kept the pager on the nightstand, alongside his pistol. Last night he'd left both with his clothes, scattered somewhere around the front door with her clothing.

He slid away from her and out from under the covers, then followed the noise to his trousers, where the pager was clipped to his belt. The number was familiar—the guard shack at the *Queen*—and so was the suffix: 9-1-1. Emergency. He went to the kitchen phone to call in. "What's up, Jimbo?"

"Thought you'd like to know that Paulie Baker turned up."

"Where?"

"He drifted into a snag about twenty miles downriver. Had a bullet hole in the back of his head. It wasn't a pretty sight."

"Oh, God." Chance closed his eyes, swallowed hard. He knew Ianucci was a dangerous man. Hell, he ran two multimillion-dollar enterprises—the *Queen* and the money-laundering operation. He *had* to be dangerous. But with all his crimes, this was the first time murder had become a part of the picture. "Any chance at all it's not related to what happened last week?"

"There's always a chance, son. Just not much of one. The guy was quiet, well-liked. Lived alone. If he drank or did drugs, he did that alone, too. Never missed a day of work until now, never had any run-ins with the law. He was about as clean as any casino dealer ever gets.''

Chance swore long and low, then took a deep breath. ''Does Mr. Ianucci know he's been found?''

''He arrived at the *Queen* about ten minutes ago. Ebert was maybe two minutes behind him. Stopped long enough to tell me to page you and tell you they want you in five minutes ago.''

''Tell him I'm on my way.''

''Give sweet Mary Katherine a kiss before you leave.''

Chance's grip tightened around the phone. ''What makes you think…?''

''Her car's still in the parking lot. I tried to call you at your place and there wasn't an answer. You're one lucky man.''

Sometimes, Chance thought. And sometimes it seemed the only luck he had was bad. ''I'll see you in ten minutes.''

''And a foolish man, if you can say goodbye to Mary Katherine in less than ten minutes. Later, partner.''

Chance hung up, swore again, then went to collect his clothes. He gathered Mary Katherine's while he was at it, then went to the bathroom to get dressed. He used the extra toothbrush he knew she would have in the medicine cabinet, then deliberately left it in the holder next to hers.

He was halfway to the door when he realized he had to leave a note. On the pad next to the phone, he scrawled a couple of words, tore off the page and crumpled it, tried a couple more and crumpled them, too, then tried again. The final note didn't say what he wanted, but it would do for now.

He was halfway to the door a second time when she spoke. ''Old habits are hard to break, I guess.''

Feeling guilty as hell, he stopped abruptly, then turned to face her. She stood in the bedroom door, the sheet draped around her. Her shoulders and arms were bare, except where her incredible hair tumbled down, and most of one long, shapely leg was exposed where the sheet fell open. She looked...hell, like some sort of Greek goddess. The goddess of lust. Of temptation. Of love.

He stared at her a long time before he finally got his voice to work. "Oh, angel, if you could get Sara to let you work looking like that, every man onboard that boat would be in love with you."

"I'm not interested in every man on the boat." Gracefully, unconsciously seductively, she came a few feet closer, stopping beside the kitchen counter. The sheet slipped dangerously low over one breast, and his mouth went dry, but she caught it, eased it back up. "Leaving without a word?"

"I left you a note."

Following his nod, she picked up the note pad. *Emergency at work. I'll be back soon as I can.* Without a change in her expression, she laid it down again, then picked up the discarded pages, smoothing them flat. They all bore the same short message. *Thank you.*

Thank you.

Thank you.

Then something changed on her face—became softer. Sweeter. More beautiful than ever. He closed the distance between them with three strides, pulled her close and fiercely kissed her. Then, before she could say anything, before she could tempt him, he left.

The *Queen*'s parking lot was deserted except for Mary Katherine's car, Ianucci's and a few others. Chance traded his usual distant-back-row space for one right up front, then stopped briefly at the guard shack.

Jimbo checked his watch, then gave him a disappointed look. "You're a stronger man than me. I couldn't have left her so quickly."

"It wasn't easy." But then, it never was.

"They're waiting in the office. Bubba's with them."

Their dirty cop friend. Chance smiled thinly. Just what he needed this morning.

Ianucci's office was on the California Deck, a large suite with a hell of a view, but no one was interested in looking this morning. Ianucci sat behind the desk, Clyde Ebert in one of the two chairs opposite. Cliff Dunigan was leaning against the wall, Bubba was shuffling a deck of cards at a table, and the assistant casino manager, a man by the name of Lawrence, stood nearby.

Casey, the casino manager, hadn't been invited to the meeting. Her job was overseeing the casino and nothing else—strictly legit. The less she knew about the rest of Ianucci's business, the better.

"I assume Jimbo told you our missing dealer has turned up," Ianucci said as Chance sat next to Ebert. "Unfortunately."

It was particularly unfortunate for Paulie Baker, Chance thought. All the way from Mary Katherine's, he'd been thinking about Jimbo's comment that, whether Baker was guilty of cheating or merely of making someone think he was cheating, either way he was guilty. And he'd kept wondering whether his murder was merely bad luck or whether it was connected to the *Queen* and who was truly the guilty party here. Now he took a stab at finding out.

"Bodies dumped in the river generally do surface," he said mildly. "Unless they're attached to something to keep them under."

Both Ianucci and Ebert looked at Dunigan, whose scowl intensified and took on a defensive air. That answered one question—or two or three.

"Wasn't there another way to handle this?" he asked, careful to sound as if he cared only from a murder-is-bad-for-business point of view.

Now everyone's attention was on him. Snidely, Ebert asked, "Developing a sensitive stomach, Reynard?"

Before he could respond, Ianucci silenced them with a

gesture. "He had become a problem, and problems must be resolved before they become bigger problems."

And the fact that the problem involving Paulie Baker wasn't his doing was inconsequential. Guilty either way.

The discussion continued, ranging from the public relations aspect of the murder to satisfying Baker's family with a generous payoff to the possibility that he hadn't been the first to find a way to skim profits, and required little from Chance but his attention. Finally, Ianucci dismissed everyone. Chance was rising from his chair when the boss looked at him. "Stay."

He sank down again. Once the others were gone, Ianucci offered him a cigar before lighting his own. Chance refused.

"Is Clyde right?" Ianucci asked. "Are you losing your taste for this business?"

"I never had a taste for killing people."

"It bothers you?"

"Yeah, senseless death bothers me. It won't take too many incidents like this to put the *Queen* under a microscope. We have a lot of enemies out there, Mr. Ianucci. If people connected to us start turning up dead, they'll put us out of business." He hesitated a moment, then asked, "What was the point in killing Baker? So he was accused of cheating. You have proof that he wasn't."

"Actually, we have proof that he was."

"But Ebert told me—"

"What we told everyone. Only he and I—and now you— know the truth. Paulie was stealing from us, and we took care of it, and the next dealer who's tempted will think twice about it." Abruptly, Ianucci changed the subject. "That new girl—the one you gave a ride to last night…"

Chance wasn't surprised that the boss knew about that. Monitoring the video-only cameras mounted in the parking lot was part of security's job. "Mary Katherine Monroe."

"Yes, that's the one. She asks a lot of questions."

A cold chill snaked Chance's spine. "What kind of questions?"

"Curious ones. Whether our games are honest. How someone—a dealer, not a player—might cheat. Whether we have many incidents like the one involving Mr. Baker."

"She...she's a schoolteacher," he said lamely. "She comes by her curiosity honestly."

"Perhaps you should point out to her that it's perfectly acceptable—indeed, even desirable—for some questions to go unanswered."

Chance had to swallow hard before he could get an answer out. "I'll do that, sir. Will there be anything else?"

"No, you can go. If you pass Clyde on your way out, tell him I want to see him."

With a taut nod, Chance left the office. He passed on the message to Ebert, waiting twenty feet down the passageway, took the stairs three at a time and then forced himself to keep a normal pace down the gangplank.

Jimbo came out of the guard shack with his clipboard to mark the time next to Chance's name. "Learn anything new?"

Though he wanted nothing more than to get in his car and get back to Mary Katherine's so he could find out what the hell was going on, Chance stopped, forcing his nervous energy into his clenched fists. There was no point in appearing overly anxious to get away to anyone watching those damn surveillance cameras. "Oh, yeah. Dunigan did it, and everyone knew except me."

Jimbo gave a low whistle. "Should be interesting listening to the tapes."

Chance nodded. While Ianucci had cameras mounted in the parking lot, as well as all the public areas of the *Queen, he* had voice-activated bugs planted in most of the private areas. In the months he'd been working aboard the riverboat, he'd taped thousands of hours of conversation—but none so chilling, or so damning, as the past half hour. "I'll see you later. I've got business to take care of."

"Yeah, sure. Business with big brown eyes and legs as long as the river."

Though he didn't feel like grinning, Chance managed to pull one up from somewhere. "Mary Katherine's not business, son. She's pure pleasure." And, this morning, business, too. The most important business of his life.

After Chance left, Mary Katherine tried to go back to sleep, but found it impossible. Her bed smelled of him—heavens, her *body* smelled of him—and she couldn't get the image of him as he was leaving out of her mind. The boots, the black trousers, the once-starched, now-limp white shirt, the shoulder holster…and the gun.

He'd looked dangerous…and sexy as hell.

As she showered, she wondered what the *Queen*'s emergency was. As she dressed, she wondered if he really would come back as soon as he could, or if that was just something he said to women the morning after.

Though it was nearly noon, she had breakfast—a toasted raisin bagel with a bottle of water—at the kitchen counter, with the four notes spread out in front of her. The first one she'd read, the final one he'd written, didn't matter, but the other three… *Thank you. Thank you. Thank you.* Those three touched her in ways she didn't need to be touched.

When the phone rang, it startled her into guiltily scooping up all four notes, then she silently berated herself. It wasn't as if the caller could see that she was mooning over wrinkled slips of paper. Still, she slid them into her pocket for safe-keeping as she answered the phone.

"Mary Kat?" her grandfather said. "Is that you?"

The guilt magnified, because other than a few questions and a lot of watching, she'd all but forgotten his reason for her being there. In nearly two weeks she'd learned noth-ing…except that she was still tremendously susceptible to

Chance's charm. That he was still the most incredible man she'd ever met. That she was well on her way to either the heartbreak-to-end-all-heartbreak…or the happily-ever-after she'd always dreamed about.

"Hey, Granddad. How are things in Jubilee?"

There was impatience in his voice that he had to take the time to answer her question. "Nothing ever changes here. You know that. What have you learned?"

"You know it's not that easy, Granddad," she warned. "I can't just go around asking people if they've ever seen any cheating onboard the *Queen.* I have to take my time."

"Take your time? I don't have all the time in the world, you know. I'm an old man—an old man who's lost his life savings thanks to some scoundrel on that riverboat."

Mary Katherine smiled faintly. There was a better than even chance that the only scoundrel involved in the losing of his money was the one she was talking to at that very moment. "Tell me something, Granddad. How in the world did you even get onboard the *Queen* in the first place? You're not exactly their typical customer." Part of Jimbo's job was to steer the small-time gamblers to the other casino a short distance downriver. Too bad he hadn't steered Paddy away. Then she wouldn't have come here, wouldn't have run into Chance again, wouldn't have had that fabulous sex last night.

Too bad? Oh, no, not at all. Too *sad* would have been more like it.

"I went as Judge Edwards's guest," he replied in a haughty tone. "He's a regular there, and he said it was a fine, reputable gaming establishment."

"And you took his word for it." She rolled her eyes. "Judge Edwards, the man you always said was lucky to be on the bench because it was the only thing keeping him from behind bars. The man whose legal career was distinguished by the untold ways he found to twist, deviate and subvert the law. The man who retired at the age of forty-five on so many family fortunes that he could burn a pile of hundred-dollar bills every day and never miss them. Oh, Granddad.''

When he finally spoke after a moment's silence, there was a wounded tone in his voice. ''Mary Katherine, I swear I was cheated. I don't know how, but I swear… Aw, you don't have to believe me. No one else does. At the market yesterday, Cleve Thompkins said I couldn't win a hand of poker if I was the only one playing and dealt to myself off the bottom of the deck. And over at the old folks' center, they said I ought to go play bingo with the kids because that was about my speed in games of chance. And your aunt Mildred said that maybe it was time for me to go live in the nursing home since I'm obviously not responsible to handle my own affairs.''

''No one's sending you to a nursing home, Granddad,'' she said firmly. ''You always said Aunt Mildred's just a sour old woman and Cleve Thompkins is an idiot. What they say doesn't matter.''

''It's what everyone's saying, Mary Kat, and it does matter. Have you even tried to find out something?''

She felt a flush of guilt because she'd devoted so little time to her primary purpose for being there. It was just difficult to think about proving something that she didn't believe deep down could be proven when there was so much more on her mind. ''I'll try harder, Granddad, but I have to be careful not to rouse suspicion. That's why I got the job for the whole summer.''

''Well, as long as you don't get caught up in having so much fun that you forget all about your poor old grandfather.''

Poor old grandfather? She choked back a snort. Though he'd lost his money, Paddy O'Hara would never be poor, and no matter how old he got, he was never going to act it. ''I won't forget, Granddad.''

After another few moments she got off the phone, promising herself she'd make more of an effort, starting her very next shift...then forgot Paddy altogether when a knock sounded at the door.

It was Chance, and he looked...unsettled. That was how he made her feel, too. Awkwardness swept over her. She didn't know where to look, what to do with her hands, how to stand or whether to sit or what to say. She settled for sliding her hands into the deep pockets of her dress, and felt the rustle of notepaper. *Thank you. Thank you. Thank you.* The notes gave her the courage to meet his gaze.

"You came back," she said softly. "I guess some habits *can* be broken." At least, temporarily. She opened the door wide enough for him to come in, then closed it behind him. "Is everything all right at the *Queen?*"

He removed his black coat, drawing her attention to the shoulder holster once more. It was still sexy, but she'd give almost anything if he wasn't wearing it. If he wasn't working a job that required a gun. If he wasn't working for a dangerous man.

When he saw the focus of her gaze, he shrugged out of the holster and laid it on the chair underneath his coat. "Since you'll hear about it at work this evening, I'll tell you now. Paulie Baker, the dealer who disappeared last week, was found this morning. Murdered."

"Oh, my God. Why? Who?" She tried to swallow, but her mouth had gone dry. "Was it because of what happened?"

For a moment he frowned at her, then he gave an exasperated shake of his head. "You have an active imagination, don't you, angel? Maybe in your schoolteacher world the best way to get some screw-up out of a union-protected, tenured position is to kill them, but in the real world, it's easier. We just fire them."

"You're saying it's just coincidence. He gets in trouble at work, disappears a few nights later and is found dead a week later, but it's all coincidence."

"Coincidence. Bad luck. His time to go."

She wanted to believe him—wanted it more desperately than she could say. But it seemed just a little *too* coincidental, and he seemed just a little too troubled. Because he knew? Because he'd graduated from saving a man from arrest to protecting a murderer?

Hugging her arms to her chest, she went into the kitchen and began fixing two glasses of tea. She dropped an ice cube to the floor, splashed tea all over the counter. When he pulled the pitcher from her hand, she let him. When he wrapped his arms around her from behind and pulled her bottom snugly against his hips, she let him do that, too.

"I want to make love to you," he murmured directly above her ear. "I want to be inside you, Mary Katherine. I want to stay there, safe inside you, for the rest of my life."

Even though she shouldn't, even though last night was supposed to be just another one-night aberration, she wanted exactly the same thing. In bed together they were safe. She could believe him. She could trust him.

Sliding free of his arms, she walked into the bedroom and pulled the shades hidden behind the sheer white curtains. She folded back the covers on the bed she'd recently made, turned on the fan she'd just shut off and began unbuttoning the dress she'd worn so briefly.

On the other side of the bed, he was undressing, too, revealing a broad chest, narrow waist, lean hips, nice legs. Smooth, tanned skin, taut muscle, and one hell of an impressive arousal. "Why, Mr. Reynard," she said in her best fluttering-lashes, syrupy-sweet Southern belle imitation, "you could bring fear to an innocent young girl's heart."

"Or pleasure to an experienced woman's body."

And sorrow to a foolish woman's heart.

He rested one knee on the mattress, then stretched out as she shimmied out of her dress. In that brief moment his voice got huskier, thicker. "But I'm not interested in an innocent young girl or an experienced woman. I only want you."

He'd told her that once before, and it had lasted less than twelve hours. How long this time? she wondered as she joined him on the bed. Twenty-four hours? Forty-eight? Maybe, if she was lucky, the remaining eight weeks of summer. But not forever. Chance with his sweet lies wasn't the *forever* type.

But that didn't keep her out of his arms. It didn't make her turn away from his kisses and his heated, tormenting caresses. It didn't stop her from welcoming him inside her body and holding him there, and it didn't even come close to stopping her from surrendering to his passion, his pleasure, his sweet whispered promises.

He was going to break her heart again, no doubt about it, but this time she couldn't lay all the blame on him. This time, even knowing what he could do, she'd welcomed him. She'd offered herself to him, to do with what he would, and she would pay the price later. The pain would come soon enough.

But right now he was giving her nothing but pure, soul-deep pleasure.

And right now she couldn't think of anything else she needed.

Chapter 6

Though his limbs were heavy with satisfaction and felt boneless, Chance summoned the energy to lift himself off Mary Katherine, then collapsed beside her on the bed. He lay on his stomach. She remained on her back. His skin was sticky and damp. Hers was flushed. He felt as if he couldn't rise from the bed to save his life. She looked the same.

"Are you awake?" he asked, his voice rusty.

"Am I alive?"

He trailed one fingertip across her stomach to her breast and watched her nipple quiver in response. "You're alive."

"Hmm. I thought I'd died and gone to heaven."

Which was exactly where an angel belonged. Not with a sinner like him.

He wanted to simply lie beside her, to savor the quiet, the satisfaction, but there wasn't time. They were both due at work before long, and he had to know what was going on before she set foot on the *Queen* again. "We need to talk, sugar."

That made her stiffen, made her turn her head toward him

and open her wary eyes. "Is this where you say 'hey, it was fun, but now it's time to move on'?"

He didn't smile. She didn't seem to expect him to. "I've been told that you're asking questions on the *Queen.*"

For a long time her expression remained blank, then she slowly blinked. "Asking questions? Someone keeps track of the questions I ask?"

"When you ask this kind of question—questions about honesty, about cheating—yeah, someone notices. Why so curious, Mary Katherine?"

She reached for the sheet and pulled it modestly over her before shrugging carelessly. "All the talk about the dealer being accused of cheating, I guess. I can see where it might be a tremendous temptation, but I don't really understand how anyone could pull it off." She shrugged again. "It was just idle curiosity."

He studied her intently, searching her face for some clue that she was being truthful. He didn't find anything that convinced him she was, but, more importantly, he didn't find anything that convinced him she wasn't. Her gaze was steady, clear. If she was lying, she was good at it, and he really didn't think she could be that good. She was too sweet, too much a real, live angel.

Deciding to believe her, he sat up, swung his feet to the floor and, for the second time that day, started dressing in the same clothes. "Forget the questions, darlin'. In the gaming business, even idle chatter about cheating can cause serious harm."

"Yeah, look at Paulie Baker," she said quietly. Accusingly.

He looked at her over his shoulder as he tugged one boot on. "Let's not jump to conclusions. The authorities are investigating Baker's death. Let's see what they find out before we start convicting anyone."

He finished dressing quickly, then sat on the edge of the

mattress, beside her. "I'm going home to shower and change. I'll pick you up in an hour, okay?"

"You don't have to."

"Your car's not running, remember? Besides, I want to." He grinned his best, most charming grin. "It's a fantasy of mine—picking up a beautiful, sweet, innocent angel and taking her for the ride of her life."

"And you do it quite well. You must get a lot of practice."

His gaze shifted from her dark brown eyes to her lips, slightly parted, inviting his kiss, and his voice went husky. "Only with you, darlin'. Only with you." With more willpower than he knew he possessed, he stood without kissing her and started away. He made it to the bedroom door before she spoke.

"Chance?"

Stopping, he turned back to find her watching him. She looked incredible lying there in bed—so well-made-love-to. "Yeah?"

For a long time she simply looked at him, studying, measuring. Then, as if she'd seen whatever answer she needed to see, a satisfied little smile lifted the corners of her mouth. "Never mind. I'll see you in an hour."

With a nod, he walked out of the bedroom, through the kitchen, out the door. The only thing that made it bearable was the sure knowledge that he would be back, and she would be waiting.

At his apartment, he showered, shaved and dressed, then sat at the table with the phone. For a time, he merely sat there, staring at the keypad, debating whether to pick up the receiver and dial. He'd believed Mary Katherine, hadn't he? She was just curious, nothing more. She'd always been curious, full of questions about things she didn't know or understand. That was all that had prompted her questions.

But when he finished debating, he dialed the number. He

had just a little doubt, just a little concern about why she'd felt the need to cover herself before answering, about how calculated that careless little shrug of hers seemed in hindsight. And in this business, a little doubt could easily get you a little dead.

Like Paulie Baker.

The call was answered on the second ring. "Jake's Classic Cars. You need a part, we'll find it."

"Jake, it's Chance."

"One of my best customers. How's the Cuda?"

"It's fine," he said absently. "Listen, I need a favor—anything you can turn up on Mary Katherine. Any ties to former employees of the *Queen*, anything connecting her to Ianucci or the customer list or…hell, *anything*."

His boss's voice changed from friendly to serious. "Is there a problem?"

"That's what I'm trying to find out."

"You think Mary Katherine is up to something?"

"I don't know. I just…*need* to know."

"If she's a potential problem, maybe you should get rid of her."

"The last employee the *Queen* got rid of was found floating in the river with a bullet in his brain. Gives new meaning to the word 'fired,' doesn't it?"

"Yeah, I heard about it. We'll see what we can dig up on her. Anything else?"

"No, that'll take care of it." They talked a moment longer before Chance hung up and exhaled heavily. He felt both relieved and guilty. If there was anything at all out there connecting Mary Katherine to the *Queen*, Jake's people would find it. If there wasn't, if she truly had nothing to hide, they'd find that out, too. And if his asking seemed like a betrayal…well, he'd betrayed her once and survived. He could do it again.

Except that this time, if she was innocent, she'd never have to know.

By five-forty, he was sitting outside her apartment. By five-fifty, they'd said hello to a grinning Jimbo and were on their way up the gangway to the *Queen*. Once they'd passed the guards stationed at the top, Chance pulled her aside, out of sight and earshot of everyone. If the security cameras happened to catch them on video, everyone would assume he'd sought privacy for a kiss, and so he gave her that first. Then, when she was still soft-eyed and breathless, he leaned close and murmured, "Remember what I told you. No more questions."

"Right," she said dazedly.

"I mean it. I vouched for you, Mary Katherine, so if you screw up, it looks bad for me."

She took a breath to clear her head, then nodded solemnly. "I won't ask any more questions. I promise."

A solemn promise from an impeccably proper Southern belle should give a man a certain sense of ease. Somehow this one didn't. Because he was suspicious by nature? Because he'd worked undercover too long? Because he was surrounded by people who broke promises as easily as they breathed? Whatever the reason, he made a promise to himself as he sent her off to the locker room that he'd keep a closer watch on her.

And he always kept his promises.

It was Saturday evening, and though the news of Paulie Baker's death had spread, it hadn't dampened anyone's spirits. There was too much liquor flowing, too much money changing hands. The crowd was having a good time and kept the waitresses busy, particularly in the Memphis Saloon, where Mary Katherine was working. Chance spent much of the first cruise in there, seated at the bar, keeping track of who she spoke to and for how long, trying to get a feel for conversations he couldn't hear. There were lots of smiles, lots of laughs, a commiserating look or two with the other waitresses. It didn't appear that anything the least bit serious was going on.

Because it *was* Saturday evening, he couldn't spend the entire night there in the saloon. He had one of his riskier jobs to take care of, and he left shortly after the late cruise began to do so.

Everyone kept busy on weekends, from Ianucci down to the lowliest dishwasher. Neither Casey nor Lawrence ever set foot in the office they shared until the last hour of the late cruise and often not even then if things were hopping in the gaming rooms. That made it the perfect opportunity for Chance to download the past week's records from the computer. Ianucci took every precaution possible—everything was encrypted six ways to Sunday—but the FBI's computer guys were every bit as good as Ianucci's. All Chance had to do was download the files to a micro-CD and get it to Jake, and the computer geeks took care of the rest.

He went below decks, past the employees' lounge and along one passageway to the casino manager's office. He let himself in and, by the light of the lone lamp Casey always kept burning, made his way to her desk.

The disk was small enough to get swallowed up in the inside coat pocket where he kept his pager. He fished it out, logged on to the computer and started the downloading process, impatiently drumming his fingers on the desk while he watched the progress flash across the monitor.

The copy was sixty-eight percent complete when a sound in the passageway made him freeze. With his right hand, he drew his weapon as he shut off the lamp and, in the faint light from the monitor, stealthily circled the desk to a spot behind the door.

The knob turned audibly, and the door slowly swung in. The intruder was just as slow to intrude, but as soon as he was halfway inside, Chance grabbed him—no, her, he realized from the softness of the skin he gripped—yanked her inside, slammed the door and shoved her against it, hand over her mouth. If this was Casey, come to check something in her own office, he was going to have a hell of a time explaining himself.

But it wasn't Casey. One breath of delicately perfumed air told him that. It also told him who it was.

"Damn it, Mary Katherine, what in the hell are you doing?" he demanded. Even in the shadowy light, he could see her eyes were huge, and he felt the trembling ricocheting through her body where it was in contact with his. He started to remove his hand, then decided she was probably panicked enough to overreact. "You're not going to scream, are you?"

She shook her head slowly, and he pulled his hand back, then returned his pistol to its holster. "What the hell are you doing here?"

"I—I—" After gulping a deep, noisy breath, she went on. "I saw you come in and I just wanted—"

"Liar." He'd been doing this too long to be so careless. There'd been no one in the passageway when he'd entered the office and no place to hide. There was no way she could have seen him.

Presumably because she couldn't give a better answer, her response was to put him on the defensive. She pushed him away, then glanced around the room, her gaze settling immediately on the computer. "I wouldn't have figured you for the computer type. What are you doing?"

"Nothing. Just some work."

Before he could stop her, she circled him and headed for the desk. The monitor cast eery light over her face and showed the curiosity that swept across her features. "You're downloading files. In the dark. In an office not your own. Why? What are you up to, Chance?" Suddenly she looked at him, wide-eyed again. "Oh, my God, are you— you're…you're a—a cop or something, aren't you, and you're trying to get evidence against Ianucci. That's why you helped him avoid arrest, so he would trust you, so he would give you a job where you could work against him from the inside.''

He wanted to shake her, to insist no, no, no, she had it all wrong. Instead, he aimed for cool. ''You've got some imagination there, angel. Do you dislike what I am so much that you have to pretend I'm somebody else? Is a cop so much better for the crown princess of Jubilee society than a glorified casino security guard?''

''If that's all you are, why are you downloading these files in secret? Why are you sneaking around in here?''

The computer beeped, signaling that the copying process was complete. He returned the CD to its case and was exiting the utilities program when the lights suddenly came on. Now it was his turn to look wide-eyed and panicked. ''What the hell are you doing? That switch is connected to the alarm system!''

''Sorry. I didn't...'' She swallowed hard. ''Are we in trouble?''

''Big trouble.'' Sweet damnation, there would be guards in the passageway before they could get ten feet in either direction. His entire body humming with tension, he verbally hurried the computer along so he could shut it down even as he tried to think of a way out of this mess.

Only one idea came to mind as he returned the CD to his pocket. He ripped off his coat, undid his tie and swiftly unbuttoned his vest and the top half dozen buttons of his shirt. Mary Katherine stared at him unmoving until he grabbed her hand, pulled her down on the couch with him and easily stripped her costume to her waist. As footsteps sounded in the hallway, he slid his hands into her hair, dislodging bobby pins and sending heavy strands tumbling, and at the same time he kissed her, claiming her mouth in a hard, hungry, demanding kiss.

By the time the door was flung open, he was sprawled on the sofa, hard and hot and too damn needy, and she was on top of him, incredibly soft, incredibly desirable. She gave a startled cry when the first two guards burst into the room. When three more immediately followed, she jerked her mouth free of Chance's and tried to sit up, but he held her tightly against him. "I wouldn't recommend it, darlin'," he drawled under the cover of the guards' snickers and laughter. "It seems we have an audience."

Mary Katherine was embarrassed beyond words. Mortified. Humiliated. Never in her life had she been caught half-naked in such a position by five strange men. No, make that seven, she corrected as their bosses—the head of security and Ianucci himself—came into the room. The guards immediately went silent. She was hoping she just might give in to the shame and go up in flames, leaving nothing but ash behind, but no such luck. When Ianucci ordered the guards to wait outside, she was still there. When he picked up Chance's coat from the floor, dangling it from one fingertip, and offered it to her, she was still alive and capable of feeling every ounce of embarrassment and then some.

With some careful maneuvering, she was able to get into the coat and off Chance without flashing anyone but him. The coat was far more modest attire than her usual costume, but she still felt half-naked and appalled.

"Uh, Mr. Ianucci, sir." Chance scrambled to his feet— no mean feat, she thought, considering how aroused he was. "I—I apologize, sir. We didn't mean— We were just looking—"

Ianucci walked past him to stand directly in front of Mary Katherine. Unwillingly she raised her gaze to his and felt the heat intensify. The look he gave her was tinged with disapproval but was, for the most part, disinterested. "As you're aware, Miss Monroe, this—" with one elegant gesture, he indicated her, Chance and the sofa "—is grounds for termination. You're welcome to whatever liaisons you want on your own time, but on my time, I expect you to work."

She bit back the insane impulse to point out that she was

on her dinner break. It wouldn't make any difference and just might convince him to fire her anyway.

"However, this must be your lucky day. You obviously weren't breaking the rules alone. If I fire you, I'll also have to fire Chance, and he's too valuable an employee to lose merely because he's developed a...a passion for you. I rarely give warnings. I find them a waste of time. But I'll make an exception this time. Consider yourself warned." His cool, dispassionate gaze swept over her again. "Make yourself decent. We'll wait for you in the hall." Once more he gestured, and Chance and Clyde Ebert followed him from the room.

Quickly she shrugged out of the coat, tugged her costume back into place, then repaired the damage to her hair. When she was as decent as the costume allowed for, she folded Chance's coat...and felt the hard plastic of the CD case. Curiously she pulled it out, stared at it a moment, then, without considering her actions, she tucked it inside her costume where the gathering at the waist helped camouflage the square edges. Whatever was on the CD was important enough to Chance to risk his job for it. Maybe it would tell her something about him she didn't know—such as that he really was one of the good guys. That, like her, he had ulterior motives—good motives—for being onboard the *Queen.*

If nothing else, maybe she could blackmail him into confiding in her to get the disc back.

It took more courage than she'd known she had to open the door and walk out into the well-lit passageway. The security guards were all gone. Only Chance, Ianucci and Clyde Ebert waited. "Don't forget, Miss Monroe. This is your first and last warning," Ianucci said coolly. "If there's a next time, you *will* be terminated. Consider it a warning to you, also, Chance. You're valuable...but you're not irreplaceable."

"I'm sorry, sir. I wasn't thinking clearly." Chance

grinned ruefully. "She does that to me. But it won't happen again."

"See that it doesn't." Ianucci walked away, with Ebert on his heels.

Taking her arm, Chance pulled Mary Katherine in the other direction. He didn't speak until they were outside and the heated, muggy air on the bow was the only thing around them. There he pulled her around to face him and gave her a controlled shake. "What the hell were you doing there?" he whispered even though there was clearly no one to overhear.

"Are you a cop?" she whispered back.

"No! Jeez, get over it, angel, will you? You're shacked up with an ex-grease monkey who works as a security guard and carries a gun. All the wishful thinking in the world isn't going to turn me into your perfect Mr. Right."

He was wrong, she thought as she gazed at him. All she needed to make him Mr. Right was his assurance that he wasn't one of the bad guys. Her heart told her he wasn't, and so did her head, but when he kept arguing with her, it was hard to be one hundred percent sure.

Glaring at her, he asked once more, "What were you doing in Casey's office?"

"Nothing."

He released her with one hand to drag his fingers through his hair in exasperation. "Damn it…don't play games, Mary Katherine. Mr. Ianucci is *not* someone you want to make angry. Do you understand?"

"You told me he was an honest businessman. A wonderful husband, father and boss. A paragon of virtue. Now you're suggesting that he might… What? Kill an employee who has the misfortune to be wrongly accused of cheating? Or one who happens to be in the wrong place at the wrong time?"

The taut look that crossed his face disappeared almost immediately, giving way once more to anger and frustration, but it lasted long enough to make her breath catch in her chest, to send a cold shiver down her spine. "You believe he had Paul Baker killed, don't you?"

"I don't believe anything without proof," he said flatly, but he couldn't meet her gaze when he said it.

"Oh, God." She pulled away from him and went to stare out over the river, hugging her arms—and his folded coat— tightly to her middle. Anthony Ianucci was a murderer, and she'd just put both Chance and herself in a dangerous position with him. Granted, triggering the alarm had been an accident, but that was small comfort if they lost their jobs— or their lives—over it.

He wrapped his arms around her from behind. Acutely aware of the CD tucked in the folds of her costume, she kept his coat where he couldn't feel a thing if he wandered into dangerous territory. "Go home, angel," he said wearily. "After this cruise, pack your bags and go back to Jubilee where you belong."

The idea was tempting, even if it meant telling Granddad he was out of luck. But leaving Chance...possibly rousing Ianucci's suspicion further... "Do you think he believed our excuse for being in the office?"

"I don't know. I think so. While we were waiting in the hall for you to get dressed, he said he admired my taste, though he faulted my judgment." He sighed heavily, stirring her hair, then asked the dreaded question yet again, this time in a worried, almost pleading tone. "Why were you in Casey's office, Mary Katherine? What were you looking for?"

She tried the same lie again. "I didn't even know it was Casey's office. I saw you go in and—"

"Damn it, don't lie! You weren't following me! No one followed me. I made sure of it."

"Why? What were *you* looking for?"

He forcefully turned her to face him. "What's your real interest in the *Queen*, Mary Katherine? You didn't come here looking to make money. You *have* plenty of money.

You could have found any number of more suitable summer jobs that didn't involve kids, libraries or reading. You could have found a hell of a lot more suitable adult companionship at any one of those jobs. You chose the *Queen* for a reason, and I want to know why.''

She stared stubbornly at him. ''You can never have too much money. And maybe I wasn't looking for a *suitable* summer job. Maybe I'm sick to death of everything being *suitable*. Maybe I wanted something *un*suitable, something wicked, different, fun. Maybe just once I wanted to feel like an attractive woman with something to offer a man besides a decent education for his kids.''

''And maybe you're a liar.''

For a long moment she simply looked at him. Then her mouth curved into a cool, disdainful smile. ''Well, you'd know something about that, wouldn't you, Chance? Everything I know about lying I learned from you.''

He stared at her, his green eyes intense. ''You're up to something that's liable to get you in more trouble than you know how to deal with. I can't make you tell me, but I can tell you this—you stay hell and gone from Casey's office and every other office on this boat, and stop asking questions of the other employees, or I'll have you fired. One word to Sara, and you're outta here.''

''You wouldn't do that.''

''Try it and see.''

''You are a smug, arrogant man,'' she said with a scowl.

''And you're in way over your head.''

She studied him a moment, then summoned a careless smile that was all fake. ''You get me fired, Chance, and I'll tell Ianucci what you were *really* doing in that office. Don't you think he would be interested in knowing that one of his valued employees was sneaking around in the night downloading computer files?''

Second after second ticked by as they stared at each other. She regretted the threat almost immediately, first because he didn't believe her and, second, because it gave him a more-dangerous-than-usual air. After long seconds he moved closer to her, backing her against the railing, leaning so near that their noses almost touched, and he said in a soft, silky voice, "Don't play games with me, either, Mary Katherine. Ianucci's not the only man around here who's dangerous when angry."

For a moment, or five or ten, she couldn't move, couldn't breathe. It wasn't that she was scared. She honestly wasn't, though she was convinced that he meant business. She was also convinced, however, that his "business" would never include doing her harm. No, she was turned on. Aroused. Hot. The man was threatening her, and all she could think was how she wanted to grab his vest, yank him closer for a kiss and find some privacy in the shadows to get naked.

For the first time in her life she felt just a little bit wicked.

Of course, she didn't follow through.

With the air around them actually humming with tension, she took a breath, found her voice. "I—I'd better get back to work." Carefully she eased out from between his body and the rail and started for the stairs. A dozen feet away, she laid his coat over a deck chair, then glanced back at him. He was watching her with a hint of resignation, a bit of bewilderment and other emotions too complex to sort out.

After a detour by the locker room to leave the CD in her purse, she returned to work in the saloon ten minutes early. She pretended not to notice when Chance came in ten or fifteen minutes later, pretended not to be aware of him, brooding at the bar, through the next three hours. When he finally left minutes before the boat docked, she gave a sigh of relief.

The end of the cruise had been a long time coming, but at last, gratefully, she headed for the locker room with the other waitresses. Too tired for words, she changed clothes, grabbed her purse and locked her locker again, then went out into the passageway to find Chance waiting, still brooding. He didn't speak to her as they left the boat. She couldn't think of anything to say as they drove to her house. When he parked out front, she gave him a sidelong look, wondering if he was going to come inside, hoping he planned to spend the night.

But he didn't shut off the engine or look at her or make any move at all. Disappointed, she cleared her throat. "Thanks for the ride."

He nodded once.

She got out, walked up the sidewalk, up the steps, to the door. The powerful purr of the Cuda's engine almost drowned out the creak of the screen door. It vibrated the floorboards in the hallway and pulsed through the door when she opened it, closed it, leaned against it. Feeling unsettled, her emotions in a tangle, she went to the front window. The Cuda still sat at the curb, engine rumbling, and Chance leaned against the front fender.

Logic told her he couldn't see her—the only light on inside was the dim bulb above the stove—but emotion told her he was looking straight at her. She could feel his gaze as surely as if she stood in a spotlight five feet in front of him.

She couldn't estimate how long they stood there, looking at each other. Five minutes? Ten? Twice that? After a time, though, he finally moved—not to shut off the engine and come inside to her, but to slide behind the wheel and slowly drive away. Regret seeped in until she was filled with it. Disappointed, she went to bed.

Alone.

Chapter 7

The loud jangle of the phone jerked Chance from a restless sleep. Rolling over in bed, he felt blindly on the nightstand before finding it and muttered a barely intelligible hello.

"Sounds like you had a rough night—or maybe a damn lucky one," Jake said in place of a greeting. "Should I call back after she's gone?"

"No. I'm alone." Chance sat up and rubbed one hand over his face before squinting at his wristwatch. If he'd guessed how long he'd managed to sleep last night, he would have said maybe three or four hours, but according to his watch, he'd been in bed more than twelve hours. It was nearly six-thirty, and he felt like hell. "What's up?"

"I understand you had a close call last night."

"Yeah." He related how Mary Katherine had shown up in Casey's office, how she'd hit the light switch and activated the alarm instead.

"The alarm system is tied into the light switch?" Jake asked.

"You go into a room, the first thing you do is turn on the

lights, right? Well, if you have a legitimate reason to be in one of those offices, you know the first switch on the plate sets off the alarm and the second turns on the lights. If you don't have a reason to be there, you assume the first switch turns on the lights and you get yourself caught.''

"So where's the CD? You didn't give it to Jimbo last night."

"It's in my coat pocket. I thought, under the circumstances, I'd better wait until today." He figured Jake would assume by "under the circumstances" that he meant practically getting caught and not wanting to risk further attention for himself. Truthfully, he was referring to Mary Katherine snooping in Casey's office. He'd thought it better to keep an eye on her and make sure she didn't pull any other brilliant stunts before they got back to port.

"What explanation did she give for being in the office?"

Chance scowled as he stuffed the pillows behind his back and leaned his head against the wall. "None at all that was halfway believable. You have any ideas?"

"As a matter of fact, I do. We ran her against the *Queen*'s guest list and got a hit."

A knot formed in Chance's gut and he rubbed it absently with one hand while the other tightened around the receiver. An investigation like this was far-reaching. The FBI's interest was not only in Ianucci and the *Queen*, but also in all her customers, employees and suppliers. To that effect, part of Jimbo's job, both for Ianucci and the bureau, included identifying every person who boarded the *Queen*. No one set foot on the gangway without getting logged in first, including vehicle information where possible.

Somehow, Chance managed to sound only mildly interested when he prodded his boss. "You planning to share this hit with me?"

"Does the name Patrick O'Hara mean anything to you? Older man? Goes by Paddy?"

"No. Who is he?"

"He was a visitor to the *Queen* a month or so ago. Came as a guest of the esteemed and corrupt Judge Montgomery Edwards. He had a bad night, though—lost his life savings of forty thousand dollars—then went home and told everyone the game was crooked." Jake paused before adding the final bit of information. "He's Mary Katherine's grandfather."

"Aw, hell." Squeezing his eyes shut, Chance rubbed the ache settling in his temple. "So that's what she's up to. Finding—justice? redemption?—for her grandfather."

"Looks like. Ole Paddy's something of a legend in Jubilee," Jake said with a chuckle. "By all accounts, he's a bit of a rascal. He's always up to his neck in something and it's never his fault. He gets misled, taken advantage of and snookered by every fast talker in the state, but no matter what the scheme, he's always as innocent as a babe in his version of it."

Chance wasn't amused. Sweet damnation, she was flirting with death merely to prove that her grandfather's gambling losses weren't his fault? He was not only going to get her kicked off the *Queen,* he was going to have Jake lock her up in a padded cell somewhere for her own safety until this case was closed. And then he was going to take on the full-time responsibility of watching over her—and protecting her from her grandfather—himself, even if it meant marrying her.

Especially if it meant marrying her.

"You there, Chance?"

For just one moment he allowed himself to consider the all-too-sweet prospect of marriage to Mary Katherine, then he took a deep breath. "I'm here."

"How do you want to handle this?"

"I don't know. Warning her doesn't always do any good." But telling her the truth might. If she knew he was a special agent with the FBI, if she understood the very real danger she was placing both of them in, he was relatively sure she would back off.

But if she didn't... That could be even more dangerous for them both.

"Well, you need to decide quick, 'cause, son, another day or so, and you're out of there. The U.S. Attorney's decided to present the case to the grand jury next week. The tape regarding Paul Baker's murder was the icing on a very big cake. With everything else you've gathered over the past fourteen months, he feels confident he can put Ianucci, Ebert and the others away for a very long time."

Another day or so. There'd been times when Chance had lived for the day he could walk away from the *Queen,* but now that it was actually going to happen, he didn't want to go. He *couldn't* go, not until Mary Katherine was gone, too. Not until she was safe back home in Jubilee.

"In fact," Jake went on, "you've probably taken your last cruise. You're off today and tomorrow, right? And the U.S. Attorney will want you in Oxford a day or two before he presents the case to the grand jury. You can start packing your bags."

Chance stared at a water stain on the ceiling. Mary Katherine was off today and tomorrow, too. He could use that time to persuade her to quit, to pack her bags and move her home or into protective custody, whichever she made necessary. And if he couldn't persuade Jake that there was a legitimate need to place her in protective custody—and he doubted he could—he would devise his own version of it. He had favors to call in, people who would help out.

Inside his coat, tossed on a chair across the room, his pager started beeping. His headache worsening with each beep, he stretched the phone cord so he could reach it and checked the number. "Jimbo's paging me 9-1-1," he said. "I'll see what he wants and get back to you."

He hung up, laid the pager on the nightstand and dialed the guard shack.

"Mr. Ianucci wants you in," Jimbo said. "The *Queen*'s doing an unscheduled private cruise this evening. Seems Mr. Hamilton from Atlanta had a free evening and decided he wanted an elegant dinner and a few hands of high-stakes poker with some of his equally well-heeled and bored friends."

The private cruises weren't unusual. Ianucci made the *Queen* available to any number of his regulars, who, in turn, made it worth his while. The short notice was a little odd, but not unheard of. The sort of wealthy people the *Queen* catered to had the ability to make things happen quickly, no matter what the price. Still, Chance felt...uneasy. And with good reason.

"He also requested that Mary Katherine come in. She's on her way. So are Sara and a few other girls, as well as a couple of dealers, one bartender and some of the kitchen staff."

"New girls don't do these private cruises," Chance said flatly as the first hint of panic curled in his stomach.

"They never have before."

"Can you stop her from boarding the boat?"

"I'll see what I can do."

"I'll be there in five minutes."

He dressed quickly, grabbed his pager and started out of the bedroom, then abruptly stopped. Something was wrong, he thought, the hairs on the back of his neck prickling. Something was...missing.

His gaze settled on the coat he'd worn last night. The coat in which he'd placed the micro-CD in the pocket with his pager. And yet when he'd retrieved his pager for Jimbo's call, he hadn't noticed the CD. Jerking up the coat, he shoved his hand into the pocket and found it empty. So were the other pockets.

He swore loudly and profanely as he dropped the coat and left the apartment. Had the disc dropped out of his pocket in Casey's office? Had Ianucci somehow palmed it when he picked up the coat and handed it to Mary Katherine? Or—he swore again—had *she* taken it in those minutes they'd left her alone to get dressed?

Breaking the speed limit and running a red light or two got him to the *Queen* in record time. He parked beside one of two limos in the lot and headed to the guard shack, where Jimbo waited alone. "I couldn't talk to her," he said, stalling Chance's question. "Dunigan was down here hanging out. He went onboard right after she did. As far as I can tell, she's still in the locker room."

The women's locker room was two decks down and clearly marked on the door No Men Allowed, but that didn't stop Chance. He pushed it open, aware of a blur of women in a flurry of feathers and sequins but saw only Mary Katherine, standing in front of a mirror, applying lipstick.

"O-oh, Chance, we'd always hoped you'd wander in here," one of the half-dressed waitresses teased as he passed her.

Grabbing Mary Katherine's arm, he pulled her across the locker room and outside into the passageway. "You've got to get off the boat."

The look she gave him was too innocent. "But they asked me to work and I said yes."

"I don't give a damn what you said. You're getting off the damn boat and you're not coming back *ever*. Do you understand?"

"You're not my boss, Chance. If you want to give me orders, you've got to tell me why."

"Just once can't you trust me? Can you do that?"

For a long time she continued to look at him, judging him, weighing her answer. After a moment, a bit of softness came into her expression and he would have sworn for that moment that she did trust him. But then she smiled gently and shook her head. "I can't leave the boat."

"Damn it, Mary Katherine—"

She touched his arm, then gestured behind him. "We're under way. We're here for the duration."

Whirling around, he stared at the receding shore. He'd been so focused on finding her, convincing her, that he'd neither heard nor felt the *Queen*'s departure. A sick feeling washed over him. Irrationally he wondered if they could possibly survive a jump, but the river was too shallow. Only a fool would take the chance.

"What's wrong, Chance?"

He looked back at her. "I don't know. I don't know what the hell you're doing here, but I don't think it's good. New girls never go on these private cruises. The money's so damn good that it's reserved as a reward for those who have been around awhile."

"That explains why they were surprised to see me," she said with a nod toward the locker room. "Do you think— do you think it has anything to do with last night?"

The mention of their little escapade jogged his memory, and he threateningly advanced on her. He'd backed her into the wall when the locker room opened and the waitresses came out. They were in high spirits—the promise of a big payday brought that out—and they whistled and snickered with every bit of the class the guards had shown last night when they'd found them in Casey's office.

"Jeez, Chance, can't you keep your hands off of her for five minutes?" one teased, followed by another. "Yeah, give the poor girl a break—and put 'em on me."

"Kiss him good-night, Mary Katherine, and catch up with us," Sara said. "We're going to the Pacific Lounge. Don't be late."

Once they were out of sight, Chance moved in close again. "Where's the CD?"

"The what?" Then realization dawned, and a flush tinged her face. "In...in my purse."

"Why the hell did you take it?"

"I wanted to know what you were doing," she said defensively. "I wanted to prove—"

That he was one of the good guys. Was it a tribute to his acting abilities that she still wasn't sure? Or a sad comment on the lack of trust in their relationship?

"Where's your purse?"

"Locked up inside."

"Get it."

"But—"

He leaned menacingly close. "Angel, you and I could be in more trouble than we know how to get out of. Get me the damn CD. When this cruise is over, we're going to pack our stuff and get the hell out of Dodge, and I'll tell you anything you want to know, okay? But right now I need that CD."

With a subdued nod, she slid away from him and went into the locker room. He waited impatiently for maybe a minute, then went in after her. She was standing in front of her locker, digging in the small suitcase that passed as a purse. He watched her a moment, then took it from her, swept the makeup from a counter at the mirror and dumped the contents of the bag.

Scattered across the counter was everything a woman could possibly have any use for away from home, along with a few oddities—paper clips, rubber bands, a battery. But there was no CD.

"Where is it?" he demanded.

"I don't know!" God knows, she'd lied to him enough in the past twenty-four hours, but he believed her this time. Her face had gone pale, and her eyes were rounded. "I put it in there, I swear. I came here when I left you, and I put it in my purse and locked it up. After the late cruise, I changed clothes and...and my purse spilled inside the locker."

Spinning around, he returned to the locker and began yanking out the clothing stored on the bottom.

"I picked up everything," she protested.

He held sandals, dress, panties and bra, a makeup bag and three slim packages of pantyhose, and the locker was empty. "You remember picking up the CD?"

"N-no. I—I guess I just assumed it was still inside. Not everything spilled."

"Then where the hell is it?" he demanded harshly.

She shrank back. "I—I don't know. Oh, Chance, I'm sorry. I'm so sorry!"

He exhaled heavily. He'd been in tight situations before, and had always survived. This one wasn't any different.

Oh, but it *was* different. He didn't have to worry about just himself this time. If anything happened to Mary Katherine... God help him, he wouldn't want to survive.

Reaching out, he wrapped his hand around the back of her neck and pulled her close. "Listen, angel, we might be in trouble here. You've got to go up there to the Pacific Lounge and act as if nothing's going on, all right? You've got to smile and flirt just as if it were a regular night on a regular cruise. Can you do that?"

Though her body trembled, her voice was steady. "I can try."

"Trying's not enough, sugar. Our lives might depend on it."

She put on a smile that he would have sworn was genuine if he didn't know better. "I'll do my best."

He kissed her hard, then turned her toward the door. "Go on. I'll put your purse up for you."

Still smiling, she hurried from the dressing room. He returned to the counter and began scooping things back into her bag. When he came to her wallet, he stopped. It had come open earlier, revealing a driver's license, a couple of credit cards and a photograph. Though he'd never seen the photo before, he remembered it. It had been taken one sunny afternoon at the garage in Oxford, and he'd been leaning against the Cuda, grinning at the first and only girl he'd ever loved. That night she had come to him, and they'd made love all night. The next day he'd broken her heart.

But she'd kept the picture.

"Oh, angel," he whispered. "I'll make it up to you. I promise."

And he always kept his promises.

The party in the Pacific Lounge was intimate. The seven guests had dinner first, with all sorts of delectable dishes that reminded Mary Katherine that she hadn't had time to eat her own dinner before reporting to the *Queen*. The Caesar salads looked fantastic, as did the lobster tails, and the flamed strawberry dessert practically made her drool.

Once the dishes were cleared away, the poker game started, and she and the other girls went to work. She did her best as she'd promised Chance, but it was hard, smiling and flirting with strangers while wondering where he was and what was going on. What if he was in danger at that very moment? What if Ianucci had found the CD and connected it to Chance? God forbid, what if he *died* because of her?

"You look like your feet are hurting," Sara murmured as she joined Mary Katherine at the bar to pick up drinks.

Mary Katherine increased the wattage on her smile a bit. "Do you think I'll ever get used to these heels?"

"Hon, I've been doing this for five years, and my idea of heaven is still a hot soak and a foot rub." Sara gave her a sidelong look. "You've really got Chance hooked, haven't you?"

A heated blush crept into Mary Katherine's cheeks. "We're just...just—"

"Oh, hon, if you say just friends, I'm gonna slap you. Chance and *I* are just friends. Chance and every girl on this boat are just friends. But Chance and *you*... The boy has fallen, and hard. You're the envy of every woman on the *Queen*—and not just because you got to work tonight."

Gratefully Mary Katherine seized the chance to change the subject. ''Why do you think that is?''

''I don't know. Maybe your gentleman friend over there has a weakness for big brown eyes, lush curves and mile-long legs. He certainly seems enamored of you.''

Mary Katherine glanced back at the table and saw her customer watching her. There was definite admiration in his look, but it did nothing for her. She just hoped Sara was right, and that her presence on the cruise tonight was nothing more than a matter of having the right physical attributes.

But it wasn't long before she came to the sickening realization that that wasn't the case.

The clock showed nine o'clock, and the night was dark, but the lounge was alive with laughter and good-natured fun. She'd been given a ten-minute break and had just stepped outside the lounge when two of Chance's security guards intercepted her. The bigger one, Dunigan, blocked her way. ''Miss Monroe, would you come with us, please?''

Not Chance's guards, she reminded herself. Ianucci's. Swallowing hard and hoping to heaven that she neither looked nor sounded as panicked as she felt, she asked, ''Where do you want me to go?''

''Mr. Ianucci would like to see you in his office.''

''But...I just have a short break.''

''He'll extend it for you. He's the boss. He can do that.'' Dunigan took hold of her arm just above her elbow and turned her in the opposite direction.

Ianucci's office was at the opposite end of the same deck. One man stood guard outside. Inside she found several others, including Clyde Ebert—and Chance. When he saw her with Dunigan, alarm flashed across his face, then quickly disappeared behind a coolly blank mask. She tried to duplicate the mask herself, but it was hard to be cool when she was scared out of her wits.

''Miss Monroe,'' Ianucci said. ''Will you have a seat?''

She'd rather not, she wanted to retort. But since she was

the only unarmed person in the room, being flippant or rude didn't seem the brightest idea.

"You've been with us almost two weeks, haven't you?" She nodded.

"Did Sara tell you about the two-week evaluation? That's where we look at your performance and determine whether to keep you or terminate you."

She did wish he would stop using the word terminate. Fire, get rid of, let go—they were all appropriate substitutes. But terminate just sounded so damn final...and she was afraid that was exactly what he had in mind.

"Clyde and I have been evaluating your performance. As a waitress, you're quite good. The clients like you. The other employees like you. But there seems to be some question of your trustworthiness and your loyalty. Loyalty is very important to me, as you can well imagine." He paused to light a cigar and was careful to blow the smoke away from her. "You've asked a lot of questions since you came here. You've called the *Queen*'s integrity, and therefore my integrity, into doubt. You were caught snooping in an office in which you don't belong."

"Sir, she wasn't—"

He raised one hand to silence Chance's protest. "Why, Miss Monroe?"

She desperately sought an answer that would sound reasonable, but came up with nothing. "I—I was just curious."

"How curious? Schoolteacher curious? Maybe reporter curious? Maybe even police officer curious?"

Mary Katherine's eyes widened. "Oh, no. No, no, no. You want the truth? My grandfather was aboard the *Queen* last month, and he lost everything. He swore he was cheated, and he asked me to get a job here and prove it. Yes, I was asking questions and I shouldn't have been in that office last night, but I wasn't *doing* anything. I was just humoring an old man."

Ianucci looked at Ebert, who shrugged. "It sounds stupid enough to be true. What's his name?"

"Paddy—" Mary Katherine swallowed hard. "Patrick O'Hara."

Ebert went to the computer, gave it a few commands, typed in a few strokes, then nodded. "Here it is. He lost forty grand."

"Interesting. But that doesn't explain what you were doing with this." Ianucci held up a small square case that, last night, had been tucked safely in her purse.

"I—" She didn't dare look at Chance for fear she'd give in to the terror rising inside her and beg him to help her out of this mess. "I—"

"Tell me, Miss Monroe, how were my money-laundering records going to help you prove that your grandfather was cheated? Or did you intend to use them to blackmail me? Or possibly to seek revenge by turning them over to the authorities?"

"I—I—"

Ianucci laid the disk on the desk, then waved her to silence. "It doesn't matter. No harm done us. Unfortunately, we won't be able to say the same about you. Chance."

Chance stepped forward into her line of vision, but she still couldn't look at him. She was too afraid of what she would see on his face, too afraid, period.

"We hired her on your say-so, and yet when we found her in Casey's office, you were there, too, providing her with an alibi. She's a stranger. I have no reason to trust her. But I have plenty of reasons to trust you—and only one to doubt your loyalty." Ianucci paused for effect, and the effect damn near sent Mary Katherine into hysterics. Her entire body was trembling, and the only breaths she could manage were shallow and terrified. The room was utterly silent except for the rushing in her ears and the pounding of her heart. Then Ianucci quietly spoke again. "She's become a problem. And problems must be resolved before they become bigger problems.'' He held out a hand to Ebert, who moved forward and laid a pistol in it. Ianucci offered it to Chance. ''This is your opportunity to redeem yourself.''

Chance stared at the gun as if he'd never seen one before. He was sure he couldn't move to save his life…but there wasn't anything he wouldn't do to save Mary Katherine's. Stiffly, he walked forward to accept the gun, resisting the impulse to recoil from its cool touch with revulsion.

''Mr. Ianucci, I've worked for you a long time. You just said you have plenty of reasons to trust me and only one not to. Don't make me do this. Don't make me—'' He glanced at Mary Katherine and couldn't go on. She looked terrified, as if she just might faint where she sat. He *felt* terrified.

''I'm looking for one more reason to trust you,'' Ianucci said smoothly. ''I understand she means something to you. That's why I consider it an appropriate test of your loyalty.''

Chance tore his gaze from her and looked back at his boss. There was no point in arguing. If he refused to kill Mary Katherine, he would fail the test and there would be two problems resolved tonight. Besides, it was probably in their best interests for him to agree. There was no way Ianucci would have someone killed in his own office—blood stains were so hard to get out of priceless Oriental rugs. Anything that got them out of the office—and hopefully away from some of these people—had to be in their favor.

He wrapped his fingers around the grips, testing the fit, then slid the gun into his coat pocket as he approached Mary Katherine. ''Sorry, sugar,'' he said as he pulled her to her feet. He'd been right. She was unsteady. She practically fell before catching herself, then jerking away from him.

She backed against the desk, shaking her head frantically from side to side. ''No, no, you can't do this. I didn't know—I didn't—''

He took hold of her arm in a grip she couldn't break, and steered her toward the door.

"Dunigan will go with you to make sure you don't succumb to Miss Monroe's charms one last time," Ianucci said behind them. "Once you're done, come back, Chance. I'll have something for you."

What did you give somebody who'd just committed his first murder for you? Chance wondered cynically. A fat bonus in his paycheck? Or maybe his own bullet at the base of the skull?

"We'll go to the Texas Deck," Dunigan said when they were in the passageway. He signaled for one of the other guards to accompany them. "It's far enough from the Pacific Lounge and the kitchen that no one will hear a thing. A little pop, a little plop into the water. Problem solved."

"The way you solved Paulie Baker's problem? Isn't that stupid? Two identical murders of *Queen* employees in a week?" Chance scowled at the guard. "Let me take her back to shore and do it there. I can make it look like a mugging or a robbery gone bad. The cops will think it's just a case of being in the wrong place at the wrong time. They'll never suspect it has anything to do with the *Queen*."

Dunigan considered it a moment, then shook his head. "Mr. Ianucci wants it done now. Like this."

They reached the Texas Deck way too soon. Some perversity led Dunigan to stop right at the place where he'd interrupted their kiss a lifetime ago. "This'll do fine. Want some advice? Have her stand at the rail, with her back to you, and put the barrel right here—" With one finger, he touched the back of Chance's head.

Chance knocked his hand away with a glare before guiding Mary Katherine to the railing. She was in shock, he guessed, too afraid to comprehend exactly what was happening. He'd never seen her so pale, or so fragile, and he'd never wanted to tell her the truth more than at that moment.

He'd never wanted more to tell her that he loved her.

"Hey, angel," he whispered as he positioned her next to the rail.

She tried to smile at him, but it was such a dismal effort that it damn near broke his heart. "I hope you have a plan," she whispered, her voice barely audible.

He couldn't tell her that nothing had come to mind yet.

"Come on, Reynard, hurry up," Dunigan said. "Mr. Ianucci's waiting."

"Knock it off. You can wait two minutes while I tell her goodbye."

"I didn't need time to tell Paulie goodbye."

"Yeah, well, you weren't sleeping with Paulie, were you?" Chance ignored his muttering and focused his attention on Mary Katherine again. Her lower lip was trembling, but her brown eyes were clear...and filled with trust. What a time to give him the thing he wanted second most in the world, he thought with a faint smile.

Slowly his gaze moved past her to the river below. Because it wasn't a regular cruise, a great many of the *Queen*'s lights were off, leaving the river shadowier, darker, than usual. It was impossible to tell how deep the water was.

It would be damn near impossible to see two people in the water.

"Come on, Reynard," Dunigan said impatiently, "or I swear, I'll do it myself."

"Keep it up, bubba, and I swear, I'll do *you* myself." Chance reached inside his pocket for the gun Ianucci had given him and leaned close to brush his mouth across Mary Katherine's. "I hope you can swim, angel," he whispered.

Confusion narrowed her eyes, then surprise widened them as he half lifted, half heaved her over the railing. As her scream echoed in the air, he spun around, fired twice at the guards, then leaped over the rail himself.

He landed in the water a few feet from a godawful thrashing and sputtering and struck out for the source. Mary Katherine was going under again when he grabbed her. Spitting water and curses, she frantically clung to him, and he held her just as desperately. "It's all right," he whispered. "It's all right, angel."

After a moment, she calmed down enough that they could strike out for shore. Once they'd climbed out of the river, up the bank and some distance away, they collapsed on the ground to catch their breath. Chance's heart rate was just settling when suddenly she smacked his shoulder hard. "What was that for?" he demanded.

"They were going to kill me!"

"Darlin', they were going to kill *us,* because there was no way I was going to let them kill you."

"Are those guards dead?"

"I don't know. I think so."

"Good." Then she smacked him again. "Money-laundering records? What the hell did you want with money-laundering records? What the hell are you? *Who* the hell are you?"

He captured both her hands and pulled her with him as he lay back on the ground. "Just a man who loves you more than life itself."

That took the edge off her emotion, made her soften a bit against him but not for long. "Tell me the truth, Chance."

"That was the truth, angel. Scout's honor."

She leaned close to peer into his eyes, then skeptically shook her head. "You were never a scout."

"Nope," he admitted, then brushed a strand of wet hair behind her ear before solemnly asking, "How about FBI agent's honor?"

She worked her hands free, and for a moment he thought she was going to punch him again. Instead she leaned forward and gave him a hard, triumphant kiss. "I *knew* it!" she all but crowed. "I knew you were some sort of cop and you helped Ianucci avoid arrest to gain his trust and to get a job so you could gather evidence against him from the inside! You did, didn't you?"

"I did. His gambling operation is pretty much on the up-

and-up, but his other business, money laundering, is *just* a little bit illegal. The bureau's been trying to make a racketeering case against him for years. Last year they got the idea to send me in undercover.''

''And you made their case for them.''

''It goes to the grand jury next week. Ianucci's going down on charges of racketeering, murder and now attempted murder.''

''So that CD had information on it that you could use against him.''

He nodded regretfully. ''We have a lot of evidence, but with a man like him, every little bit helps. Too bad we lost that disc.''

''You mean—'' with a smug smile, she reached immodestly inside her costume and pulled out a plastic case with a flourish ''—this disc?''

Chance stared at her. ''Where did you—? How did you—?''

''Remember when I pulled away from you in the office and said—'' she pressed the back of one hand to her forehead and breathily whimpered, '' 'No, no, you can't do this'? It was sitting on the desk. I put my hand down on top of it, scooped it up and slid it inside my costume.''

After staring at her a moment longer, he burst into laughter. ''I thought you were about to faint. I thought I was going to have to carry you out of there, and here you had the presence of mind to steal the CD—*again*—when I'd completely forgotten it. You're an amazing woman, Mary Katherine.'' Getting to his feet, he offered her a hand up. ''Come on. They've probably sent someone to find out why I haven't returned. Luckily, they don't know where we jumped, but they'll be beating the bushes for us. We'd better get back to Natchez.''

She glanced at the river behind them and the woods ahead, then gave her heels a woeful look. Once more laying the back of her hand to her forehead, she fluttered her lashes and said in her best helpless-Southern-belle voice, "Oh, my, all this excitement has been more than my little heart can stand. I feel faint. I do believe I need a big, strong FBI agent to carry me out of here."

Chance looked at her in the pale moonlight. She was muddy and bedraggled, strands of hair had come loose from her chignon, her feathers drooped and her sequins had lost their shine. She looked…well, like something that had crawled out of the river, and damned if he could remember when she'd ever been more beautiful. With a laugh, he swept her into his arms, but they didn't make it far. She wrapped her arms around his neck and pulled his mouth to hers for a long, lazy, sweet kiss.

"I love you, Chance," she murmured before kissing him again.

"Enough to forgive me?"

"Yes."

"Enough to marry me and spend the rest of your life with me?"

"Oh, yes."

Feeling the heat, the arousal and the need start building, he kissed her and was surprised they didn't steam. "I love you, angel, and I'm never, ever leaving you again."

After one more kiss, he put her down and, hand in hand, they started through the woods. "Did I mention I was thinking about quitting the FBI?"

"Considering what happened tonight, that might be a good idea. I'm not sure my heart could take it. What would you do?"

"Besides make love to my beautiful wife? I could do a lot of things. I'm one hell of a mechanic. I could work as a security guard. Or a cop. Or, hey, how about this? I could actually put that college degree to use and be an accountant. Do you think Jubilee could use an accountant?"

"You bet. My granddad could be your first client. You could teach him how to live on a budget." She smiled up at him. "Imagine that—an accountant and a schoolteacher. How much more normal could we be?"

A brief walk through the woods took them to the highway, where lights shone at a house a few hundred yards down the road. They were directly across from it when Chance stopped and gazed down at Mary Katherine. "When did you decide to trust me?"

She smoothed the lapel of his coat, brushed a spot of mud from his vest. "Oh, about eight years ago. The day I walked into your garage. When did you decide you loved me?"

"The same day."

"I always knew you were one of the good guys."

"And I always knew you were the one for me. Come on, angel. Let's see about getting home." Clasping her hand, he started across the highway. "Did I ever tell you my nickname is Lucky?"

Her sweet, clear laughter echoed in the night, and she did a credible imitation of his most charming drawl. "Oh, sugar, you certainly are."

And he knew without a doubt she was right. To be alive and in love and loved by her....

He must be the luckiest man around.

* * * * *

USA *Today* Bestselling Author

SHARON SALA

has won readers' hearts with thrilling tales
of romantic suspense. Now Silhouette Books
is proud to present five passionate stories from
this beloved author.

Available in August 2000:
ALWAYS A LADY
A beauty queen whose dreams have been dashed in a
tragic twist of fate seeks shelter for her wounded spirit
in the arms of a rough-edged cowboy....

Available in September 2000:
GENTLE PERSUASION
A brooding detective risks everything to protect the
woman he once let walk away from him....

Available in October 2000:
SARA'S ANGEL
A woman on the run searches desperately for a reclusive
Native American secret agent—the only man who can save
her from the danger that stalks her!

Available in November 2000:
HONOR'S PROMISE
A struggling waitress discovers she is really a rich heiress—
and must enter a powerful new world of wealth and
privilege on the arm of a handsome stranger....

Available in December 2000:
KING'S RANSOM
A lone woman returns home to the ranch where she was
raised, and discovers danger—as well as the man she once
loved with all her heart....

COMING NEXT MONTH

**#1039 THE BRANDS WHO CAME FOR CHRISTMAS—
Maggie Shayne**

The Oklahoma All-Girl Brands

After one incredible night spent in the arms of a stranger, Maya Brand
found herself pregnant—with twins! But when her mystery man
reappeared and claimed he wanted to be part of their lives, was Maya
ready to trust Caleb Montgomery with her expected bundles of joy—
and with her own fragile heart?

#1040 HERO AT LARGE—Robyn Amos

A Year of Loving Dangerously

SPEAR agent Keshon Gray was on a mission that could ultimately get
him killed. So when his one and only love, Rennie Williams, re-entered
his life, Keshon wasn't about to let her get too close. But knowing she
was near forced Keshon to re-evaluate his life. If he survived his mission,
would he consider starting over with the woman he couldn't resist?

#1041 MADE FOR EACH OTHER—Doreen Owens Malek

FBI bodyguard Tony Barringer knew he shouldn't mix business with
pleasure when it came to protecting Jill Darcy and her father from a
series of threats. After all, Tony was around for very different reasons—
ones Jill *definitely* wouldn't be happy about. So until he got his answers,
Tony had to hold out—no matter what his heart demanded.

#1042 HERO FOR HIRE—Marie Ferrarella

ChildFinders, Inc.

Detective Chad Andreini was more than willing to help beautiful
Veronica Lancaster find her kidnapped son—*but* she insisted on helping
with the investigation. So they teamed up, determined to bring the boy
back home. But once the ordeal was over, could this unlikely pair put
their own fears aside and allow their passions to take over?

#1043 DANGEROUS LIAISONS—Maggie Price

Nicole Taylor's business was love matches, not murder. Until her dating-
service clients started turning up dead. Suddenly she found herself
suspected, then safeguarded, by Sergeant Jake Ford. And falling hard for
the brooding top cop who no longer believed in love.

#1044 DAD IN BLUE—Shelley Cooper

Samantha Underwood would do whatever it took to help her eight-year-
old son recover from the loss of his father. And thanks to sexy police
chief Carlo Garibaldi, the boy seemed to be improving. But when it came
to love, Carlo was a tough man to convince—until Samantha showed him
just how good it could be....

CMN1000